The Bloody Tugboat and Other Witcheries

THE BLOODY TUGBOAT
and Other Witcheries

Robert H. Waugh

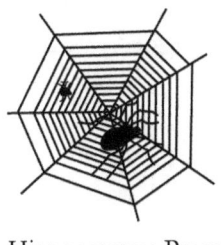

Hippocampus Press

New York

"Iceboy," first published in *Weird Fiction Review* No. 2 (2011). "In
Her Eye," first published in *Weird Fiction Review* No. 3 (2012).
"The Bloody Tugboat," first published (as "The Tug") in *Weird
Fiction Review* No. 5 (2014). All other stories are original to this
collection.

Published by Hippocampus Press
P.O. Box 641, New York, NY 10156.
http://www.hippocampuspress.com

Cover artwork by Mike Dubisch copyright © 2015 Mike Dubisch.
Cover design by Barbara Briggs Silbert.
Hippocampus Press logo designed by Anastasia Damianakos.

First Edition
1 3 5 7 9 8 6 4 2

ISBN 978-1-61498-131-2

CONTENTS

The Bloody Tugboat and Other Witcheries

THE PORTRAIT OF MISS CONSTANCE

Her name was Constance, and she did not approve of her cousins when they called her Connie. Especially she did not approve of her cousin Matthew when at Christmas he attempted to snatch the last delicious bite of pork from her plate. Faster than thought, faster than a bolt of purple lightning, she pinned his hand to the table with her dinner fork and forced him to open his fingers. We do not need to belabor the point that she was adroit with cutlery.

"Aw, Connie, I was just joking," he complained, sucking a tiny drop of blood from the back of his hand. She ate the bit of pork very slowly as she smiled at him with her greasy lips.

No, she did not approve of her cousin Matthew; she did, however, approve of the back of his hand, spangled in blood.

Her parents spoiled her; no one in the valley had any doubt of that, but it was very difficult for her parents not to spoil her, the only daughter of a father who had done quite well by his farm and could afford to lavish much on her, the only daughter of a mother who skipped rope with her and who garbed her in the clothes that she would not have worn on her own back, being of a frugal nature like her husband; but neither questioned their expenditures for the sake of their darling girl. Her three brothers, older than she, were in awe of her and begrudged her nothing; jealousy was unknown in the house.

Constance purred. Day by day she purred, her self-love pouring through the valley. "Willful and winsome," remarked a wit in the village.

The valley was out of the way of the turnpike from Boston to Albany; three generations of families had lived on the banks of the small river since Jonathan Edwards had preached to the tribes that built their long houses along the river but slowly passed away in the face of the Puritan tide.

Before Constance was born that tide had begun to ebb. Her parents would not have accepted the covenants of the early settlers, and only a few of their neighbors sniffed their long noses at Constance's dresses. She had a bombazine dress dyed in scarlet; most bombazine is dyed in black for mourning, but she had decided on scarlet. She had nothing to mourn, other than the death of a great-aunt; and scarlet was the most wonderful dye. The cousins laughed and pointed their fingers as she walked to the meeting with her parents, and Matthew whistled. It did not matter; she triumphed, her head held high, as she walked and ruffled. Constance wore her scarlet bombazine to the meeting, of course with her parents' permission and her brothers' allowance, and no one in the congregation dared say a word about the Scarlet Woman. They would have paid dearly, but no one felt moved to such accusations; the Book of Revelation was a trifle passé. Many women cooed about the dress as they left the meeting; the men saw red, and several wondered how they could approach her father for her hand.

A few of her cousins wondered the same and felt hopeless. She gave no indication of her own desires as she sat in the winter, her feet on the fender watching the play of flames, and as she sat in the summer in the apple orchards. The bees hummed around her to the despair of the cousins.

It was at the time of the scarlet dress and its fine vibrations that the painter arrived. His reputation did not precede him, for he had none, and had he had a reputation no farmer in the region would have bothered to pass it along. He had to create his reputation wherever he found himself, though unfortunately he was always ill at ease in putting himself forward.

At first he found himself in the cousins' home where he split wood and undertook the plow, all with a good will. But slowly he informed them—the mother who stood in a significant relationship to Constance's mother and the cousins as he worked the axe and the saw—that he was an artist, yes, an artist, and willing for a small bit of cash to make a portrait of any of them eager to partake of immortality. At the tip of his brush it was no less than immortality, no less; and, he intimated more quietly, it was an immortality that had nothing to do with the heaven or hell of the ancient covenants.

Of course they put little stock in his claims. The cousins were not of the breed that would have believed any such rigmarole—their belief in heaven and hell was firm but vague. Nevertheless, the claims he made, that he was indeed a painter and not bad at portraits, began to percolate through the valley. Several times folk oohed and aahed as he showed his paints and easel to their entreaties.

So it was not long before Constance's mother began to consider that nothing more became Constance and the position of her husband than such a portrait. Constance, of course, was far ahead of her mother in this matter.

"Please, mother," she said, flopping on her mother's bed one morning and tickling her under her chin. "Won't it look simply perfect in the parlor? I would wear my scarlet dress. Mamma, mamma, do listen!" and both of them laughed.

In no short time her mother yielded, and in no short time her father yielded also. They had no portraits in the house. They had not been that kind of family, but with three generations beginning to weigh upon them the father felt it was time to record their lives. And it was Constance. They loved her so much. There was no one better than Constance to carry their features and their world into the next world; and whatever she wanted they would give her.

The name of the itinerant Titian was Harry Scrubbs. Hardly an artistic name, but one must do with what one has—not a sentiment that Constance agreed with when it thundered from the lungs of the ministry, but one she found she had to take in stride when matters were as they were. Harry was short and stout; he did not eat as he ought unless he was doing his odd jobs, splitting logs and painting barns if he could not find a nabob who required a portrait. Hand to mouth, that was Harry.

He took the portrait seriously. He and she and her mother consulted about the dress she should wear and decided at last upon the famous bombazine. When he heard the story of the fork he insisted upon her holding that instrument in her right hand, not as a symbol of gluttony—she was not at all fat—but as a symbol of her will. She agreed proudly. She would sit at the fender, a small heap of wood flickering at the hearth and through the window the river running south.

The work took three days. A good model, she sat for an hour in the morning and for two hours in the afternoon. The only disturbance came on the second day when Matthew and his brothers came to gawk and comment; but her mother, whom they all loved and obeyed as their own mother, soon turned them out. Constance's own brothers kept a holy silence, and out in the fields it was nothing they really thought about; this was their holy silence.

On the last day Harry dabbed the last strokes on the portrait and Constance was permitted to see it. She found it acceptable. It was not as beautiful as the young woman she met in the mirror in the parlor, but it did get under her skin; it revealed her in ways that surprised her—what more could she want? She, however, knew from her first viewing that she was more than the portrait. But her parents' pride beamed from their brows, pride in her it goes without saying and pride in themselves as the first owners of a portrait in the valley. The parents' pride for a short time, however, exceeded the glory of their daughter, who in the portrait represented the glory of the family—yes, even the glory of her brothers and cousins.

They had not thought of the question of a frame until Harry pointed out that the portrait could not hang as it was in the parlor. He explained the mechanics to them and also insisted that the frame needed to be worthy of the painting. "Oh, very well!" Constance's father exclaimed, so Harry drew a sketch of the frame and listed the specifications of its material and dimensions that they could send to an artist in Albany whom he knew. Though with a heavy heart Constance's father felt that the cost of the portrait was extending beyond anything that he had expected, he agreed to everything Harry suggested; so in a few weeks the frame, a heavy, ornate oak structure, arrived and the portrait was duly installed and hung in the parlor. Everyone in the family was ecstatic, but Constance's ecstasy exceeded all bounds; the oak frame had the effect of a halo, indicating her sainthood—not that Constance was any saint.

And so the portrait hunt through the various vicissitudes of the family, a record of its past and a challenge to its future. Constance still gripped the fork.

Anne, from the perspective of the twenty-first century, recognized the portrait as an example of the American Primitive, neither very good nor at all very bad. The texture of the scarlet dress was striking. The chin, square and firm as most of the chins of that period seemed to be, had Anne only known, was not in fact an example of the style of the period but Constance herself. Harry was a more revealing artist than anyone might have expected; but by Anne's time his name was quite forgotten. To a few scholars, not many, he was known as the Westfield Master. The grandchildren and great-grandchildren knew of Constance of course, but Anne with no shame called her Connie.

Connie, the willful young beauty, a wicked hand with a fork, who died young.

Influenza took her, as it took many in the valley that winter. One early afternoon she became weak, weak with a weakness that floored her, and took to her bed, an action utterly unlike her. A bad cough shook her, it would not stop, so bad that speech became difficult. Three hours before her death she whispered to her mother, almost singing, "Make it long and narrow."

The words seemed unaccountable. It was only fifty years later, when people began to notice that her cousin Matthew had not married and was not likely to, that her words were remembered. "Significant," said the town scribe, tapping his nose, "significant." Matthew lived to the age of eighty-three. One day he stopped with his plow in the middle of a furrow, sat down leaning on a stump, and passed away with no fuss and no comment. Well, that was who he was.

Something odd happened to Constance at the instant of her death. She found herself seated in the parlor in perfect health, watching her family draping the mirrors. "That is not necessary," she tried to say, but the words would not come from her mouth. Her mouth would not open. She was not uncomfortable, it did not seem that she was paralyzed, yet not a finger, not a toe could she move; and her heart did not beat.

This condition, she was certain, was not heaven, it was not hell, and she was too comfortable to believe she had fallen into a papist purgatory. She resided in her portrait. She was dead, oh yes, but she was not dead either. No, that was not right, she was dead because she had heard the men in the hallway, her three brothers and her three cousins, Matthew at their head, admonishing them to be careful as they carried her coffin to be buried in the family graveyard. She would be near, near to the family, near to the graves, and she cried out (but her lips did not move), "Don't bury me in that cold ground!" But they had to. They talked about it in front of her in the parlor taking tea. Matthew left, but the boys talked about cutting the ice-cold clods apart to make room for her in the ground.

So she was dead.

Many years passed as she watched her mother age and die, her father age and die; they were hardy folk. Her brothers, heavier and much more serious than in their youth, were married; and suddenly children, when their mothers allowed them, crowded through the parlor breaking family heirlooms. Their mothers told them in solemn tones the story of the beautiful Constance, and the children giggled.

Across the room hung the mirror, in which she saw herself in the portrait. Not a wink of the eye, not a twitch of the lip, betrayed her deep presence. She was not given to speculation; nevertheless, given the years she sat in the portrait, she did think long and deeply about her condition. To her surprise it dawned on her, after some years, that it had something to do with love. Whether it was her love of the portrait, which was rather corrupt through her pride, or her love of the family, corrupt also, was beyond her. Either she haunted the portrait or she haunted the house. Perhaps this was purgatory and she had something, perhaps this pride, to work out. She had something to look forward to and only her love could save her.

Listening to the talk in the parlor and the hallway she witnessed the growth of the family; her grandson Jonas, a man very like her father, had five children and was forced to buy new land and build an extension on the house. She also watched the family's decline. It became painful not to intervene as the great-great-grandchildren diminished and lost land and acreage and barns—one of those barns Harry had painted! It was painful not to intervene in the decisions of the men as they debated what they ought to sell, more often than not getting drunk and losing the argument and the land for a penny. So it seemed to Constance, raging on the wall in her scarlet, imperious dress.

They were also destroyed, though they did not know it by their persistent tillage of the same crops. The land was leeched and ruined. Most of their neighbors moved on but they did not, watching the trees grow up once more upon land that had once been cultivated meadows. They had a fidelity to family that embraced the land they had worked for generations and ruined.

At last the house, only the house, the meadow that stretched down to the river, and a few outlying, scrofulous fields came down to Anne. She was a true sprig of the family. Her husband, a distant cousin, did his best to save the holdings and failed, muttering his apologies on his deathbed. Anne snarled at his apologies and Constance, down in the parlor, heard her snarl from the upstairs bedroom and snarled her voiceless snarl in accompaniment. Neither woman felt the house shake.

After ninety years had passed the fender was removed, the fireplace stopped up, and oil heat introduced to the parlor. Had Constance had any say in the matter, as she had not, she would have screamed once and then have held her tongue. No more of fantasy and play in the flames. No more fantasy at all.

Anne and her feral cats, sometimes two of them and sometimes three, settled into the house to die slowly. It helped that she was a frugal woman, and it helped that she held long sessions with her cats. She spoke with her tabby often. She also spoke with her Connie.

"What are you smiling at? You think you're some Mona Lisa?"

"Whatever became of the scarlet dress? Did they burn it for fear of contagion? Or did they bury you in it? You would have insisted on that, wouldn't you? But you never believed you would die."

"Yes, I did."

"What am I going to do?"

"Not much, not much."

"You think you're some Mona Lisa?"

That was her refrain at morning tea and afternoon tea. Her grim humor seldom varied. You can imagine, however, that she had much else to say.

"I wish you could advise me on these tax forms. You were never one, though, for calculations and percentages, I bet not. Look at this!"

She held up to the portrait a swatch of forms, flapping them in the face of Constance, forms that no one could have read; and in any case she was quite right. Had Constance the ability to deal with such forms she would still have hurled herself back in her chair. But she could not do either. She could only sit there, blinking the eyes she could not blink and crying for Anne the tears she could not cry.

It was most unsatisfactory. Each in her own way was stymied.

"Tell me this," Anne would ask, very late at night when the cats had snuggled at last to bed. "Were you ever in love? I do miss Philip. I do miss him, but we must soldier on, mustn't we? You think you're some Mona Lisa?"

She had a last sip of Catawba wine and stumbled up to bed.

Constance smiled a smile in her fashion, edging down to her heavy chin, trying to discover eternity, and kissed her descendent to bed. She kissed her brow, but she was not in the bedroom of course, and her lips could not kiss.

Several years passed in these conversations before Simon entered the house and began his negotiations with Anne. The nub of the various possibilities was that Anne, who was now in her late eighties, should leave her house for a comfy cottage, yet to be built, leaving the house to be demolished. In its place the consortium planned to erect a mall, very handy for the people in their cottages. In time a large senior estate would be built with pools and saunas and tennis courts, complete with the latest medical facilities, doctors falling over each other's stethoscopes, and much greenery.

Anne saw Constance wink and ask several questions that left Simon speechless and sputtering. The main point, to which she returned often, was the well-known fact that greenery sucked up oxygen.

Simon dodged that point. "No, ma'am," he said. "That's not the intent at all, and no that is not a death room we have in mind—no, ma'am, not at all."

He left without anything signed and Anne saw to her cats. That afternoon she sat with her tea in front of Constance and initiated their accustomed conversation.

"What are you smiling at? The point is that I am old, older than I would confess to anyone but you. I'm terrified of tripping and falling. We wouldn't talk much after that. You're my dear, aren't you, Connie? But there's no money, very little at all, and we'll go no more a-roving. So if I can't do anything I'm afraid it's up to you, you'll have to do something. What are you smiling at?"

The great secret was that Constance was smiling, quite beyond anything that that rare puss, the Mona Lisa, was capable of. She smiled because her spine was beginning to itch and the backs of her arms. She was waiting for something, just as she had always known she was, because at the bottom of her life was this profound love for family, incarnate in Anne.

Simon came the next day, his briefcase overflowing in new forms that he was convinced Anne would sign. The cats greeted him at the door, purring and slinking past his cuffs. He was well accustomed to these cases. If the cats are for you, who can be against you? He laid a hand on a back that lifted itself and took a long, deep, slippery roll beneath it. They were his beasts, not hers. The tabby then ripped the back of his hand open.

Anne showed him into the parlor nursing his hand, brought in the teapot and the cups, sugar and cream, and sat down to hear his presentation. He now said that his consortium would offer her a good deal of money for her house and property, more than he was speaking of yesterday, and in addition they would offer her an annuity that would pay for a great spread of medical difficulties. She would be dead ten times over, he said laughing, before she came to the end of that annuity. Anne, however, as she sipped her tea to the dregs, knew that he lied, and Constance from her special perspective within the frame knew also that he lied. She had a long, disinterested experience, watching people from her enforced disinterest, since she could not intervene; but never had she so wished to intervene.

Anne rose, took the teapot, and went to the kitchen. Simon rose and turned to the mirror, adjusting his tie and admiring his aplomb. Never had he felt so capable. And Constance, looking at his face and his face in the mirror, realized that he was not simply a liar; he was evil. The two sides of his face were exactly alike. Most people have faces that are asymmetric, but evil people have symmetrical faces that reveal nothing in their perfection.

He was evil. She ripped herself from the frame.

The sound made Simon turn. He saw the portrait tearing itself apart, like wallpaper tearing itself from the wall, but it was Constance who ripped and tore herself apart from the only thing holding her to the canvas, her blood exploding behind her one-dimensional body. Bloody and ghastly she tore from the frame, gripping the iron dinner fork in her hand that she plunged into Simon's heart.

His blood followed the fork as she drew it out, then plunged it in once more and drew it out. Once more and once more. Simon collapsed and she collapsed; and as she collapsed her blood became what it had always been, the dry paint that represented her scarlet bombazine dress.

Anne was shocked when she returned with the teapot and scones. She stood long at the door before she walked into the study and called the hospital and the police.

Nothing could be made of it, of course. Anne's fingerprints were not on the fork that had caused such horrible and knowing wounds. The portrait had shattered, probably due to its age and the low humidity of the season. No one wished to present a comprehensive theory of the event.

The consortium backed out of its proposition, and Anne settled into a life of greater frugality. She got into touch with distant cousins and welcomed them to the house.

She died in her bed. The nurse who was sitting out in the hallway said that five minutes before her death she could hear Anne chuckling.

When the estate was auctioned off the frame fetched a very good price.

The distant cousins established a foundation that assured the survival of the house.

"What are you smiling at?"

ICEBOY

They had driven very high that morning. The sky was as spotless as water in the mountains. They had driven so high that the deep blue in front of Martin's face shone almost black; the sky seemed to rest on the long line of shimmering snow. He suddenly remembered that sky as he nodded in the waiting-room, two o'clock in the morning, and forgot it again. But later he would remember the sky, pristine as black snow, as clear-cut in his mind as ever, the time they had always been happy. Eden above the snow-line. It is very quiet at first as he and Gerry step out of the car. They only hear quick, sharp, small sounds. The wood is eating itself, breathing through charcoal.

But the Berkshires are no more than 2,000 feet high. How could the sky have suffered that extremity of blue-black emptiness? Only the dazzle could have darkened it so bleakly. The thick vinyl he sat on in the waiting-room creaked as his bodily discomfort settled itself to his left side. Gerry got up on his right hand, brushed his shoulder clumsily, as though she were unaccustomed to his presence or as though his shoulder were sore, and walked out of the room.

Married for only a year, they had been driving over the Berkshires above Westfield to visit some of her acquaintances, a husband and wife, a sister and brother—he was not clear what they were, the Stauntons, and he couldn't try to remember them now, but it was her, the wife or the sister, that Gerry had known in college. They were driving to visit the Stauntons, and it was late April. The crocuses had begun to wilt, beaten down in the face of the taller, greener daffs; the rains were harder. Every cloud passing by fell in a great earth-shaking shower of rain. But as they drove along that winding, dipping, swooping country road that he was convinced would bring them to Barrington sooner than the highway, the rain turned to a cobwebby mist. The world became darker; it was only late morning but darker and darker until they came round a rock cliff and out into the sun, the snow, the black-blue scorched sky, and the ice. Gerry gave him his sunglasses. The bare black rocks next to the snow turned a fuzzy dark brown glazed in the shine of the ice.

It's two in the morning, sitting in the waiting-room, in that unnatural half-brightness that hospitals drape themselves in at that hour. Ricky is dying down the hall, but Martin still has the ice at the top of the Berkshires in mind. He was thinking about ice as hard as he could when a nurse asked him to speak to Director Asquith.

The director's office was very white, and she was very black, hunkered in her seat behind the desk like a bear. She began by asking him how they had found Ricky.

"It's just that Gerry, my wife Gerry, always looks in on him when we go to bed, and she knew that his breathing wasn't right." He wouldn't tell her how his ten-year-old son was hugging his teddy bear; and he wouldn't tell her how the other stuffed animals, the fox and the lamb and the lion, looked down on the scene of his son's sweat-drenched bed.

What did he think of Ricky's breathing? He thought—he didn't know, what could he think?—that maybe it wasn't right, but he wasn't sure, still hugging his teddy bear tighter than anything despite his loose, ragged breath. But Gerry must know, he figured.

How had Ricky acted the last few days? Martin thought he was pretty much the same. He wouldn't take out the trash. Ten-year-olds get awfully stubborn. He wished he knew what gets into them.

What did Martin do then? Well, he yelled and made him stand in front of the trash can for an hour. That didn't help. Then he yelled some more.

Did Martin hit him?

His answer was in his throat; he stopped. He realized what that woman Asquith was really concerned about, and he spoke very quietly, very carefully. No, he hadn't hit Ricky, he knew he hadn't. Who doesn't hit his kid? Who isn't ashamed? But none of that mattered if Ricky was dying, and they said that Ricky might be dying. It was a lot of aspirin he'd drunk down before he went to bed. Was he that unhappy? We're unhappy, so unhappy. When the director let him find his way back to the waiting-room and asked Gerry to speak with her for a few minutes, he walked out with his face hanging off his neck like a cow that the butchers had just discovered they didn't have room for in the slaughterhouse that day. It wasn't reprieve; it was just so late at night, 2:30 at least, damp and chilly this February, and his bones were sagging inside him. When he sat down his eyes closed before his head slipped off to the side; he was asleep before he was awake. No, he was awake.

After a short drive along the crest of the mountain they came to a deserted rest-stop, where he pulled off and idled the engine for a few moments before Gerry let her breath out. He let his out. "Oh look, oh look, oh look," she said. He turned off the engine. Then they stepped from the car and walked beside the low stone wall that enclosed the rest-stop. One moment they were talking too loud, the next too soft. An ice-storm had swept through the mountains that night, then snow, and then a thick moist air that froze to every speck of green. The milkpods leaned over in diamond casques; green ferns brightened like scallions in grocery-store sprays. The ice in the woods crinkled. Each stem, each twig, each bud of maple and needle of pine, each blade of grass exhibited and stood by its selfhood to shine in a sheathe of ice. What small wind there was had no effect on the shining world. The organic world twinkled like crystal.

They walked for some ten minutes at the edge of the woods that lay beyond the wall. She threw a snowball at him, but the ice didn't make for good packing; they smoked a cigarette. Then Gerry said it was too much. She yawned crocodile-jaws, yawning so wide and so deep that her jaws almost cracked from the effort she made not to yawn. They laughed. She went back to the car, bent down to the passenger-seat, and fell asleep while her head was still leaning back onto the headrest. He could see the dear top of her head over the dashboard.

He turned to look at the woods again. Tum tum, tum tum-tum-tum tum, tum tum, his tongue beat out a rhythm against the roof of his mouth as he watched the sunlight skipping through the branches. A bit more wind was up, not enough to make it colder. It was warmer, a little after noon, and the sun behind him shook through the trees like soft lightning.

Winter returns, he thought, winter returns. But the final return is the most beautiful, the most fair. Light shatters on the shoulders of the pines, tinsel flimmers, flares. Ice folds into the black folds of the ice, ice holds out, ice stutters, ice speaks, the considerate ice of the fallen, material air. Ice takes you along to its secrets. And looking at the soft lightning he saw something else. If you go into the woods today, you're in for a big surprise.

He looked across the gleaming room at the white wall that faced him and wondered how they could be taking up these hours talking to Gerry. Didn't they know that Ricky was dying? Wouldn't anyone come out of those discrete doors and tell him something, at least tell him that Ricky was dead, and then he could cry? Ricky was hugging his teddy bear like death. Martin remembered his own teddy bear, but he had never loved it like that. He would hit it and see how high it would fly, watch to see if it hit the ceiling, and then he would hug it. By the time he was five years old his teddy bear was in shreds. He looked at the twig-thin molding of the door; he had noticed its aseptic pale wood when he first sat down two hours ago.

In the back of the woods some glint of light moved like a soft lightning, shaken full of pieces of wine glasses and black glass, moving like the whisper that ice makes when the wind stirs through it on a cold cold day, this cold cold day at the top of a mountain that's ridden out an icestorm and come again into the sun. The light flicked light from its shoulders; it was dapper, thin, and small. It flirted with its own elegance.

When it spoke its voice tinkled and chimed, "Daddy."

"Child," he said, "child."

It was a naked boy, no more than ten years old, standing very lightly on the ice-spear grass that his feet did not press down. The light pierced him full of yellow sunlight because his flesh and skin were shards of ice.

"Don't go into the woods today, Daddy. No no no." The boy shook his head back and forth solemnly, very self-important and solemn and impressed with the message he had to tell. He had a secret but he couldn't tell it. His hoar-frost hair fell to the side of his forehead stirred by the secret.

"No?"

"No no." But when the boy turned and went into the woods, Martin followed without thinking. He was humming and smiling and very frightened.

The vinyl couch creaked as Gerry sat down beside him and took his hands. He didn't offer them.

"They told me how this happened."

"The aspirin."

"No, at school, Ricky had fallen in love."

He's ten years old and he's fallen in love. It is so simple. You fall in love and you want to die.

"And Michael took the girl away from him."

"Michael's his friend. And what does that mean, took the girl away?"

"I don't know what it means. They told me what Ricky said when he responded a little to whatever they're doing in there."

"Did they ask you about us?"

"Yes, that's routine, and they know we didn't do anything."

Ricky is in love, he wants to die, and they know we didn't do anything. I'm tired, Gerry is tired, I hit him, I rub his face in the food he won't eat, but we didn't do anything. We don't do anything. We let him fall in love.

"What are they doing?"

"They pumped his stomach. Now they've got him breathing through charcoal."

"Oh."

Gerry leaned her head back, the way she had leaned her head back in the car and fallen asleep the day he had followed the iceboy into the woods. He couldn't make out whether she was asleep now or not. In a few minutes an older man came into the room and sat down in the corner. Martin nodded slightly; so did the stubble-bearded man. They examined the walls, the tile floors, the clock on the wall. A quarter to three. Martin picked up a *National Geographic*. A snow-thick covered bridge in Vermont offered itself. A black gash showed where the snow had begun to peel away in the sun.

The woods flashed and flared. Every detail burned behind itself in a layer of ice that lit up the sun-drenched world in transparent flames. The red tips and lithe red branches of the juniper bush were redder, the yellow yearn of the forsythia was yellower, the flat green leaves of the mountain-laurel greener. The black and white sheaves of the birches coursed down the trunks like ice-floes down the black waters of the Hudson that he and Gerry had crossed that morning. There was still time to get to the Stauntons. All the colors were sweeter caught in the ice. And all weighed down. All the branches bowed down to him and fell before him as he high-stepped through the crusts of the old snow. An icestorm clears out a woods; it brings down the deadwood, the impossible straggles of vines, branches, and trunks that the owls and woodpeckers have filled full of holes. It is exhilarating to walk through the litter that the storms have brought down.

The woods became thicker. The boy was nowhere to be seen. Martin was not lost, his footprints led back the way he had come; he was not fearful, not even anxious anymore. The woods were not so thick that he couldn't still see the blue-black, carbon-black sky that hung there ice-still beyond the branches, untouched by the small wind and the small cracklings and hisses far away. There was a shake like a jitter of ice-cubes in vodka from the freezer. The world had become thick, syrupy. Though the air in front of him was cold and spacious, it was becoming hard to breathe. It was too cold, too black. Something brown and black eyed him from behind an oak.

He gags but can't stop filling the air in front of him with Ricky's breath. He has to breathe through charcoal. Isn't that what Gerry said? What does that mean? What does that do? How many ways can you aspirate soot? They don't, he's sure, stuff the child's nose and mouth and throat in elegant powdered ink. But what do they do then? Is it a gas mask, its jowls hung in blocks of coal, that they hang on the small face? On Ricky's small, thin face? Does it leave the gums black like licorice, a shattered Halloween mask to stare down the world forever? Does it leave hotdog buns blackened? Does it hang on a little girl's cheek after the first kiss? Do failed suicides recognize the mask in each other's face? Ricky already wears the charcoal smudge in his eyeballs. He's just a minor for a heart of death. Do they throw a soot-soaked black bag over his head, the bag of the hanged man, and tell him to suck for the little breath he deserves? He can't imagine any of the work that's going on behind the swinging door.

The clock on the wall showed a quarter after three; its hands did not move, but they moved. It made you wonder, so early in the morning before any light showed in the East, where any motion existed in the world. Gerry had gone to the bathroom. He had pressed her hand limply as she stretched out of the couch.

"These waiting-rooms are the slowest places," he said to the stubble-bearded man across from him.

"Yeah."

He could use a cigarette. Good thing he stopped. He could use a drink.

"I could sure use a drink. Course I would nurse it." He offered the man the joke, knowing that it wasn't very good.

"My daughter," the man waved his hand, "she's like . . . Her mother's on the plane from LA, maybe she'll get here. Friends will pick her up in Albany."

"Sorry," Martin said. He picked up the *Geographic* again. Something brown and black eyed him from the other side of the covered bridge. He walked on. He remembered walking on. If you go into the woods today you'd better go in disguise. Something had hulked away from the other side of the oak, quietly, with no fuss, and made for a patch of brighter light off to his left. He followed the sound of its breaking through the brush. Now he could see its black back fixed for a moment against the snow like the shadow of a tree on the snow on a night of the full moon. He felt that the iceboy was following him too but would not be in sight if he turned.

It was a picnic in the clearing. The ice, the last of the ice before the sun finally warmed it all into a tremendous fall and crashing, sang and winked and clattered around them, the chandeliers and prisms and diamonds and pendants of the woods, the hall of mirrors at Versailles, the peace of the world proclaimed to us all. In the center of the clearing the bears sat on their butts at logs and stumps where the picnic was arranged. They growled, spoke, purred, and hummed, slavering honey on their meat. It was hard to hold the meat in their clawless paws, but they did; the cloth helped. The buttons of their eyes stared out black at the ice and snow and meat. Blood stuck in the seams of their armpits.

Black teddies, brown teddies, cute teddies, big-headed teddies, lovable teddies, chewing away at the carnal remains of the children. Love is our feeder.

"Daddy."

He turned and saw the iceboy standing to the right of his tracks.

"You have to go home now, Daddy. I'm sorry. You didn't have to see that."

"They're eating the children." Flesh hung from the blunt teeth of the bears. White teeth, black tongues, tongues black as charcoal. "They have teeth."

"Yes, Daddy."

"You never see that."

"It's a surprise."

Turning his back on the carnage of the teddy bears, he followed the child back. As they walked, the boy on top of the snow, Martin shoveling through it, the sun was warming the woods. The branches dripped. Crackles of ice fell. Ice sweated. And the iceboy began to fall into pieces.

Martin had seen once in the Peabody Museum in Cambridge an exhibit of glass flowers that displayed the old-fashioned elegance of late Victorian science: green glass stems, lavender glass petals, purple glass stamen and sepals, yellow glass beads of pollen, all unfold their splendors, organs of increase, shadows of ghosts in the high-ceilinged, unfluttering papery room. The flowers were dusty, as though they had withered but would not turn brown. He thought of those glass confections as he watched the iceboy come apart, stumble, shred, and shatter. It was no good to offer any help; flesh was water, flesh was pale green grass beneath the snow. An ice liver, periwinkle-blue, sank into the melting snow. Willow-yellow ice kidneys straddled the path, garlanded in grass-green viscera of ice. Ice lungs, black-black, flowed into black water, and between them lay an ice heart blushing dusty rose. Martin's footprints stepped around the slush of the fading rainbows. When he reached the car Gerry was still sleeping.

She said, "It's all right. He'll be all right."

"All right. You mean he's safe?"

"He's safe."

"Safe."

The man in the corner was still sobbing, the nurse had come out and told him, he was still sobbing great, jagged sobs as though his throat were caught in ice.

After they came down from the mountain the Stauntons weren't at home. You forgot things. That night in the motel they made love. Nine months later Ricky was born in the afterglow that still dazzled them in the heart of all that ice.

In Her Eye

The only trace of the event that Barbara can find today, now that she is ready to go home, is a fragment of pale bone through which a mesquite spears its bitter branch; each desperate green leaf in that desert casts a sparse shadow onto the gnawed bone. The bone will not be folded into mud to fossilize, it will not be found. Nothing will be left when winter comes. Roger Kensington had showed her much more bone and flesh at the beginning of the summer. Coyotes and vultures, flies, ants, bacteria, in their various cleanly fashions, have gorged. She had not meant to cater the feast, but she does not begrudge them; they never eat too much, none of them. The most marginal beast knows better than to eat too much; but it eats enough.

She still wonders what she had actually been doing when the earth shook. Roger was quite clear about the time. For her it was ten minutes after two o'clock in the afternoon of the second Friday in March. But since she only learned of the event three days later when Roger called on Sunday night, she finds it difficult to recall where she was, what she was holding, what she was looking at, what was in the air, what was the set of her mind. Most probably she was sitting at her desk, dissatisfied with the numbers Mr. Olsen had provided on the screen, her cold fingers poking at the empty in-out tray, or staring across the Charles at the pyramids and mortuary domes of MIT. But she could as well have been on break, reaching for her bottle of water from the refrigerator or in the bathroom, squatting and waiting. Though she had been sick to her stomach that morning, she had seen no reason why she shouldn't go to the office, and the walk had invigorated her. Her work is perfunctory; forms come in, bearing the heading of the plaintiff, are manipulated, and depart transformed. When she came home in the afternoon, walking with her usual economy past the station on Huntington Street, past the church, stopping in the grocery-store and the yarn-shop, she found the end of the day as satisfactory as she had found the morning. She ate and worked and went to bed. This is satisfaction, this is enough.

So she wonders what she could have been thinking at that instant. And was it prayer?

She doesn't believe it was prayer. She was finished with prayer since the day she came back from the Vineyard and told Joshua that she couldn't see him anymore, that it was dangerous. Because prayer, she knew, could do nothing.

"Listen to yourself," his voice had said calling from Newton that night. "You're not a child anymore, you really aren't. You can't expect that something that big can be saved when it comes rolling in at high tide. And you can't just cut someone off like this, out of the blue."

But Joshua didn't understand how little she wanted. She hadn't expected anything more than a gesture from God. Not even when she was a child did she expect more than the smallest brightening of the tip of the candle on either side of the altar, and when she was older she expected no more than the usual acts of kindness in a day, just the sight of one person giving one penny to a beggar. One penny.

So now both she and God had to pay for the dismissal they had suffered in those weeks last summer when the right whale had come ashore east of Gay's Head and heaved its helpless lungs beneath the weight of its tossed up flesh. The experts from Woods Hole along with volunteers from up and down the island gathered on the beach but could not repeat the successes to which they had become accustomed in earlier incidents. Incidents. Its size, forty-four feet long and eighteen shaking tons, was too daunting to handle gently. The polite meadows upwind stank from its decomposition for days before the authorities determined that the only way to remove it was to call in butchers to haul off the slabs of blubber and thick cords of bone; the beach still stank for weeks.

And no one knew why. Perhaps whales follow a migratory track that existed across this beach millennia before the land silted and lifted; perhaps their sonars are distressed and disrupted by the increasing cacophony we make as we re-enter the sea. Every season a new theory comes into fashion to explain the gross waste and death on the beaches. That was the way of it again. This whale stank and died, and no one knew why.

The waste was more than she could bear. And the fact that it was the carcass of a right whale made the waste all the worse, the more desperate. It was right for the butchers who multiplied on the land, right for the lamps that shone on the enterprise of human use until now, as she had heard with Joshua on the whale-watch boat off Hyannis the summer before the beaching; the right whales of the North Atlantic are reduced to a community of barely three hundred. The seas and the songs are drying up, and few of the whales can hear a thing that the others are saying as they roll along scattered, murmuring to themselves the trivia of their private isolations, homeless in the dead seas.

After standing on the beach where a few hacked bones still lay in the dunes, after finding her way to Newton through the bustle of Boston, after eating the appetizer of the meal Joshua had prepared for her return and she couldn't eat a bite more, she couldn't help herself from suddenly saying that she had to create her own retreat, though she shrank from uttering the word solidarity. But it was a solidarity of flesh without fuss. Because so little was left.

That meal was a year ago. So she was in no way prepared for the significance of Roger Kensington's story, a story meant for her alone, when her phone rang that Sunday night. And her phone never rang.

"But I don't know you at all," she protested, after he allowed that a call from West Texas was nothing she ought to expect.

"Ms. Matthews," he said with that *Ms.* of the South, she could catch the difference in the slight lilt, "I can't begin to tell you how I know your name. I don't know what connection you have to what's happened out here. But you listen and you judge. If you think I'm crazy you hang up, change your number, tell the police about me, whatever makes you feel safe. But me and my wife's seen something that you can be sure concerns you. I mailed this letter today, you'll get it real soon. But I'll say this now. I've seen your whale."

Then he said, "Must be your whale. In West Texas. In my front yard."

After the call she sat for an hour next to the phone trying to re-member what she had been thinking on Friday at ten minutes past two. It was not a prayer. What had come out of her heart? Hurled itself out of her heart without her knowing? Help? Increase my heart? Feed me?

Roger Kensington had told her something else. She wouldn't believe him, he said, if he didn't tell her. "After you got home Fri-day, you opened the second drawer of the desk in your bedroom, lifted out some pieces of glass on a handkerchief, and cut the inside of your arm. Not much. Then you put the pieces back." She wouldn't have believed him, no.

She'd bought the figurine two years ago in the booth in front of the whale-watch office. A clear-glass whale, no bigger than her palm. Joshua offered to buy it but she shook her head—it was her purchase, her whale; then he smiled and passed the tips of his fin-gers lightly across her belly, and she rippled. He'd never done that before. A year later, back in her apartment with the smell of the butchered whale still thick in her hair, she had taken the figurine down from the bookcase and smashed it circumspectly in her folded handkerchief. Then she sat down to the absence of prayer.

But her year-long retreat had at least the character of prayer in its single-mindedness and the meager means it sought for itself. There was only so much she could deal with: the papers at the of-fice, the grocery-store, the yarn and the knitting, the Center off

Commonwealth, paying the bills, pulling on the quilt, the necessity for sleep. Labor's more itself without pretense. Joshua had learned that it made no sense to phone or to visit; she taught him that. When he sat beside her the last time in September next to the river she had not said a word and not missed a stitch as he blamed her for the end of the world. That ended long before she was born. When her mother phoned she said that she was doing well; she was. She was intimately in touch with the very center of what life there was as she became more spare in her space, more in control of what it meant to be in solidarity with the flesh of the displaced world, more mute in the hands of her needles as they gave away the little warmth that she could find to Rebecca or Kathy or Falla, sitting exhausted at the Center. They told her the worst was their families were scattered; they were scattered too, in their heads. They were cold. But what they looked at, she looked at: the street was the street, the rain was the rain, the stink of their flesh was the stink of flesh. Her mother in Ohio had no way to know this, the street or the rain or the flesh or the stripped-off oceans around us, and she had no way to tell her.

"Mother, I'm fine. No, I don't see Joshua anymore. Yes, he was very nice." He was. He was quizzical, light. His blond hair slopping across his freckled face made the world much better than it was. His barbecued chicken, rolled in the pungent rosemary that he grew in his window-box at the side of the bed that faced the morning sun, filled the empty parts of her body that obeyed the tongue. But the nice world protects you too much. The spice overlays the carrion.

Joshua had insisted that they go on the whale-watch, but he hadn't understood how shaken she was when that smooth skin of the ocean had lifted itself gently from the swell of the waves as though that darker wave were a dark organ the ocean displayed as it turned itself inside out and said *Love me.* In the wide forehead of the whale letting the water pour off it the ocean had said *You can love me.* It said *I don't care what the wound is.* And the whale was too big for any such words to sound perverse. As that powerful smooth back of the beast slid below the surface and the guide began chattering the statistics again, the statistics that you knew would kill the beast with well-meaning, Barbara had burst into tears and run for the door of the toilet where she could throw up her shame with as little fuss as possible.

Joshua thought she was seasick, but she wasn't. It was the shock of the animal's enormous, bodily generosity in the midst of its desolation that had shamed her. The beached whale the following summer had shown her that such generosity meant nothing, nothing at all.

How to respond to Roger Kensington's summons perplexed her; she was living on the edge of her means as it was. But Jane, when she told her that she had to fly to Texas—and she could tell the truth, that much of it, to Jane who was totally incurious—pointed out that someone who lived the spare life she did and always paid her bills must have a very good rating with the credit union. They were happy to lend her more than she needed, and left her bemused at this easy trust in a world that was getting by on less. And she had never taken as much vacation as she might have, especially this last year. She called Roger and asked him to pick her up at the Lubbock airport.

But all those days as she planned her trip she kept seeing in front of her eyes his account of the event that she had received in the mail two days after the call. As the plane began to lift off from the runway at Logan and bank over the Atlantic, her stomach and breasts could feel the event like a slow turn in the air.

"I've lived man and boy in Slayton for forty-five years. My wife says we just passed our silver anniversary, and she must be right, she always knows what she's saying. I work in town, we farm a bit too. It's bleak as anything all year round, but you get a living. My wife Lurlene saw this herself, like me.

"We were sitting on the porch at noon at 12:10, heard the day's weather on the radio, just had lunch when we saw it rushing up, rising up from the ground fifty feet away across the drive, real near the other side of the flowers. It didn't come out of the ground, and it didn't just flash appear, didn't come out just head first either, then the rest. It was like it come surging up from that heat line you sometimes see out here hanging ten feet from the ground, like it was leaping from the waves; maybe it thought it was. So the thing, this huge thing, flung itself into that hot noon sun and took a slow turn in the air like it was going to circle for the rest of its life like some hawk. And then it fell smack on that flat desert floor, and from fifty feet away where we were sitting the porch shook beneath us. That was it. Must have died like that. But Ms. Matthews, I know it's your whale. Not that there's anything anyone can do about it."

When she walked into the Lubbock terminal he lifted his hat to her at once; he had no doubt who she was, and as she looked at the gray bare slope of the scrub across the tarmac she knew that she stuck out among all the other people landing in this small airport totally off the end of the world. He was not her picture of him. He was large, pot-bellied, weathered, soft, and his coppery face was washed out above his buttoned-up shirt. She flushed to think how she looked to him, slight, pale, fair-haired, sullen, and airless.

"What do you do, Mr. Kensington?" she asked in his truck.

"I work for an appliance store in the middle of Slayton. I repair air-conditioners. That's a good job here." He almost laughed. "I used to go out hunting sometimes." He gestured vaguely to the country he was driving through that to her eyes bled off lifeless as the seas off the Vineyard.

"Where's your tribe?"

"And some things I just don't talk about much at all."

"I'm sorry." She had felt so clever for a flash, had to show off, had to show him that she knew something too. Because he knew things about her.

"No need to apologize. It's just, people get this notion, you're a Native American," he spoke the phrase as though it would taste queer in his mouth all his life, "you're into something that's going to save the world, or's going to do nothing, that's shoved off. My wife's real easy about the Indian thing. My tribe, well, we get together. Now I'll tell you this. What I saw, what she saw, what you're going to see, I didn't see it because I'm what I am, and I didn't see it because I was drunk either. Don't touch the stuff."

She didn't see the shape from miles away; that was a fantasy. One moment they were driving along the main road, the next Roger had turned off up a hard dirt track that circled a small rise, pulling onto his land where dusty hollyhocks were blooming next to the house, flowers she had never expected that took her breath away with their sweet nodding to the wind under the wall of the suburban house; dusty blackfoot daisies and zinnias edged the walk, and the doors of the garage opened as Roger drove in. None of it was Texas. So when she turned to look through the garage window the mass of the whale struck her as no more out of place than the garage and the house and the flowers, no more out of place than the man sitting next to her who repaired air-conditioners with his dark rough fingers, and no more out of place than Lurlene in her polyester apron getting up from the rocker on the porch to welcome her. So they had to talk and Lurlene had to go off to the kitchen for the iced tea before she could turn to the whale.

"You like sugar?"

It was not as big as the whale beached on the Vineyard. It was diminished; she hadn't taken into account that a week had passed since it fell to earth and shook the Kensingtons' porch as they rocked in the noon-time heat. Roger didn't call in the butchers; he only called her. But the scavengers had heard the news, the coyotes and vultures and the hound down the road that belonged to the Kensingtons' neighbors. Every night it was becoming less and less. The tail was gone. The vestigial legs, long as her forearm, longer than she thought possible, showed teeth marks. The long ridge of the fin above the tail was shredded. The broken ribs jutted out of the mottled flesh that draped the remaining mass as though it were an old brown suit that the whale was about to contribute to the Good Will.

In this dry distant air the stench she had smelled at Gay's Head disappeared.

"It's a female," she said at last, after a long walking up and down, bending down, at last placing her hand on the stiff flesh.

"Yes. Hard now to see."

"Why's she lying like this?"

"When she came up like that, wet, breaching you know, she was looking to fall back into whatever ocean she'd come out of. She came up turning, the tail came up and tossed out, the water spraying off her, and she lay there flat in the air for the damn longest time like she'd just come out of the belly of the sky—it was blue that day, the way it is here for day after day this time of year—and then she just fell that way, flat."

"Shook the ground in your backyard."

"Yeah."

"What comes eating?"

"Coyotes, vultures, ants. They all smell it. Nothing lasts very long out here. But they didn't get everything, her eye is still here. That's the surprise. The birds won't touch that eye for nothing."

Barbara looked into the clouded blue surface of the eye and thought she saw something move, a reflection.

"Anyway, we wouldn't let anything near it."

As she lay in bed that night next to the fireplace they'd lit for her against the March chill that started to seep through the walls, she tried again to make sense of it. Was it effective prayer, was it her prayer? Was it just a gasp, her breastbone grunting *The seas die?* Was it about the right whale whose carcass she could not forget rotting on the Vineyard, or about the one whose generosity she could not endure the summer before that? If the body out on the Kensingtons' front yard had been a right whale she wouldn't have been able to bear the possibility that she had somehow drawn her out of the depleted oceans. But she wasn't a right whale; and after he had examined some articles and a book or two carefully in the local library, Kensington had discovered that no kind of whale like her swam on earth today. Not today.

West Texas wasn't always a desert. The inland sea once rolled here where she was trying to sleep, where she'd never get to sleep. She rolled over in bed, tucking up her knees, hugging herself tight, it was so cold. At the dawn of the world in that great hot humid world where the waters flooded and the first great flesh stood up in the leafy sun, the sun had poured through it all and the first whales had returned to the first home of us all. That soon dried up. Effective prayer. The attention of us all now in the world, listening to the hum of our air-conditioners, scattered through the sweaty streets, looking out our windows across rivers, it's our attention that hankers back for the first flesh. It's the weight of our pity that brought the flesh forward, to this sun, to this place of the emptied seabeds, breaching time. The weight of our pity, the force of our exhaustion, the plunge of our working hands.

Standing beside the mouth of the whale in the late afternoon light, she had felt an awful tenderness rush through her, bending down to stroke the black, fine threads that lined her lips, long, silky, tough, soft, pressing.

"But how did you know it was me, in Boston?" They were sitting at the table after supper; she felt unbalanced, forced. The setting sun lit up the wall of the family portraits that Lurlene had explained to her in detail. That's family, pictures going back to the turn of the century.

"I saw you in her eye."

She made a gesture as though pushing something off her face.

"When I first saw you, I could look at nothing else, I was just so dumbstruck. Lurlene too. You sat at a metal desk not quite your size, not made for you, maybe not made for anybody. When your face turned the eye turned with you, so that it was always looking just straight at your face. And then we saw the nameplate, Barbara Matthews. There you were, sitting in her eye."

"When we looked the next day," Lurlene added, "well, the eye was starting to film over, but you were there, silvery, sitting on a bench like on the side of a river, knitting, and behind you there was a big skyscraper. Well, even out here in Slayton, Texas, we know what the Prudential looks like, and that that was Boston where Barbara Matthews lived."

"That first night after the whale fell out of her leap from the sky we saw you in your brass bed, sleeping by the light of the streetlamp outside."

"And that's how you knew me at the airport."

"Wherever you were, walking, waiting for the subway—"

"The T."

"—it didn't matter, you were still in her eye, no matter how cloudy it was getting. You're still there."

Lurlene got up and asked her to come out to the back porch where they couldn't see the body, "It's a good time to hear the whippoorwills. Roger, you stay put."

"Yeah, you ladies go talk."

Out in the warbling darkness, after they'd stood there for a time listening, looking out, Lurlene whispered, "You've got to forgive us, honey. We didn't know what we had here, we still don't. All we could do was watch. And we did watch, wherever you were, at the office, at your home. All the time. We saw you in the bathroom. We saw you throw up. Saw you crying. You've just got to forgive us, because that's why you had to come here, what we couldn't tell you on the phone. That we were perfect strangers who knew stuff about you that nobody knows."

How long does it take that massive body lying on the ground under the stars while the coyotes are gathering again, gathering hungry out there, how long does it take to die? How long do the thoughts take to pass through the brain in that dying? How long do the thoughts last that hold her? Lying in bed on her back, her hands at her side, she felt the tears press against the tissue of her throat again, her sore breast starting to hiccup, because it didn't matter. She would never pray again, she didn't need to; she couldn't get out of the sight of the dead eye.

Two weeks later, staring at the bone in the mesquite, she was still in her eye.

THE HOT TUB HORROR

You will not want to believe this story, in part because so many people, old and young, men and women, the profoundly ugly and the fiercely beautiful, behave in the gymnasium as though it were their home, and especially in the hot tub. Nothing bad happens in this space. This story occurred in front of everyone, and nobody said boo but me. Now as for me, I am an oldish, married male who has spent too much of his professional life behind the computer. The pool and the sauna relax me, and the hot tub lays me out in bliss; it is the hot tub that I want to tell you about, but I want you to believe my story because truly it all happened, all in the daylight, the sunshine pouring through the two sides of a spacious room built from glass walls and glass doors, mirrored from the white tiles, a world of transparent crystal: every way you looked a transparent, sunny, bright world. Nevertheless, you won't believe me—maybe all the more you won't.

No one wanted to sit with him in the hot tub—though they had to perforce.

No one.

Let's start there, with the heavy recognition that everyone carried the guilt of saying no to his horrid example.

For he was a horror.

It had little or nothing to do with his appearance, though many did not like it. They were repulsed.

He was muscular and hairy, black hairy stalks sticking out in a thick pattern upon his back and chest, thick black hairs sprouting from his armpits, a thick black beard, and on his forehead a swathe of black and white hair that crossed in a widow's peak. It was very dashing, and it turned my stomach.

I'm ashamed to say that, but he was frightful. In addition, it was worse because he reminded me of someone I knew, but more of that later.

You could never excuse him, whether the men were talking in the men's shower room or the women gossiping in the women's shower—so my wife told me. I must say, however, there was nothing to excuse. He was perfectly well behaved, and he was frightful. It always seemed that the water around him was chilly.

Perfectly well behaved? Yes, he was the most pleasant man in the gym. Amicable, obliging, considerate. His ferocious black beard utterly belied his meekness. "Excuse me, please," he would say if someone bumped him, but he never bumped anyone. He was very careful about that. He was leery of touch. But it was never odd that anyone did bump him, because he was only in the whirlpool, it seemed, when six or more people were there. He was shy, oddly shy, with smaller groups. It was a large hot tub that held at least ten people, ten people legally. It was deep, coming up to two inches above most men's belly-buttons, and a bench of various heights surrounded the tub on three sides, upon the fourth side sporting a staircase of six steps and a sturdy railing. He had a lot of room to be free in.

So it passed after some time. I am not in fact sure when he joined the gym. For years he had not attended, as had my wife and I, though she spent more time in her garden, and suddenly he was there. I first became conscious of him in the mid-autumn. The red and gold leaves had begun to litter the ground and there he was, his heavy torso and his widow's peak, his black hair stalks and all.

When we began to open up to each other, as happens to many people after some weeks, sitting for some time in the hot tub, I began to know him a little better. Other people were talking about problems at work, and he admitted to me, as though he wanted to be one of the boys, that he had difficulties, problems, embarrassments. He could not describe them at any length, and as he spoke of them his language became vague. He laughed softly, and his laughter became vague.

And he, as people began to leave the pool, disturbed by his language, his muscular torso and hairy chest and back—he began to soften. I did not notice the effect at first. We were not that often in the whirlpool together. But when we were, the temperature beginning to rise to 105 degrees, together with some five or six people who were beginning to leave, I could see the softening, a skin like a soft curd that had not been returned to the refrigerator. Say it was like tallow or lard long past their prime. Long past—then he truly became a horror.

After that day I began to pay attention. If we were six or seven people in the hot tub, it was all right; but if it was a smaller number, that made the horror all the more—what should I say?—all the more something we bathed in. His horror was our horror, his body our body.

We did not leap from the water, but we took to the stairs leading out of the pool, one after another; and as we did so his features slowly lost cohesion, a bit like curdled cheese, yes. We were exhausted, as though we had just made love, and we spent much more time in the showers. We did not look back.

No one confessed to any of this, but I could not deny it.

I needed to know more about this man with the widow's peak, so one day in a crowd of seven or eight men and women I offered him my name. It had the proper effect. "I'm Benjamin," he said, and then more warmly, "You can call me Benjy." He offered no family name, and it would have been too evidently prying on my part to ask. A person does not pry in the gym. But I was prying of course; very oddly, I thought it would have been irresponsible of me not to pry.

But at my laptop that evening I put in these tags: [the gym's name, which I do not mean to reveal], his name, and the words "whirlpool," "jacuzzi," and "hot tub," and came upon this curt obit in the local newspaper. The date was August 28th. "The body of Mr. Benjamin Trent, forty-three years old, was discovered this morning drowned in the whirlpool of [the gymnasium's name] where he was an employee. He had been in the pool for at least eight hours. The police suspect no foul play. He seems to have slipped on the side of the whirlpool and fallen in, knocking his head on the side. He leaves no kin."

"No kin," I whispered. Is that the reason he holds on to the social world of the hot tub? But even as I whispered the words I would not believe it. I do not believe such things. When people tell local ghost stories, like the one that took place in our museum that was once an old stone fort, I do not believe it. In that story the old woman who now manages the museum and cooks small boxed lunches in the gift store—one night as she walked up the stairs a young woman in an old-fashioned dress walked down and without pausing walked through her, leaving a chill air behind. A fine story, simple, believed by many because it occurred just down the street in the center of the historic town. No one asks the old woman about the story, of course. I admire the story, but I neither believe it nor any of the other stories people tell me, stories that happened to them. So why should I believe this story because it is printed in the newspaper?

But this was different, in a way that made me almost believe it. He was a ghost in the broad daylight. We talked to him, bumped into him if we had to, and never recognized him for what he was. Did he recognize himself?

I did, however, recognize him at last, when I read that he had been an employee of the gym. The face was familiar, yes, though when I knew him with a nodding acquaintance at the gym he had no beard. But I don't remember anyone talking about his death. I imagine that the management demanded of its staff a complete silence. Don't want people thinking about sad or violent things when the whole point of the gym is a studied relaxation and self-improvement. The ideology of the gymnasium and the ideology of the ghost are wide apart. And the gymnasium is firm in these matters. Don't want people thinking hard about the blood, sticky, smelly, dripping blood, that must have flowed into the hot tub when Benjy cracked his head on the tile.

So now I knew who he was, and I had a doubtful suspicion of what he was. It was time to talk with him again.

Before that, however, I had to confess to my wife the nature of the obsession that had begun to grip me. It was impossible for her not to see that something was wrong. So I told her the whole story.

I don't know what I expected she would say. She was a red-diaper baby, with a healthy distrust of the supernatural, a distrust that most of the time I would have concurred with. But what she said certainly brought me up.

"You should have confessed to such beliefs before our wedding!"

"A good thing I hurried you down the aisle." So I tried to brave it out, but it was no good. I was shaken and never brought it up again. He was my ghost, certainly not hers.

It was in late November that I made my decision to confront him. The first snow of the year had fallen, five inches deep, so I drove to the gym with some caution.

I chose a time when we were sitting next to each other in the whirlpool with some six other people. I wanted support if anything happened—I had of course no idea what could happen. For some time, in fact, I hesitated how to begin. The steam of the hot tub seemed thicker than usual, curling in the shape of the double helix where the sunshine shattered off the snow.

"I was reading old newspapers," I said, "and came across your name."

"Did you?"

"Yes, to my surprise it was in the obits section."

"Well, I don't see how that could have been me then."

I said nothing then for some twenty seconds, playing with the froth that whirled on the surface of the water.

He coughed then and said, "You have to believe me. I had nothing to do with it. I have no family, and one night I was standing next to the pool. I should have been swabbing down the tiles, and I had done a part of it. The tiles were soapy and sloppy. Then I slammed the button that starts the hot tub, its jets spouting from its sides. I came over, thinking of the wonderful time people had in it, talking and warm and happy. I can't say whether I meant to do what happened next—maybe I did. Anyway, I slipped—then my head hit the side of the pool. It hurt bad, like a fiery iron ball that hit my head, and then I was dead. I didn't know anything about it at first; I was dead but I didn't know anything, until the next morning when they pulled my body from the water but I stayed. That was the wonderful thing, I, whatever 'I' might be, stayed where I wanted to be." He laughed then, his soft laugh, and looked at me. He was almost pleading.

"But if no one saw you then, how does it happen that I see you now, and where did you find your swimsuit?"

"That's a secret." I cannot tell you how childish he could seem.

"What is the secret, your skin or your suit?"

"It's nothing that I can control. People walk into the whirlpool and without being aware of it give me flesh. Not in gobs, of course not. But what they are flows to me, builds me up and suits me. But I don't have a suit. These black hairs on my chest and belly and back—I can see people's eyes flickering up and down me—and the widow's peak, all of that comes from other people. You of course. But my swimsuit? Well, the froth of the whirlpool helps out a lot in shielding me, but the swimsuit is simply more hair. I am very manly around my prick."

"Do you have a navel?"

"Of course not."

"And when we leave, what happens to you then?"

"We all share around. I have no idea how it happens, but my flesh, which had been the flesh of everyone in the whirlpool, comes around again. They are remade, almost from the moment their foot rests on the first ledge of the stairs. I become the ephebe you sometimes see, and you don't recognize me."

"But at last I did."

"This is my second life, and it's so much better than my first. Let me enjoy it."

"Of course, of course," I said.

"And for all I say, I don't understand any of this, any more than you. I was not an engineer, not a biologist, not anything until now. And the people are so sweet."

"Of course," I said in surprise, not daring to tell him that people thought he was frightful and finding myself shaking his repulsive hand as I stood up and walked to the stairs of the hot tub. I put my hands on the rail and pulled myself up. I felt unclean, I was unclean, every inch of my flesh. People in the whirlpool waved to me and I waved back, unclean, unclean, every well-fed person among them, unclean. We were his body, his oily, witchy body, unclean.

What were we to do about him? But no one could believe what I only in part believed, so the question was really what I was to do about him. The question preoccupied me through December. Through Advent and Christmas, the Slaughter of the Innocents and Epiphany, I worried round what I was to do. I felt called on and unclean.

I couldn't stake him out as though he were Dracula. What would Dr. Van Helsing do? I have to think outside the hot tub.

It was not simply that my flesh was unclean; it was sexual. I had rolled in him, he had rolled in me, and I could not escape his odor, his touch, his intimate parts, those hidden behind the horrors of his pubic hairs. He was coral and barracuda. Something had grown into him that would not let him go, would not let us go. The churning hot tub was contaminated, even though the tub was drained and scrubbed twice each week—what could recall it to its primal, innocent state before the fall? Benjy's fall? I paid no attention to his absent belly-button.

Did I have to destroy his haunt, the ghost that was his essence? If I left that question aside, as I thought I had to, for though I was high church I had very little hope or belief in exorcism. Imagine me waving the cross and the missal above the whirlpool! What, then, was left? How to forbid him our bodies?

I went to the gym a few times as before and met him looking at me questioningly. In time he felt reassured. He would brush his widow's peak as though everything was all right. The few times we talked he was quite confidential; he treated me as his best friend. It was almost as though he had discovered his long-lost kin.

Then I noticed something at the gym, and that sparked an idea. It did not seem a brilliant idea, but it was all I could dredge up out of my shallow brain. I drove to the gym one Tuesday morning when few people would be present. Tuesday morning they cleaned the hot tub, so on that day it was always cold, bone-chilling cold in the morning, and few people attended it that day—a few natatory masochists yes, but not often. The sun shone brilliantly through the light snow that had been coming down since early morning. The snow was not heavy, but it did make all the more certain that few people except the staff would be there. Eric was the lifeguard as I knew he would be that day, but he seldom paid much attention to anyone, not even a beautiful woman, after he signed the clientele in.

Near the hot tub on a stable tripod was a large fan that the management used sometimes to control the heat. I don't know what voltage it carried, but it was certainly strong enough to move the air through some 90,000 cubic feet of space. It was now going full blast. When no one else was in the hot tub I slapped the button to start the jets and stepped into the cold, whirling waters. In a few minutes the enervation flowed through me as Benjy began grudgingly to take shape. I hardly provided him all the flesh he needed.

"Hello," I said, and he nodded.

"It's really very kind of you." He was so polite. The widow's peak on his forehead nodded, and his thin black swim suit fluttered beneath the cold foam.

I stayed in longer than I would have normally. After fifteen minutes I was tired, oh so tired and cold, and Benjy was as muscular as ever. I drifted to the stairs. Then, as swiftly as I could, I pulled myself out of the whirlpool, step by step, and staggered against the fan, staggered in such a way that it swayed on its tripod and plunged into the water.

It crackled and burst and the smell of electric rot, the fry of a foreign flesh, filled the room. I fell into one of the plastic chairs. It was just as much as I could do and I fainted, perhaps for ten seconds, and recovered consciousness to see Eric running over to pull the plug on the fan; but being Eric he was much too late. Whoever was in the hot tub was fried, and no record of who it could have been was written on Eric's board. When the police questioned me I denied ever knowing the man in the pool. So Eric was fired in no short order after he admitted that he should have told me not to stay in the whirlpool so long. Ten minutes was the maximum written in bold letters on the board of regulations—not that any of us had ever paid the board any heed. So it was Eric's fault, not mine. I was almost sorry, but he was never that good a lifeguard.

The county closed the gym for a month. It took the officials three days to clean out the hot tub and weeks to come to the decision that such fans should never be used again. People flocked to the hot tub thereafter, but I never approached it again. When many people were in it I watched, but the widow's peak never appeared. I would limp away, unclean.

That is all I can say. Don't believe me.

THE BLOODY TUGBOAT

There is not much that I can say in this short time, but when my friends find my body in a few days, unspeakably mutilated no doubt, you will know that there was a reason for my death. I would like to have a reason for it. It is not that I understand why my death is necessary. I had seen something. Perhaps I did something. That was all.

You might like to have names, but my friends know my name. I am Richard Broadbent—that's it, no need for my name again. The other names in this story I don't know, mainly because they were out of my hearing. I do hear reasonably well, but most of what happened this afternoon was too far from me. Having retired from my labors as an historian and an academic, I devoted most of my idle time watching the river that moves back and forth as the tides and the moon would have it. It is a remarkable river, one hundred miles from the ocean and still obedient to the ocean's tides. I had a wide panorama that spread beneath the French windows on the west side of my cottage. I no longer launched myself onto the river. My father, who owned the cottage years ago, took me out on a rowboat to go fishing. We used a cove that lay at the end of a stone footpath that leads down from the kitchen. Later I had a canoe, splendid for middle-age flirtations after my wife died, and later still a kayak. I had no children—that is an important detail of this story—pay attention. Now my legs are withered, I'm eighty years old, so I don't get out as much as I used to. I live alone and watch the river in its slow surge left and right at my feet.

Yachts and sailboats you see most frequently in the placid seasons. For no reason I can account for I am fondest of watching the tugboats. They have work to perform in the summer, nosing long, lazy barges up and down the river. Perhaps it's the very strength incarnate in the small snub-nosed tug that attracts me, sitting here in my wheelchair—where I won't be sitting for long. And they are painted so gaily, orange and blue and green. A tug has more pride than you can see in a servile yacht or a sailboat that has no use about it. It turns to its use.

In the winter the only boat you see is a tug, hacking and breaking the ice apart. It's bitter cold here in the winter, so the ice grows thick out in the river. It's tempting ice for skaters, but no good because of the tides that are still in the ice, under it, gnawing away at it. Sometimes you hear it, crack, crack, the dull cracks made by a sullen giant's boots. So every day after a deep freeze the gay tug in its green and orange and blue paints, its chimney puffing for a fare-thee-well, will be chugging out in the middle of the river, slowly beating the ice apart, the sun shining and the shattered ice shining. It's a fine sight.

But one late afternoon in a very bad winter it was no good sight at all. I had not been at home all day, because some good friends in that horrid cold—when you're a withered cripple your real friends show themselves, ostentatiously—well, they took me here and there, mainly to the grocery. An expedition, following the chill paths of Shackleton and Scott! So I had seen nothing of the river through the short January day. I wheeled up to the French windows, approaching them on the diagonal after a stop at the bar—a double whiskey, thank you, and I topped it off. A great, thunderous crack of ice on the river turned my head. So then I saw it.

But not at all what I expected. No gay tug sporting on the cold, frivolous waters, no.

It was a brutal, dark-red tugboat that I saw, dark red streaks like dried blood, but not dry, rumbling through that late afternoon on the river. It was larger than any tug I had ever seen on the river to that day, larger than any tug I had ever seen. It was not as large as a dingy, pitted destroyer, but it seemed that large—compact violence, framed by the tattered trees of our two banks and framed by the taut, bowed, cantilever railroad bridge that stretched from bank to bank. Larboard or starboard, this imposing tugboat gave the world no mind. But from my first skew-eyed look at it I could sense that it was my boat. Don't ask.

In one glance it scared me, everything that it carried uncanny like a bad dream.

Much of what scared me I couldn't see at first. There was no sense to its motion, lumbering and grinding away at the ice it was made to beat down. Its prow was pointed west upriver. As though foiled it backed down slowly, five feet and then down ten feet. Water gushed from its stern, the chimney gushed black smoke as the tug lunged forward, plowed through the shards of ice it had mashed down, and once more began to edge downstream so carefully. It made no sense.

Man overboard! That was it! This roiling, dark, grinding ship could only make sense if it searched for a man it had lost. Lost in such awful ice. That spoke to me. They were looking for the corpse of a man dead for too long, too long. I can't tell you how long it's been.

As I thought of how hopeless it was, despairing for the sake of the men who had no time to despair, the sun edging close to the horizon now streaked in scarlet, a man shouted—a small, weak shout from such a distance. Now I noticed him and the rest of the crew, who until this moment had been dwarfed to insignificance by the giant, grotesque ship. The man held a rope that plunged beneath the ice. He was pulling it in slowly, arm after arm, pulling up a body dangling in a grapnel, its arms and legs and head pulling back to the ice as though the body was made of iron that the magnetic ice would not release, water pouring from the corpse's mouth. The man at the rope was exhausted, pulling against that magnetic field.

Despite everything that fought against the dwarfs, at last they pulled the body over the tires on the hull and the rail and spilled the stiff flesh of the body on the stone-cold deck. Dead men feel nothing, but despite their deadness we treat them like living, substantial flesh.

I had a glimpse of the man. By this time I had pulled my binoculars out of their cabinet and set them to my eyes to watch at this great distance the silent men. I focused the lens. The tug rolled sideways, lifting the dead man and dropping him, dead from my eyes. His cheeks were pocked by the time, by the ice, who could say? His skin was gray, almost green. He wore a shock of red hair, a high brow, rapacious, sharp cheekbones that the river mud had preserved. He was the man you did not want to meet in your nightmares, but you always did. Well, in my dreams, and I drowned in so many.

Who was he? He should have been a member of the crew since they knew how to search for him and find him—the tug knew how to find him—but his clothes suggested otherwise. It is not that the clothes of sailors change very much over the years, but the ineffable cut of his jib made him older. Much older. Not even decades of summers could warm his bones that the bitter winters had drenched him in.

Then this dead man's eyes flashed open.

He rolled onto his elbow as more water poured from his mouth, reached up to take a purchase on the rail, and stood up—but he did not let loose his hold on the rail as he stood and swayed with the waves.

He looked at the dwarf sailors, men so much smaller than he—questioning them with his imperious look one by one.

It was easy for him to discover the man who had saved him from the icy slosh.

The corpse, the man returned to life, had no gratitude. He took up the grapnel, ran its flukes against his hand, testing the edge of their keen blades, and flicked them out, the rope singing through the palm of his ice-hard left hand, jerked it and eviscerated the man who had brought him out of the cold darkness.

The man fell forward, screamed, knocked his knees on the deck, and died as his forehead ate his guts.

I heard the scream like a wrench of deadened blood, a scream from far away though through my binoculars the death was in my hands.

If the crew had been insignificant before, dwarfish, ant-like, they were doubly small now as the tugboat fattened above their caps and under their boots. The dead man laughed, ripped the grapnel from his savior's belly, and took out the life of another victim, snatch and grab.

It would make no sense to tell you how this dead man walked up and down the tug, up to the wheelhouse and down to the galley, destroying many and releasing a few. But those few men he released, for no clear reason I could grasp, he forced to clamber over the side and find their way to the shore across the ice floes. Often those small islands cracked or slipped aside and pitched the men to a swift, cold death. And the men who reached the shore still had to shove through the snow and the trees to reach the highway a hundred yards away. It was Sunday, and no traffic showed.

I watched this debacle through my binoculars, horrified, adjusting the focus. No, 911 never occurred to me—but how could it?

At least a half-hour had passed since the dead man had made of the tugboat a slaughterhouse. Bloody, iron stripes in the air hung draped on the freezing sunset, and in that dubious light the tugboat flickered. With the last of the crew accounted for the dead man dropped the grapnel onto the deck in a great clatter and began to climb to the wheelhouse once more, passing the name of the ship next to the ladder. *The Bildad Bruiser.* In the wheelhouse he took up the body of the captain and swung it to the deck below.

I fell asleep at the wet slam of the captain.

When I woke less than an hour had passed, but much had changed. *The Bildad Bruiser* had turned, its flanks larboard and starboard bumping at the masses of ice, turned and turned until its prow pointed downstream, chugging down from the west. Looking at its massive structure swollen from the deaths onboard it, I remembered my dream, though not enough of it to make any sense. I saw the tug heaving out of the river. The muddy waters streamed from its blood-wet iron sides. Unbelievably its furnaces roared, burning to burst. I saw men shoveling coal, but they were all dead—the tug could not be stopped. It was a boat that should have had no room in that broad, shallow river, but it was my boat and my river—it was inescapable, framed by the banks and by the iron railroad bridge that humped to the sunset sky, and me in my wheelchair, withered legs and all. I shook myself awake, trying to pierce the dark sky. I lifted the binoculars from my lap and focused.

Did I give birth to this?

In the wheelhouse a shock of red hair peered out. The dead man, starting to disintegrate in the cold, fresh air, his flesh slipping off his bones, waved to me and tempered his touch on the wheel. Part of his middle finger knocked off, but his touch never wavered. The tug straightened, prepared to ram the cove.

And it did. Its engines flared and gushed as it slowly ran up onto the ice, resting upon the ice of the cove for only three seconds before the ice collapsed beneath it. The floor of the cottage shook and shook beneath me, the chair hunched and scrabbled, wheeled, caught in the rag rug. My whiskey glass spilled on the floor empty. I was awake, never before so awake. And the dead man, piecemeal, dead and green, nodded to me. He saw me, backwards as it were, through the complicated lenses that revealed me to him, far away and small. He watched me as though in a cross-hairs.

I cannot escape, he has me now, and he's clambering up the side of this bank. It is difficult and slow, his ascent. He is coming apart, but he still holds onto the grapnel that he picked up as he left the tug. He will be here soon, his faith to meet me is so great.

He is knocking on the kitchen door. I understand him. He will not take the easy way through the French windows.

He is pounding on the door with his grapnel.

THE BRIGHT THIN ROOM

I

I don't know if this is the story of the house that wasn't there, the story of the unborn, or the story you hear every Christmas, that there is no room in the inn. Since it's my story as well as Marion's its boundaries are very confused. Writing the story after more than fifty years have passed, sitting in my office beneath the domes of central Philadelphia, now that the city is at last rationalized as far as Benjamin Franklin would be concerned, whose glass ghost house floats only a block from me, I can't be sure where the story ends or where it begins or what purpose it might serve. Let's say it's our story.

Whatever story it may be, it started long ago, considerably longer ago than my father believed. For him and for Marion it began that morning when she looked out the window of her class and saw that house, five miles across the valley. In the late-summer haze it shimmered as though through a scrim, caught in the climactic moment of a transformation in a fantasy drama, set on a provincial stage of the early nineteenth century, somewhere off the map in Central Europe; and the house never ceased to have for her that air of the antique and faërie, the place of ill-defined borders. It was a comedy, but deadly serious.

"At first," she told my father, setting the tea-cup carefully on its shelf, "I was only struck by its pale gold wood in the isolation of the muggy light. But it looked so near, I could have put my hand out to touch it, like that phrase of Lamb's in 'Old China': distance cannot diminish it, figuring up in the air." Doing the dishes with him after supper she was struck again by the sight that had preoccupied her for those few moments before she turned to her students and began to lecture on the dry delicacies of Elia. "It was so fragile in the middle of the woods."

He looked at her, a slight, dark woman who for a moment dipped her jutting chin, a simple woman who wore no jewelry. "You talk as if that was the first time you saw it," he said, handing her a pot to dry. She wasn't very good at washing.

"You'd think so. I've taught in that room three semesters now; and since I can't bear to talk with anyone before I start a lecture I stand at the window, not really looking out to see anything, but looking out anyway, and you would have thought that I'd have taken in all the details of the valley from that angle. But I can't remember the house."

"The way you describe it, it must have been built around the turn of the century."

"Oh it's older than that, Teddy, it has to be."

She would call it later the house that is not there. That morning it was a two-story brown-wood, late Georgian house without any gingerbread she could make out from that distance; it was severe. From the high steel, brick, and vinyl classrooms of the college that rises on the hills east of the river, she could see the house shining like a small, narrow fire in the haze that lay above and below it. The house did not float, fixed firmly in the underlying granite, but it seemed to have the will to float, from the distance of the classroom looking like the balsa model of a clipper-ship, dry wood, airy, papery. In the gloom of the August haze a massive labyrinth of oak, boxwood, maple, and pine slowly receded. The morning was very still. The house was bright, steady like a flame in the sunlight. It was an accusation. No odor of roses that rose from the many gardens of the valley pervaded or impeded its bright freedom—or its accusation.

Talking like this about the house that night fixed its image in Marion's mind and prevented its floating off to join the host of the other losses she daily surrendered to habit. The house and its third-story square tower recurred to her that night as she was falling asleep, a sudden bright spot of invitation in the slumbering dark of their bed, and she remembered it next day after lunch as she was walking down Adam Street to their apartment and noticed catty-corner to the diner a house that might have been her house's young cousin four times removed, without the tower and the sober porch, that airy sight on the tide of trees. She suddenly realized it was her house; it wasn't Teddy's, my father's, though he listened to her attentively.

The distant cousin to her house was having an addition put on, probably to room students at exorbitant rates. Details now stood out that for years your eye had ignored; you see then they've changed, and they carry with them for your inspection everything else that has changed while your back was turned, getting on with your life. It wasn't her town anymore. At the college she was engaged in a work of consciousness that will-she nil-she was aimed at the demolition of the town's accepted worlds.. She could not evade her small shame. It was not the same river that Henry Hudson had sailed up to meet the Lenape Indians.

But that was the last time for some weeks that the house that is not there came into her mind with any intensity. The summer session ended in a gnarl of papers and finals, and immediately she and Teddy left for the mountains. The spare cabin they had reserved, below them the twenty other cabins precisely like it, the ceaseless pace of the pines, the spruce lawn she quipped, and the lake with its narrow pier—all were something else than the house. Only from the edge of her eye did she catch a look at the house before it glided off.

When the fall semester began and she returned to the same classroom, this time for a seminar on Keats and the dry splendors of *Hyperion,* as the students were coming into the room and shyly meeting each other again, she looked for the house on the first day but could catch a sight of it, not even the sparkle of its windows. At first she was sure she was missing it. It was very small, very tiny from this distance. It was so far away to see such a thing; it should occupy no more of the field of her vision than the arc between the

Pleiades in the hump of Taurus, potent and fugitive. But as she looked up and down the few miles of the valley where the house had to be and became more convinced that it was the house that is not there, a cold ache of loss began to hurt at her side. "Deep in the shady sadness of a vale," she whispered, turning to her students and beginning the lecture, putting her house away. But the ache would not stop.

Beginning to wake up that Saturday she could sense the house somewhere nearby, in her. She was walking in the fields, but she couldn't see the house because ceaseless pine trees and the one big willow at the edge of the field had overgrown the path that led to it. Her feet were wet; her shoes were inadequate, she hadn't worn her walking shoes. How could she have been so stupid to come out walking in her sneakers? She had to wade the stream. Then she was looking up at the house.

My father was still sleeping, his blond head tousled on the pillow. Rolling off the mattress she crept into the living room and called Joanne.

"I'm looking up at the house because it stands on a slope that rises as if to hip-level of the trees. I don't know what kind of trees those are, they're very old; but the third-story tower doesn't rise above the trees that are standing behind the house. I think I only saw the house from the college because the front yard where I'm standing on the stone walk is long enough. But the yard is narrow. The walk is made from flat stones that must have been carried from the stream. But the stream was deep and strong; it must have been deep for my shoes to get so wet. I don't know what possessed me to cross it."

"Can you see yourself crossing it?"

"I don't know, Joanne." For a moment Joanne's round bear-face rose up in her mind across the seminar table in New Haven and hid the river. "I must have seen myself crossing it; yes, there's a big stone in the center of the stream that thrusts itself sideways like a locomotive. The porch is on the narrow front of the house, not the long side that looks across the yard to a strawberry patch. The porch is high, with a single straight-back chair looking down on me, it's painted a light green, a late summer green. You're there, I think."

"Do you go in?"

"I don't think so. It's really just enough to stand there. I'm very happy, deep-down content you know. There is gingerbread, but it's very restrained. It's that degree of ornament that will not call attention to itself. It's only there to soften the lines of the house so that the house stands on this side of severity. The gingerbread doesn't obscure the strength of the house. It's a narrow house but deep. I'm very happy."

"How are you and Teddy?"

"We're fine. You do like him, don't you? He's sleeping now, otherwise I'd have told him the dream first. I had to tell somebody, right now, or I'd have lost it."

"Well I'm always up at this hour. It's a fine time before things become too loud in the streets, not that it ever stops. I like it though. Something always going on in Denver, the air's clean, and it's never like the woods where you live that strangle you with their growing. But folks will live anywhere. And the library's down the street."

Marion laughed and told Joanne about the reception where Edward had cut off the latest bore in his department by exaggerating all the budget paranoia of the college. The faculty would be fired en masse, the students leave in disgust, town revenues dry up, the new fire station cancelled, the president incinerate the administration building and run naked through the streets (yes, he's an arsonist, didn't you know?). And she told Joanne what she had cooked two nights before that.

"The house is like the old china cups in that Lamb essay you made me explicate ten years ago; and Teddy and I are like them, just an old couple, thirty years for them, precious little Bridget and Elia, three years for us—and we're none of us married!"

"Don't press your luck, dear."

With the house fixed in her mind she began to look for it again, but with almost no success. The house seemed to be moving ahead of her, always slipping off into a space prepared for it among the trees, a new space where the ground had been sown, tilled, and harvested. Just once one morning did she think she saw it two miles down the valley from its place in the china cup, its tower just peeking up from the slow roil of the season of mists below it; but when the mellow fruitfulness had risen there was nothing there. And after that it was hardly surprising that she couldn't see the pale house, probably lost in the fierce change of color that had overtaken the trees in the frost one implacable morning. For a number of weeks because of the hurt in her side she couldn't bear the disappointment of looking for the house that was going ahead of her.

"Fair youth beneath the trees, thou canst not leave thy song." In one of her notes she writes, "I ache for the little town emptied." Dressed in a berry-red tunic he was turning away from her the moment she heard his throaty song, "J'ai trouvé l'eau si belle," he was singing, "que je m'y suis baigné," and very far off in the woods, deep in the shady stillness of the vale she heard, "jamais je ne t'oublirais," because she had forgotten the house and she had to find it. Years before she had memorized the Québeçois song of national loss. They were walking around the corner of the house at the border of the land, and she had allowed it to be passed on, but not for love as he thought. None of it was for love.

But she admits that Teddy does remember the stream of the builder and the bank where the small purple flowers grow. He remembers the bright imagination in which memory grows and the stream in the haze and the thick roiling mist.

As she woke up that afternoon and put the book down she knew that she had to start looking for the house again, with more hope of seeing it because the leaves were starting to fall and because, after all, it really wasn't the house that is not there. She had seen it that morning in early August, really, as my father knew. When he told me the story he emphasized that it must have existed for her to have been both so clear and so off-hand about it. And the dreams that she told him or, when he had to leave so early in the morning or when it was Saturday, that she told Joanne, they were simply that, dreams. And one morning the next week, just before she was going to turn from the window to her notes and her lecture, she saw it. And a great peace fell upon her.

No mist was rising from the river or the orchards. The weather had been clear for days, rehearsing the clarity of winter; you could see the mountains thirty miles off in a detail that was impossible except for two or three days every month since the air was so bleached by a continent of smokestacks and acids. She had to admit that Joanne had some reason for preferring the urban sobriety of Denver. So there was no surprise. It was simply that the house sat in its foundation waiting to be seen by anyone who knew where to see it. The impediments to seeing it were the minute particulars of the landscape which she could only appreciate in the sparkle of the air that revealed the world itself for the first time. There were fields that she had never noticed, gray threads that were old stone walls and white threads that were fences, oblique lines to the tops of the trees that indicated hollows or streams that lay behind them, openings that might be dirt roads, other houses nearby—one in fact to the right, a gray frame house with a red barn, its far side starting to sag, that might be less than a mile from her house, the house that was there, and route 82 lying a mile perhaps below the field that led to the barn. She could remember that.

The light was so clear that she thought she could see on the porch the green straight-back chair. The house was narrow, narrower than she remembered but deep, thin and fixed in the granite rise like an axe-blade; at the bottom of the yard poked a tree-stump. In the window upstairs someone sat on a red chair sipping a glass of water. In the window downstairs a gold light filled the room.

"I don't believe it," my father said that afternoon as he sliced onions for the casserole. "Not at that distance, whatever Lamb has to say to say about china cups, you couldn't see such a thing. You're making it up, or your eyes did."

"I probably am. I'm sure I am. I want someone living there, taking care of the house. No one takes care of things anymore. That barn on the next farm is falling apart, and they'll build some monstrosity, probably a slab of a condominium with mown grass and dead trees. But I did see something red in the window that was probably a chair and a glint of light that must have been some sort of glass floating above it."

"You don't have to worry. If it's as perfect as you say, someone must be living there and taking very good care of it."

That weekend she drove up route 82, looking on the left for any road that might go off in the direction of her house or the gray farmhouse with the barn. It seemed that she had driven too far, but she reminded herself that that's the way it always is when you're driving an unfamiliar stretch of road looking for an unfamiliar address. She had asked my father whether he'd like to go too but was not surprised when he begged off. She was relieved. He wasn't interested in houses, and this was her house.

She'd said to Joanne that morning, "It's not like I want the house."

"I understand, I'm the same way. Men don't know about houses anyway. We're the ones who wash the dishes and put them away, fold the clothes, put up the linen, hang the curtains, appreciate the light and the closets, sweep the floors."

"It's the space, it's knowing that the space is proportioned, that it both sharpens your attention and accepts your body. But I don't have to own that, I just have to know it's there."

"The fox has his hole," her former professor intoned, "and the birds their nest."

"Please, Joanne!"

So this was her mini-vacation, her hike by herself. And when she found a dirt road with a mailbox that said Carpenter she drove up it some two miles (she confessed to Teddy that she'd failed to note the odometer again) before the woods opened into a field of cows immobile in the stored-up heat of the late October morning and across the field the red barn itself, sagging with an illegible chaw sign that she could only make out from its size. No one would repaint that sign; the company was defunct and the side of the barn invisible from whatever bend in the road they had painted it for fifty years ago.

Mrs. Carpenter came to the door with a cleaver in her hand and two cats nuzzling her fat slippers. She stood at the door for their entire talk, but she knew nothing of the house. "That land," she gestured with the cleaver, "hasn't been used for years. Our boundary line's in there, it abuts George March's on the other side of the gully, near as anybody can remember. But it's all overgrown. Bad ground. Rattlesnakes down there too. Mr. Carpenter, he doesn't mess around down there, and I sure don't neither. But you go ahead if you want to."

Walking around the edge of the yard to the field on the other side of the Carpenters' house Marion could feel Mrs. Carpenter's eyes on her the whole way until her head disappeared in a field of faded loosestrife. Thistles and wild carrot grew there too, and chicory, the red spear-heads of sumac leaves, brambles and wild-grape, and everywhere the mustard-yellow loosestrife.

She couldn't push her way far into the woods. Mrs. Carpenter had been right about the rattlesnakes which seemed to lie on the other side of any rotten tree that had fallen, not that she minded snakes. The wild grapes pulled and weighed on the trees, but not many trees fell. It was precisely that kind of exuberant growth that had made Joanne flee the East Coast; but this was late October, the end of the growing year. Everything lay in each other's arms, *birds in the trees, those dying generations,* every green stem and trunk grew out of each other's fall. Free ground was knee-deep in leaf and branch and quagmire. The walking-stick which she had picked up before she had gotten very far in came up brown muck every time she thrust it into those spaces. Then she had to try evading them by picking out a path around, which every time seemed to sidle off from the direction she wanted to go. She was Alice, and Mrs. Carpenter was the Red Queen, not an idea she liked, and she wondered why she hadn't brought a knife or a machete, and boots.

At one point she came to a small pond. On a log half sunk at the end of it, half-fallen on the bank, sat a snapping turtle perfectly still and alert. She bent down. She must have waited there motionless five minutes watching the turtle, while the turtle and its slab of nose waited watching nothing but the glare of the day and the place of her shadow in it. The shell was thicker than the nail on Teddy's big toe, she told Joanne later, and wondered why women's toenails are so amiable, men's so admirably hateful. Dull reds and dull dark greens checkered the shell. She waited five minutes breathing no more than the adepts at the Zen Center in the next county. When she moved she was for an instant as light as the house resting on top of the sun's light. Then she shoved on. After a half hour, when she could still see off to her right the sunshine that lit up the way to the Carpenters' field she was struck by a panic that if she did find her way further into the woods she'd never find her way out again. When she floundered out scratched and flushed, she could feel Mrs. Carpenter's satisfied eyes far across the loosestrife field, watching her failure. The color had leaked out of the late afternoon. But before Marion retreated she saw ahead through the thickest tangle of underbrush a creek, small purple flowers on its bank, snapping turtles sunning themselves in the late light, and set square in the middle a rock larger than she'd have thought shaped like some kind of locomotive; and the coalman waved.

When she pushed into the tangle again and came to the bank of the creek, she saw on the other side an old rock wall. More like the trace of an old wall, for stones lay jumbled on all sides. Through the branches she could just make out a stone post at the end of the wall, but the stone post was walking. It made no boundary clear. Boundaries flicker through the woods, and you don't know where you are. She backed out into the field.

To avoid Mrs. Carpenter's eyes she circled the field in a great arc to the west and north, though it didn't help; she could feel the woman's eyes breaking through the barn. On the top of a hill silhouetted against that lavender-peach sky hulked the gross black bodies of a dredger and a crane deserted for the night, motionless. Dead but not without peril, the implacable shovels, plucking the earth up to outlive us.

She was pleased when she came into the kitchen to find a note from Teddy saying that he was doing research at the library. She didn't want to face him yet with her story. Instead she dialed the name she found in the telephone book. Because every townie knew about old Mr. March, though no one ever saw him. His voice was dry like a rattlesnake's skin, dry and interested.

"Ms. Hornbeck"—he really did know to say Ms.—"those woods you tried to enter present some of the most difficult land this side of the Great Swamp of Satan Himself Almighty. I'm gratified to hear that you extricated yourself. But I can't tell you much more. On my side of it the cliff drops down, it's like a fifty-foot fall or so. It's harder on this side than on the Carpenters'. So you saw Mrs. Carpenter? Does she still exhibit the cleaver when you approach the premises? I haven't seen her, her husband either, for thirty years. You didn't see him? Makes sense; he was buried ten years ago. You don't want to see him. I made sure I never saw him when he was alive. No, far as I remember from the survey that was made in my father's time, there never was a house standing between our land and the Carpenters'. Nobody ever lived there but the snakes." She imagined him living in that four-room house of his, stepping through the aisles of old newspapers and catalogues stacked shoulder-high, tilting his glasses on his face trying to find that survey map from his father's lawyer which he'd looked at twenty years ago and put aside somewhere. The walls oozed age and stories; and he didn't know whose stories they were.

II

"So what do I do now, Teddy?" she said on Sunday morning as they lay in bed passing the *Times* back and forth and squabbling over the crossword. "It's getting more frustrating than you can imagine."

"Check the claims in the county courthouse."

"You are so much brighter than you ever let anybody know."

"No, it's just that you literary people are weak on the possibilities of hard research. Textual analysis can't hold a candle to the intricacies of documentary evidence. One other bit of advice though. Take an ordinance map with you. And 27 down is *albescence*."

She looked at him for a long while as though he had just manifested one of those simple forms of brilliance that touch on heaven. He later told me, long after I was a child, that that's the kind of look you can live on from a lover all your life.

She said, "I love you too."

So on Thursday she drove the twenty miles to the county-seat with an ordinance map my father bought her at the hiking shop. She didn't like going there anymore. The old courthouse, once the center of the valley when the life of the state was country, no longer stood lit by its secular stained glass in which nation and labor strode side-by-side, with a staircase deep and broad for farmers' boots, glass doors opaque to the slide of graft. The new courthouse was plastic, like the parking lot, its automatic ticket machines shrewdly sticking their tongues out; everything was visible, reasonable, perfectible, in place. In the old courthouse every angle and surface was too large for her to absorb, for anyone to absorb she presumed, and not only because she could only remember her child's-eye view of the resonant rotunda from behind her father's knees, not daring to look up at the copious dome glowing above her and the quiet click of her heels. The farmers walked quietly; the bankers walked quietly; it was more than anyone now deserved. In the new courthouse the revolving doors, the front lounge where you wrote out the new forms for the car registration, the central hallway, the two elevators, they were too small to bother absorbing because they were constructed for merely such purposes and nothing more. The information desk was nugatory, the gumballs were stale. Her father was dead. Only the minutiae of government extended beyond comprehension.

The woman at the survey office explained this and that as she opened the first ledger for Marion and pointed at the material for the Carpenters' property.

"The complication with these papers is the fact that with every sale they are researched again, so that the definition of the property or the procedure gets refined every thirty or forty years. Each time the official is different. It doesn't help, either, to attempt to legislate the procedure. Every lawmaker and every clerk knows better; I know better." She laughed and showed her brown teeth.

"So it's as though the land was always *there*, but we're less and less sure where *there* is the closer we look for it?"

"You got it."

No thicket is as impenetrable as that which legal language and geodetic language beget when they lie together; I know that professionally, so what hope did Marion have of understanding the compaction before her? At first the only obvious fact seemed the occupancy and possession of the land by Carpenters and Marches for as long as the town where she had grown up could remember. None of the evidence seemed to say, however, when the most recent survey of their two lots took place; it was that long ago. Most confusing of all was the existence of a spring which in some documents belonged to Marches, in other documents to Carpenters. In 1871 Mr. Bevert Carpenter, great-grandfather to the present Mr. Carpenter deceased, laid claim to the irrigation and water rights, that is to say to the headwaters, which no survey specified, of the ancient Vanderkill plantation; but Mr. Bevert Carpenter's father, or uncle, had sold those rights, or rights that certainly appeared the same though rights become slippery in the language as it shifts year by year, to Caleb Marsh [*sic*] in 1838, who paid $10 down for the occupancy, a further unspecified amount due in five years, with no evidence that the species was forthcoming.

But once she had gone deeply into the documents they expressed no more than the fascinated despair of the surveyor, cartographer, and lawyer to ever get it right. The strawberry hedge sprawled; the oak was broken in the storm and slowly rotted, the fungus and lichen ate it up. The stone rolled off. And the steady pressure of the earth turning over changed the look of it all. The indigene lied, the invader lied, the heir lied. And behind all the mutations and crumblings was only the will for a home. A room. A habitation. Where to live, in what materials, next to what hill? The documents only meant that we wanted to settle.

Adding to the confusion was that point in the 1830s and '40s when the boundaries, the land itself, shattered under the impact of a host of sons, half-sons, stepsons, and cousins who inherited smaller and odder parcels of land from a series of mad fathers. The daughters you could only hypothesize from the words. Feuds, elopements, murders, reconciliations failed to clarify the land. The families were too close in the summer, too far away in the winter, ever to come to any clarity, and the land suffered their uncertainties. Not that the families were totally endogamous. Other names appeared in the documents and sprouted across the land, Vanderdonks, the old Vanderkills of course, Beviers and Dubois and Ten Broucks; the old Dutch and Huguenot strata, and Hamdons and Mercers, the more recent English overlay. The Mercers were peculiar though; only one family of them appeared, the father Gyles and his daughter May, owning a small rhomboid of ground near the north peak of the March land somewhere near the headwater of the Vanderkill spring, appearing for a momentary flicker of time in the long history and vanishing, and Marion couldn't determine whether a March had sold them the rhomboid.

By the time she had arrived at this point the late afternoon was seeping into the ledgers; she could feel it in her heavy body though the long fluorescent files of lights above her never blinked. Her neck was stiff in a way that literature simply couldn't cause. Messaging her shoulders that night Teddy laughed, "Only historians know the back-breaking weight of the old manuscripts and their feathery writing." Heaving to her feet now she thought of how little she had found in the lightly dusted pages. The old graveyard at the edge of town might tell her more about the people, she hoped, but it would tell her nothing of the house. Only the house mattered; the people went through it.

The next morning she found Mr. Carpenter's stone and the stones of the other names too, the Marches and the worn-down Vanderkills, several of the stones cut in the curls of title-pages or the grand prosceniums of minor houses where the curtain is always postponed. Sara Brodhead [*sic,* she whispered] lay under a weeping-willow that languished above her like one of Blake's foolish virgins. She found no stone for the Mercers.

Her head knocked back from her dream, and she woke up. She looked at the pad and pen in her hand. She had been walking in the house, it must have been the house. The air shook, vibrating under the pressure of the dream, but golden as though it were sifting flakes of the sun or that thin warm chaff that lit up the light in her mother's brother's barn; she was three years old, and the horse shifted the mass of its brown body next to her, hidden in its stall. Her mother's brother had the same mass. She had been walking in the house, on its bare pine floor and the hallway, it seemed like a hallway, and in a long narrow room; Joanne was there. She wasn't there, she had been; the scent of her handkerchief hung in the air. Outside they were walking, they were still walking outside, she and Joanne; and someone else, the wrinkled man in the overalls down the dirt road who brought her there in his four-wheel drive; and someone else, her sister. But she didn't have a sister. Outside they were still walking.

Laying down the pen she stared at the acid paper. She never loved the books of the nineteenth century the way that my father did. To her mind they were too bulky. The print and the pictures never matched. The world of those writers of manifest destiny clot-

ted the page; if not an exercise in self-glorification, American Stud-
ies became a conscious effort to escape itself. You had to read
through it, and that was too hard. The books were ungainly and
made anyone reading them ugly. She was ugly; she swallowed her
spit and reminded herself never to say such things to my father.

Before the Dutch sailed up the river that Henry Hudson had
simply called the River of the Mountains—they called it the River
Mauritius, and some of them called it North River—the Lenape
tribes were tilling the flood plains of the valleys all along it and
hunting in the upper reaches of the mountains. They raised gourds,
acorn squash and summer squash, planted beans in the maize, hunted deer and cinnamon bear, trapped muskrat and beaver, dug out
rabbits and groundhogs; sometimes they snared pigeons, hawks, and
turkey-buzzards. They fished for sturgeon, bass, and shad. The river
swelled. By the time the Dutch set foot in the valley the influenza
and the small pox had ebbed so that the swannekens, the salt-sea
bitter people, confronted a swarm of tribes, beasts, and trees, not the
clearings that gratified the earlier settlers' sense that the land was
opening up for them. The Dutch had to deal with powers still manifest in the shape of the land. Someone was there before us. It was
another house.

The Vanderkills had bought the land, that ill-demarcated land
to which they later laid claim, from the Wanomanas Indians,
though it is very doubtful that the name of the tribe should in any
way be accepted as authentic; they bought it for a schepel of pipes,
two ancres of wine, and thirty fathoms of black wampum. The Vanderkills multiplied and thrived; the Wanomanas dimmed.

Standing up from the desk and thanking the young woman from
the Midwest who had become the archivist of local history two
months earlier, she left the library thinking that it was time to visit
the woods again. It was the end of December. My father was at-
tending a conference where he was beginning the difficult task of
interviews. Classes were finished, the year was finished, the trees
and the leaves finished, the swamps sunken and dry or blocks of ice.

The woods ought to be open to the clearing where the house stood. But not through Mrs. Carpenter's cleaver this time.

Mr. March's papery telephone voice was reassuring. "But of course, Ms. Hornbeck, yes I do remember your call." How many calls did he receive in the steep maze he had made of his house? "It would not discommode me in the least your taking a stroll through my grounds; I don't allow hunters you understand. You will forgive me for not accompanying you, I'm not so young; but you're very welcome. I do appreciate your calling ahead. Do be careful at the cliff."

"Is that what I've heard called the gully?"

"Some people before my time would call it Gilly's Gully, but in my considered judgment and my father's before me it's a cliff. It does, I do recall, drop off less sheer downvalley from me. You go east from my house."

"Thank you very much, Mr. March, it's very good of you."

"Not at all." Already she could hear his thin voice losing interest, slowing down, pulling back, pulling in to the baffles of his mind again. "You take care. Goodbye." The click of the receiver was inaudible; it took her seconds to realize he had hung up.

The next morning was clear. As she drove out route 319 and passed the right fork of 82 that led off to the Carpenter land she appreciated her luck in having such sober weather, a bit above freezing but with that dry air that would not chill you more than a day that was colder or damper. And the high cirrus blurred the winter glare. The driveway to Mr. March's, she was surprised to find, was flanked by a freshly painted white gate, and his name in serene Roman letters stood sentinel beside it. She parked near his stone house, buttoned her red eider vest, and looked with satisfaction at her boots as she swung her feet out of the Accord. This time she was ready.

At first the ground was all she had expected. She could see further; it was as though the leaves were no longer laughing in her face the way the scarlets and flashy yellows had done in October, and the undergrowth no longer grappled her knees. The ground was dry, not the sucking muck; but, she reminded herself, walking in from Mr.

March's she was above the quagmire she had blundered into from the Carpenters' fields. She had not hiked for a half-hour when she came to Gilly's Gully.

She agreed with the judgment of the March men; it was a cliff, a steep fall-off of branches, rubble, and bare granite that she could climb down, doubtless, with another person, the two of them reaching each other a hand, but not alone. Teddy wasn't there, and it was her house; he needed to find a tenure-track, and she was, she had to admit, just that little bit dizzy from the half-hour walk, not confident enough to try the cliff. So she began to find her way east, following the edge of the cliff and now and then approaching it again to see if it had yet reduced itself to a gully. But now it all became more difficult, whether because the trees and deadfall were more frequent, crouching closer, deeper, closing in, or whether because of the time she had to spend steadying herself on a limb or a stone at the edge and leaning out, it would have been hard to say. When she had lost all sense of the time the cliff came down to the ground beneath it. Was this the gully, or was that higher up? A breeze in the east started up, blowing cold in her sweat-streaked face. She began to pant and loosened the collar of her vest. She looked at her wrist, but in the pleasure of vacation she had deserted her watch on her bureau.

She had no idea of the time when she stumbled out of the woods onto a broad unexpected path. She felt like she could fall on her face. Sitting down on a stone that apparently marked a turn in the path she leaned down exhausted for some time before pulling out the sandwich she had brought and was still sitting there exhausted a few minutes later when she heard footsteps and lifted her head, helloing in case it was a hunter, to see a woman, her hair done up in a bun, walking up the path in bib-overalls, her wrinkled round face nodding.

"You look done in," she called out.

"Well, I am."

"I'm Mrs. Ten Brouck," she said as she stepped in front of Marion. "I live down this road not far and, you'll excuse me for saying so, you're on my land."

"I'm Marion Hornbeck. I'm sorry if I'm trespassing. George March gave me permission to hike on his land but I must have wandered off."

"Oh that's all right. I was just remarking. George is fine. I haven't seen him for years but George is fine." It was at that moment that Marion realized she had been seeing Mrs. Ten Brouck in town, off and on, all her life. The assertion of the woman's nose was not to be mistaken. Marion wasn't certain what the woman's relation was to the other Ten Broucks, to Marjorie or to Richard, but she was town. "George is a gentleman. And I know you Hornbecks. But how'd you come to ask him?"

"I phoned. I was trying to visit a house that I've been seeing from one of the classrooms at the college, but he and Mrs. Carpenter deny that there's any house in there. I understand of course. It's thick. I doubt that anybody's been in that jungle for a hundred years. But there is a house in there."

"Well, Mrs. Hornbeck—"

"—I'm sorry, if you'll just, Ms.—"

"—if you'll just wait a few minutes I can help you find the house. You wait right there." She turned back down the path and vanished before Marion could answer. In a short time a four-wheel drive Cherokee rumbled round the corner scraping frozen branches on both sides of the path.

Marion laughed as she clambered in, "Luxury in the middle of the forest primeval!"

"Hold on and be careful of your fingers."

Mrs. Ten Brouck drove up the road. When they came to a creek and the Cherokee forded it Marion realized that it was a lower part of the creek where she had seen the turtles and the ancient locomotive. Splashing through they drove up a narrower path; really she was astounded, she told my father a few days later when he returned unsuccessful from his interviews, astounded that the beak-nosed woman at her side was able to shove the car through the woods that now flanked them like a cold gray wall in the slight decline of the light, woods possessed of their own slow motion. Then they came out, and she looked up at the house that is not there.

"And it is not there," she said to my father, bewildered.

It had been there. Despite the rise she could see the flattened, rectangular patch at the top of the long yard where the house had once stood. From the end of the path where Mrs. Ten Brouck parked the Cherokee near the stump of a tree the yard made a slow ascent of some hundred and eighty feet through the center of which large flagstones from the creek were set, once straight as an arrow but now shaken about by the frost heaves of more than a hundred winters; the winter upon them now would heave them another inch off kilter. Behind the rise where the house had imposed itself the cliff, Gilly's Gully, lifted itself to the southwest; in the late afternoon the house had darkened early. But to Marion's right hand, as she turned slowly, absorbing the hurt in her ribs again and tilting her head back to hold up her tears, she saw a southward-facing bank where a vegetable garden must have grown on the other side of a dried-up stream. Brambles sprouted there, black-berry bushes run to seed.

But there was no doubt as she and Mrs. Ten Brouck walked past the useless flagstones, the house had been there. Twenty feet wide by forty feet deep, it had been larger to the eye, to her eye she silently amended, than to the measuring-rod and plumb-line. Because it had been high, and the tower took it up even higher. You could feel the mass of its absence in the cool air. More than a century had passed, but the trees didn't yet have a mind to put themselves forward into the space it had formed.

Mrs. Ten Brouck chatted beside her as they paced around the foundations. "Mr. Giles Mercer built the house in 1840 they say. He had come from England and bought this bit of land from Mr. Vanderkill; that was the only Vanderkill still alive who had a bit of the patent left that old Josiah Vanderkill had sold away to the Marches and Carpenters. Then in the crash of '47 he left, just left, some think he went into railroads, and nobody's sure who took the house then, some March or Carpenter with no good in mind, until it burned in the 1870s."

"He was no farmer I take it. I mean, you can't farm this land."

"No, he had a shop in town, pharmacy, dry-goods, anything to take your fancy. And clever they say, a morning, noon, and night man. Light on his feet. Oh he made an impression."

"What was the house like?"

"Here." Mrs. Ten Brouck sat down on a rock outside the foundations and began to scratch at the ground with a twig, after her boots had scuffed away the desiccated grasses. "You came in the front door of the porch to this central hallway, a big window on each side. The hallway had a grand stairs going up to the second floor, the four bedrooms there, the servants' rooms in the attic; and at the front of the hallway a stairs that went up to a tower room. There was a tower on the right as you faced the house."

"But on the first floor, how were those rooms laid out?"

"Yes, there were these two rooms on the right of the hallway. On the left, that southwest side, that was one long narrow room stretching from one end of the house to the other, like it was a long house all to itself, with three wide tall windows looking down on that sheltered space between the house and Gilly's Gully. That's where"—here she looked up—"I'll show you."

Walking carefully around the foundations, she looked up and down a dense clot of weeds.

"Look here." She held up a bramble from which a fat blood-bulb bulged. "This was Miss Mercer's garden. She was Giles's daughter. Rose-hips. This"—she reached down digging with her fingers—"this is ginseng. You see the mints over there. Sassafras you must know about. And the woods are hers too, the walnuts, oaks, locusts, chestnuts, and dogwoods. Bark-brews. She favored them all. The roots and petals she'd hang in the tower to dry." She sat down on a stone. "Now look at that," she said and pointed.

Marion looked past the foundations, following Mrs. Ten Brouck's grimy finger. She hadn't liked to look yet, feeling like the trees that she didn't have a mind to put herself forward. Now as she looked little bits and pieces and flakes of gold sparks held forth in the air of the house. Mrs. Ten Brouck was pointing at a small depression at the west side, back of the house. The ground was pulling itself in, like a navel, like the earth was girding itself for a great effort.

"He built the cistern there. You see that dry run, where a creek was? It ran down to join the stream we crossed, the Swartkill. Giles capped the spring and installed a handpump, imagine. Ever since that time the spring has waited on us."

"It must have been quite a house," Marion said helplessly.

"Yes, it was."

Mrs. Ten Brouck got up and began to walk down the yard again. Marion followed her. During the entire time they had looked at the site neither of them had stepped inside the foundations. "It's all honey-dew," she said to Joanne that night, "sacred, perilous, inviolable." As she walked down the yard, though, one happy thought struck her as she looked up. She couldn't see the college. Even on this late December day with the trees bare and the sun shining behind her, the college was not in sight. Her classroom was not in sight. And if the classroom could not be seen from here, how could this space be the space of her house? Then the house that is not there must be elsewhere.

But sophistries didn't help.

At the party that their friends gave that winter, Marion and my father celebrated a bleak New Year's Eve. She drank too much, something she did not often do, and rode home on his shoulders, singing and drumming on his head.

"Diddle diddle diddle, my man Ted, runs his mistress off to bed," she sang in her thin soprano.

The next morning when she woke and walked to the window and the window got in her face too fast she said, "I want a house."

"I understand that."

"That's bullshit!" Suddenly she was angrier than she'd ever been. It poured out of her. "You don't understand because you don't need a house, you never needed a house. You had a home, you left it. All in good time. You can do without because you've had it. So that's bullshit, you're bullshit, it's just bullshit what we're doing!"

"What am I supposed to do? Stay here, hang out, write articles? Is that going to get you a house?"

"No." She didn't even have a right to her anger. "Just listen. When my father died and we moved out of our old house, the new house wasn't a house, much less a home; it was just a place to be, just a roof and just walls. Then my uncle died too, the barn was sold, all that hay-filled light-filled room," she started to cry, "and the horses!"

"Are you sick?"

"No. Yes."

III

In February my father left her. Just in a manner of speaking, of course. Not for good, he thought, but I suspect that she knew better than he foresaw. A job that would take him two states away meant the slow loosening that most relationships suffer in even the best circumstances. When you find a tenure-track position and begin preparing for the move your attention starts to drift. You're at home but you're not, and your desire is elsewhere.

That night Marion called Joanne with the news. "Yes, we're very excited. It's just the break that Teddy needs. It'll be hard of course, but we both know that and can prepare for it. We can have Tuesday/Thursday schedules for our classes and use the long weekends. It's Interstate highway all the way. And we'll both still be looking for jobs near each other. We think we can marry next year, maybe at the beginning of the summer. Anything's possible."

In her diary Joanne wrote that it was after that particular call that she began to worry for Marion. She rehearsed again, retired in Denver, why she had never married; she wrote a few lines about someone named Carl, and scratched them out. She reminded herself to call Marion more often. After a few of those calls she cried.

So I don't need to be heavy-handed or coy or explain what the reader has surely concluded. Marion never had a child. It was more than two years later that Edward—her Teddy—met and married the woman who was to be my mother, whom I love very much, but this story isn't about her. It's about Marion, who was never my mother. It is nothing that I suffer from, never to have met and never to have known the woman Marion, who might have been my mother but who never was, it's nothing I suffer from. But I ache for it now, the mother who was never my mother, the paps that never gave me suck, that emptied, passed-by place. The house that is not there. To know of the woman that your father loved before he loved your mother, and no father ever did not, is to know you're unborn. You were never born by intent, not like our houses.

When George March died a few weeks after my father's success the town knew at once. Alert to his imminent translation, perhaps it was the thaw in the air, George telephoned the mayor, the chief elected official of the region as his whispery voice put it, to announce his decease; when the ambulance arrived he was dead. At his burial a representative of each of the old families was present. Mrs. Carpenter attended, without her cleaver, and so did Mrs. Ten Brouck; and ten days later she began her spring-cleaning. The boundaries began to loosen. That Wednesday as she was lecturing Marion broke into a cold sweat and had to sit down. She dismissed the class when her stomach began to heave; she hardly had the strength to look from the window and see the house come forward from its clearing like a Shakespearean actor about to begin a self-conscious monologue. It was the first time the house displayed bad taste. Marion left the classroom before the sentiment, "Now is the winter of our discontent," had found its first measured pause.

For a week she slept in the tiny bedroom of the apartment or lay crowded on the couch behind the coffee-table. The room is bright and breathless, and the scrubbed pine floors pale in the sun like crushed honeycomb. In the bright room the thin air invigorates and stirs, looking ahead, not unknowing, virginal, for no one has ever entered the room, no one has built it. And of those who did not build it, you cannot say they built the house either, with its single third-floor tower and complex stench of plants, its green wicker furniture and chaste gingerbread, its cold cistern in the cellar. No one contemplated its ease.

There are plans of the house, that seem dated after the death of the builder. But the date of his death is doubtful, and the date of the plans may be 1841 rather than the spidery calligraphy of the 1820s.

When she walked into the bright thin room the third time, just leaving it at the other end a small woman turned for a moment. Her small figure, her narrow fox-face panicked Marion for an instant. Between her breasts a necklace of feathers drooped, from it a small hide bag like a pendent. Speaking into the hallway she said, "Come see the spring."

Finding her way through the woods she heard the throaty song again, soft, finding its own way through the spring leaves, "Jamais je ne t'oubliais," and turning she caught a glimpse of the berry-red tunic again, or maybe a splash of blood. A scarlet bunting spun through the heat of the branches. The cleaver was stalking the bank of the creek.

After a week the thaw passed. Then it rained, torrents and torrents, the river rose and flooded the flats, and then it turned cold. A few skiffs of snow fell, not much, but the temperature grew colder and colder till the flood began to break up across the flat in great blocks and sheets of ice. It was time, Marion felt, for another hike out to the house, especially in the early Easter vacation when my father left to find an apartment; nothing he said could persuade her to accompany him. The wreckage of the ice was too strange, she had to explore it.

She decide to approach from a totally different angle this time, across the flats between the Ten Brouck and Carpenter lands. Again she paid careful attention to her boots. She waited three days for the mists to dissipate.

On the third day she began walking.

It could not have been the winter air. A late morning you remember for its clarity, so bright you would have said that the bare
tips of the maples effervesced, if that were not to say too much and
exceed the sobriety of the day. But what were you to say? No shim-
mer. No shaking of the air from the cold. The air lay beyond even a
flake of snow shaken from the high air that not a tissue of cloud revealed. No stir, it was so bright, so clear.

The point of the day that became the occasion for Marion to see
the house close up for the first time, she would say this to Joanne that
night, was its clarity. The line of trees across the fields seemed miles
away, while above them the mountains thrust forward; the slabs of ice
she was about to navigate were monstrous. The world was flattened;
far was far, near was near, and nothing hung between them.

The ground was porous, as though it had absorbed the mist that
hid it yesterday, swelling and voiding it, a part of the general
groundswell doing the earth in, frail and terribly solid. It crunched
underfoot, crunch, crunch like a dead hornets' nest; the blocks of ice
stood up on a splayed tip-toe where the sides had melted and petri-
fied. Dark mud shone in a bit of transparence, small glints of pale
green light fled to the interior and sulked. The river had risen and
shook itself out like old glass.

Placing her feet gingerly step by step she was attempting to digest the research she had accomplished at the local library during
the past few days. Mrs. Ten Brouck's mother's mother was a sister
to May Mercer. But their maiden name wasn't Ten Brouck or Dubois or Bevier. It was Fontaine. Perhaps they had wanted to assimi-
late the Vanderkill name, or perhaps the Vanderkills had co-opted
them; Marion could imagine anything. But as she read further, up
one shelf and down another, flipping through this book, reading
more deeply in that, she noticed that none of the books about the
Native Americans—the indigenes, the people—forced out and driv-
en out and cajoled out and shifted and drifted out, by the last years
of the eighteenth century erased, none of the books could come to

the point. Anthropology makes rigorous demands of itself. The ethnography was impeccable. The authors meant to be responsible to the facts of the people. They agreed that the Algonquins behaved according to the structure of a matrilineal system; but no one breathed a word of that descent.

To her left on a low hill Mrs. Ten Brouck's house stood safe above the flood. When she and Marion had parted in December she had offered nothing more. They had met, they had talked; that was enough. Marion had no intention of imposing; she would not invade the woman's small space that remained from the Vanderkill plantation.

Claire and May Fontaine were sisters. No record existed of their mother. Nor needed one. The headwaters that Giles Mercer capped was their record. He capped that in order to build his house. Marion gasped. She had always known that house. Except for the tower and the porch it was Fanny Brawne's house, the house that became hers in the myth of our literature and the demand of the tourist brochures, the house where Keats began his job of dying. That Giles Mercer built in order to have a bright thin room banked above the herb-garden, ensconced in his red-gold pine-walled autumn. Watching the death of the year drop by drop, spots of blood spattering the linen. That night when she phoned Teddy and afterwards when she phoned Joanne she told them both about Keats. Very little about the house. In the frizzling light of the deep freeze glare of the morning, the miniaturized woods where Gilly's Gully snaked along lay at the foot of the mountains. Her lungs labored from the bite of it. The growing pain at her side made her briefly consider the chance of pneumonia. Could that bide in you, not appear but silently tear at you?

She had to be careful. The valley caused more allergies, people claimed, than anywhere else in the country. Even her parents, native to the valley, had asthma. The hay she loved in her uncle's barn glowed full of a gold disease; she had to be careful. Her mother died of pneumonia, and her father had not lived much longer. The cemetery they lay in was an extension of suburbia, an unrotting lawn in which one square stone was no different from another. Suffocation.

When she came to the end of the path she saw the house.

Now that she saw it up close she knew why it sat there at the top of the clearing. It had taken the woods up into itself; it was pine and oak, it was birch, it was the cherrywood and elder. It was the maple syrup crystalizing inside in its cupboards; it was the sun that had soaked through them and the rain that had soaked to their roots. It was like the snapping turtle's shell that had focused the dark lights of the creek bottom and bestowed an enduring structure. The gingerbread fretted its sweetness. Nibble, nibble.

When the door opened she saw the hand on the knob, but she didn't see the face.

"Now that you're here, you might come in," a pleasant, cultured voice said. His breath clouded the air behind the door. It was warm inside.

"I don't like to trespass."

"It's no trespass. Mr. March told me of your polite request for permission to step on his land."

"You don't have a number." She choked down the giggle that rasped the back of her throat. "You don't have a phone, do you?"

"No, but I heard. Please come in. My daughter could brew some bark-tea. It's very healthy."

"I'm sure, yes, I know it is." *She's not your daughter, she's not your daughter.* She spoke the words as clearly as she could in her mind; she was almost afraid she could hear herself uttering the words out loud. "But I can't, I have to get home."

"Goodbye then," he said as the door closed. "It's nice to have a home."

She walked down the scattered flagstones as deliberately as she could. When she reached the path at the bottom of the yard she ran and ran and ran till she could run no further and threw herself down on the sheets of the ice. In a few days, after Edward returned with news of his apartment, she explained how she had slipped and scraped the palms of her hands.

To understand later what happened my father and the police

looked into everything, even the shorthand notes that her students were anxiously scrawling in her courses, more anxiously than usual as her lectures became increasingly elliptic.

"'Dear Reynolds, I have a mysterious tale, and cannot speak it.' What was unspeakable? What he had said in *Hyperion*. For it is not true. Keats had misunderstood, fundamentally, not true 'that first in beauty should be first in might.' Are the white Americans, the swannekens, first in beauty in comparison to the Algonquins? In *Lamia* is the casual seduction of Mercury more beautiful than the writhing of the snake? But Keats learned. If the aesthetic will to power is not true, what is true? What did his ugliness teach him, little Master Johnny Keats, all five feet five of him? 'Deathward progressing to no death was that visage.' In the narrow room I don't know who she is, I stand shocked, full of shock, uprooted 'in her benignant light.' You're held up in eyes that you mean nothing to. Before Rilke's insight that every angel is terror, that beauty begins in terror, no other poet than Keats came as close to the indrawn brutality of godhead, 'all breathing human passion far above.' Unspeakable. Godhead, power, whatever that is, it even speaks a different syntax, and it tempts us to believe that we've almost understood it; prepositions become enclitics, participles are impartial, they're nouns. For there is no abiding, there's no place to live, to settle, where such a gold and lunar light looks down on you, where the sun sweats its disease. Though in mid-May health might come, at the beginning of the month we suffer from 'a sickening East wind,' we fever and suffer. And May was a daughter of the rebel Titan, Atlas."

The small woman at the blackboard spun and jabbed at it. Somehow she had become smaller, the students thought, shrunken and darker, the intensity of her thought burning her up inside.

The course was rigorous, but at the end of the semester they recognized that she read their essays with great care. Her comments were lucid. Joanne examined their notes for the police and shrugged; Marion left so much implicit, but she had always identified with her subject.

In late May after Marion had graded all the essays and the finals and handed in all the paperwork, when she was free, she took her final walk.

That morning she woke early. She had not dreamed. My father says that when she woke at that hour it was from a deep sleep from which she returned, awake instantly and clear-headed, with no dreams, no baggage. It was night, not five yet, but a shadow of the dawn lay on the wall at the foot of the bed, out of the window shaking the birds up that filled the last great darkness of night in a squabble of cheepings and brightnesses. The lightning-bugs were occasional and dim. She slipped out of bed and dressed. Did she look at his blond head? She ate a heel of bread and cheese and drank the chilled coffee from the night before. Then she drove out 319 and parked the car off the shoulder of the dirt road some fifty feet from the March house; she must have felt that between Mrs. Carpenter and Mrs. Ten Brouck he was the neighbor least likely to be disturbed by her walking the old Vanderkill land again.

I imagine her walking in, a dark, slight figure in that fresh early light. The land was changed again, and not just the same as the spring before because this was the year that the tent-caterpillars were hanging their homes out, draped and clogged in the gray cloth webs as though summer were the time for hibernation not winter, thick as a great gray caravanserai that the pilgrims would strike in the night and be suddenly gone again, if the caterpillars didn't do so much damage. Like the earth had a long breath, seven years long, and she had breathed out their homes. Marion walked in the way she had in December, apparently clambering down Gilly's Gully and rejoining Mrs. Ten Brouck's road below the pool. A woodthrush bubbled off to her right. Then she walked up the road to the yard of the house. That's where they found her letter.

She vanished in May, "rich in the simple worship of a day"; she would have put it that way if she had thought to write it down, but she didn't. When they searched for her they found a letter placed neatly on the stump of a tree, wrapped in a bit of plastic sandwich wrap and weighted down by a rock, at the bottom of a long narrow clearing. She wrote it in the neat hand that Edward, my father, and her colleagues and her students were familiar with, though a bit shaky with the pain that she must have been feeling in her ankle. There was no other sign of her, and there was no house. It was still the house that isn't there.

"Dear Teddy. I've sprained my ankle, maybe it's broken. I slipped on one of the flagstones walking up the yard. My shoes were wet. I never wear proper boots. As I waded the stream the man in the coal car waved again. Cheerily, cheerily. The engine spouted smoke laced in butterflies. There was no engineer. Mrs. Ten Brouck is in the house talking with another woman. I can hear their voices but I can't understand the words. I've called but they don't hear me, they're pumping water in the kitchen, so I'll have to hobble up the porch and knock. They'll take me in. Goodbye."

When the police showed the note to Mrs. Ten Brouck she could only say that she had been in town, at the farmers' market and the drugstore. "The poor woman," she said.

The police looked for Marion a long time; search-parties combed the woods, where there was no house. After that my father couldn't stay in the town, of course; he had his job to go to, and he didn't much want to come back. But he always told me that the town was peculiar. New York City is not far away; and the town it-self is a comfortable place to live, not ever growing too fast, the old families of the town who still live there won't allow it, and the mountain ridge on the other side of the valley has a lovely line to it. It's as though, my father would say, the bowl of the valley had its own gravity well, so that it was just that little bit harder to go up and over and leave. So if he never returned it's not too surprising that I came back, though it's an odd way to talk since I wasn't conceived or born there. He hadn't met my mother yet.

When I came back I was precisely the sort of man that Marion never wanted to see in the town, because I came back with dredgers and cranes and contractors. But I would have told her, the way that

I told the Onderdonks and her distant Hornbeck cousins, that the condominiums I was building were good for the economy. And where else are the old people, the snowbirds who love that community, to live if someone doesn't build these homes for them? You need to settle, she said that to my father. They are built well; we're careful for the land. I wouldn't be the son of my father, I wouldn't be the son of Teddy who was in love with Marion, if the houses were a disgrace to the land. But it doesn't matter how well I build them, no; I'll have to defend myself to her all my life.

Because I build well, as she would have had me do, I think that she and I know the same thing about houses, that they have a double life and exist beyond us. We intend them to. Unlike us, who are so small and who move about and who change ourselves daily, eating and loving, defecating and pissing, pouring ourselves out and taking ourselves in, never the same and never in one place for good, unlike us, I say, our houses put themselves down; relative to the great mass of the planet they're fixed. Unlike us, swarming and shoving. So houses exist beyond us, shaping the space of the world to the cant of their beams. In some places on earth, in our older places—but what place on earth isn't old?—they intersect. Their organs touch. If well built, well thought out, well balanced, they could go on for ages without the need of the material in which we first made them manifest.

But that's all just a manner of speaking. I am the field manager for Condominium Modulars, Inc. I am fifty years old, married; my two children, my son and my daughter, have begun their own lives, they live in Boston and Pittsburgh, and I'll be a grandfather soon. Houses live beyond us but I don't know how.

Our consortium bought the land from the descendants of George March and Mrs. Carpenter. Mrs. Ten Brouck's niece was a bit of a holdout until I suggested that her house could stay on the land, that we could build around it and that in a number of years we would apply for historical status. We wrote that into the contract. The Ten Brouck House will stay, at least for ninety-nine years, a long time as we reckon time now, and longer than that we can be sure. Then we tore down the Carpenter house (the March house had fallen in long before), and began the survey in earnest. After a few months we brought in the caterpillar tractors and dredgers.

That's when we found the skeleton.

The ankle was broken. Marion was a small woman, no more than five feet tall, and the bones were small; the dental work matched. But I still hesitate to say it could have been Marion. They were old bones, and a necklace hung on the ribs, deer-bones and feathers and bits of pierced onyx strung on hide; drooping between the ribs hung a small bag with a hawk's claw, a fox tooth and a snake tooth, scraps of fur, and a bit of turtle shell. According to all reports Marion never wore anything like that. Still, there was no mistaking the dental work. The forensic results were quite unambiguous.

But there was a further problem. As far as I and the other workmen could tell the body had lain within the foundations of an old house, twenty feet wide by forty feet deep, in the back where a cistern and an old rusted-away pump had been built. But the body wasn't in the cistern. It lay under the brick floor of the cistern. It had lain there for at least four hundred years.

A body needs a house; but a house needs a body.

I don't know what to say. I do feel very certain that the woman who never gave me birth is dead. There is no room in the inn. So some things you don't know. Mr. Mercer gave no sign of himself; we don't know where he went. Light-foot. It's very tricksy. Your desire departs you. Bodies and houses hang on.

Yet Here's a Spot

It began as a spot on his left index finger, nothing more. It was late summer, almost the end of August—at the beginning of the second week in September his courses at the college would begin once more—when Andrew discovered the spot, and he wondered how long it was since it had first appeared. A small, dark, scarlet-brown, oval spot, on the left side of the finger near its base. A spot as you're only too liable to find in late middle age, but no other such spot had appeared yet. He was not that old, not much past forty and still counting. A spot that had nothing of interest about it, but still there it was. He first saw it there, standing naked in his bathroom after his shower, defenseless. For a reason he could not fathom he felt dreadfully uncomfortable, standing there naked, the small spot looming before him. He had a different feeling, however, as he turned his hand back and forth, almost to admire the spot, comparing it to the spot at the top of his left palm where a friend of his in high school had stabbed him with a lead pencil, its point breaking off in his pink flesh. He no longer remembered the name of his friend or his face or the reason for his anger, but the pencil point had snuggled in his flesh for thirty years, still a cause for his suppressed pride and rage.

Four days later as he was shaving he saw the spot again and now with more than a touch of pride showed it to his wife, Francine, but she was not impressed by the display.

"Oh, that," she said in her flat voice that she reserved for situations of little interest. "That's been there for ages. You just discov-

ered it?" Well, yes, he admitted, feeling a bit foolish, he had just discovered it, but didn't she think he should find out what it was?

"You know we talked about the spot seven years ago, on New
Year's Eve when you were stuffing yourself into your tux. And very
good you looked. It was a success, and you did look rather dashing,
but you kept going on about the spot."

"Did I?"

"Yes, you became very boring."

He laughed. "Well I won't do that today."

Nevertheless, he knew he should show the spot to his doctor.
Yes, he decided, he should, and forgot about it for months. It was
something about him hidden, which had to remain hidden. How
little he had that was hidden. At least he had a spot.

Three years later he noticed the spot once more. It was hardly
any larger than it had been, and he remembered that he really must
ask his doctor what to make of it.

So two months later in November, at the end of his routine
check-up, as he was buttoning up his shirt he looked at his finger
and said, full of apology, "Just one more thing, sorry to ask you:
there's this—don't know what to call it—this spot." He waved his
fingers, which his doctor snared adroitly.

"Where is it then, this spot?" The doctor was palpably impatient, tugging at his unruly forelock, impatient to leave so that the
nurse could give Andrew his flu shot.

He stopped flapping his fingers and pointed at the base of his
long middle finger. "There," he said, "this spot."

"Oh, this? It's not cancer, I can tell you that. Nothing to worry
about. You're fit as a Cajun catfish." He laughed. "See you in a year,
right? Call me if there's anything, but don't worry about . . ." He
floated out the door.

Following the advice of his doctor, Andrew tried to forget the
spot, but now that he had showed the spot to two people, his wife
and his doctor, he found it difficult not to pay the spot attention,
and a rather obsessive attention at that.

And the spot responded to his attention. He could not escape it.

At this point he was not sure what followed, whether he demanded a dermatologist or whether his doctor, before he floated out, suggested a dermatologist—whichever it was, he found himself two weeks later in a weak, half-naked body, confronting a brusque gentleman in a flapping white smock who examined his spot, cooing and brooding like an anxious hen above a sickly egg. The doctor took a sample; he did the best he could. The spot was tough and would allow no more than a miniscule cut.

The doctor said he would be in touch in a week.

So in a week the dermatologist's office called to say the sample was benign, at least as much as they could ascertain in the amount they had received. Good news. But the doctor wished to emphasize that he still had no idea what the spot might be. He was amiss. Better safe than sorry. The doctor would like to remove the spot.

Fastidious as he had always been, Andrew now wanted nothing more than his spot removed, so in two weeks he drove to the dermatologist's office, undressed as a patient must be for a dermatologist, and submitted the skin on his left hand as the doctor anesthetized and burned it, and burned it once more and two more times. He could feel and smell the burning, pressing deep under the skin. He breathed deeply, he breathed more than deeply, and at last the doctor stopped and studied the spot moodily.

He sighed. "It's as though the thing will not let me come in any further. I can't burn in any further, no matter how deeply I try. I'm really sorry." Andrew had never heard a doctor apologize. He shook his head. "Come back in a week and we'll use the scalpel."

And so he did. He had no doubt that something was wrong in the spot, and he yearned, desperately yearned, for the doctor to remove it. So he returned in a week and the dermatologist once more anesthetized the area around the spot and began to flash his scalpel, one-two and one-two. It was as though something vital in Andrew was being scored by the silver blades.

Nothing could remove the spot, the damned, stubborn spot. As the doctor explained the situation, the thing was rooted, and no blade was sharp enough to cut it out.

But its stubborn roots would not prevent its questing. Not long after his visit to the dermatologist he realized that the spot had begun to move around his body, engaged in its own complex quest as though to find a skin on which it could rest as it grew slowly, slowly, for it was growing. It never grew at a great pace, perhaps just to find a tasty place. More important for the spot was its quest. First it slid further down the left palm, sinking for a time on the point of the lead pencil. For a few weeks it took an arduous journey up his left arm to settle on his cheek.

Now everyone knew, his friends, his neighbors, his students. They stared at him surreptitiously, in sympathy and horror and bewilderment. The classes he taught at the college were unbearable. "What is it?" he could almost hear them ask, but no one breathed a word. "What is it?" the question wafted in the fans and questioned the windows. Pope asked the question, as did Swift and Johnson and Blake. Every time Andrew looked in a mirror he almost breathed that question "Yea, slimy things did crawl with legs," he whispered.

For a short time the spot came to life on the right eyelid and then on the left. If they were able to see past the dark glasses he now affected, people asked him if he had fallen or been in a fight. Soon he was wearing dark swoop-around glasses. He had no protection from these questions, however, when the malicious spot settled for three weeks on his nose. His nose was a run-of-the-mill nose, rather squat in fact, nothing like the nose of a braggart, but nevertheless the nose seemed larger when it sported the dark scarlet-brown spot. He was worse than absurd.

When it moved to his back he did not need to ask that question, "What is it?" any more. He felt it crisscrossing in his spine and shoulders. Somehow the question was worse now, as the spot held him in ambush.

Before it found itself on the spacious land of his back, however, it paused at his heart, where it picked up the habit of the pulse, which it never surrendered. He did not know why it found the pulse so satisfying. Was the spot a musician? Did it syncopate as it picked up the beat? Like the heart, which we never hear of course unless our knowledgeable fingers can pick up the subtle beat at the wrist—like the heart, it began to pulse. It wanted the heart's double chambers where it performed in a mocking pantomime. When he met a good-looking woman at a social event she could see his spot beating just at the left of his breast bone, at which she said it had been a lovely evening and left. Francine laughed and that night they made love. There are, apparently, compensations for the spot, but not many.

Francine reacted in a variety of other ways to his distress. She bought only organic foods, free of allergenic nuts and wheat and shellfish. She regularly attended the cathedral in the Square and partook of the mass every Sunday. Every fall she insisted that the doctor's office give her a flu shot, pressed him to have a flu shot also, and insisted that they would soon provide her and Andrew the vaccination for shingles; all this she did and more, but the spot never appeared upon her clean, white skin. She bought a large, stiff loofah and a coagulation of sea-salts with which she rubbed Andrew down ferociously every other day.

Meanwhile the spot undertook its own program of purity. Whatever skin the spot touched in its odyssey across the body is purged, painlessly burned, and purified. It could not, however, change the look of the lead pencil, where in retrospect it paused for a long time, but his cheek was cleansed of its red splotches, and his doctor attested that his heart was in fine shape, comparing him to a Cajun catfish and floating out the door. His white robe fluttered behind him.

Andrew's pride had been washed away at last, for now after so many years, ten years of the spot roaming up and down him, Andrew became utterly ashamed of the spot. He could not bear its size, though it was hardly any larger than it had ever been, but ripe in its willfulness. In the summer he wore long-legged pants and long-sleeved shirts that he buttoned to his chin, but he could not prevent the spot from peering coyly, only a small nub of it, from the top of his neck. It smelled. If you placed your nose near to it you discovered that it smelled of blood and excrement and of whatever else is vile in the world. His larynx, the root of his voice, croaked in the spot like a frog before it moved on. Years had gone by, and other spots had joined that spot, his first spot, no doubt the sign of his age but much more the sign of himself, that by which he could say, "Yes, that is me, that by which I am glorified. A spot, nothing more than a spot and nothing less." As we might guess he did not voice these words, nor voice them *sub voce*. He could not help himself because now he was truly old.

Sometimes he spoke in a stern, commanding voice, "Go away, Spot, down, Spot, down, damned Spot," but nothing happened except that once more he had given evidence of his horrid, childish age, caught in the ancient dilemmas of Dick and Jane.

Sometimes the spot could not be hidden, not in the least. One day as he sat at his laptop, typing out the midterm exam, he suddenly noticed that the fingernail stretching out to strike the "o" was blackened. Any moment it might drop off—is this leprosy? He froze in horror, but quickly recognized it was his old friend the spot, occupying that space for a time, in its own good time. In a few weeks, after it had slid away, once more on its quest of his body, the fingernail never looked so healthy. But he could not bear the invasion.

At last he was exhausted, the result of a growing, inescapable lassitude that prevented him from going to his classes. He did not want to give up totally, so he asked his doctor to provide him with a medical leave. The man did and went out of the room in a solemn flutter; even the doctor felt the drag of age.

When Andrew could bear it no longer he took the subway to the cathedral and knelt in a confessional, putting himself in the hands of a young priest, pouring out his sins, which besides nonparticipation were rather small in number, and his fears and terrors, much larger in number but more difficult to describe. He had also no idea, as he confessed to the man, whether to visit the box of the confessor or the couch of a psychoanalyst, but at last chose an institution with a wide and ancient preserve. Then his tears could not be restrained. "Madness, it's madness," were his only audible words.

After this explosion he thought he might as well have gone to a priest of Freud's persuasion, for the confessor spent a good deal of time asking him about his father and mother and siblings, the two sisters with whom his relations were distant, about his dreams, and about the reason for his work. Only in a slow manner, touching the subject and swerving from it, did he ask Andrew about the spot.

"May I see it?"

Both men stepped out of the confessional, looking up and down the deserted aisles. Andrew hitched up his shirt, lowered his pants and underpants, and turned to reveal the bottom of his spine, where Francine said the spot peeked out now.

"May I touch it?" the confessor asked.

"Yes, go ahead. What else am I here for?!"

He turned his back to the confessional. Lightly the confessor touched the spot where it darkened at the bottom of Andrew's spine, then petted it as though it were an agreeable dog. Andrew could not feel how the spot responded to this attention. Run, Spot, run?

"You may dress," the confessor whispered. After Andrew did so, silently, the priest asked, "When did the spot first appear?"

"I don't know. My wife claimed that it first appeared after a New Year's party. That was seven or eight years ago I think. Perhaps ten years."

"What happened there?"

"Well, I got drunk. I had some harsh words with the chair of the department, but we made it up later in the evening. I quoted the famous lines from Pope."

At the urging of the confessor he stood and recited the lines.

"Lo! thy dread Empire, Chaos, is restor'd;
Light dies before thy uncreating word:
Thy hand, great Anarch! lets the curtain fall;
And Universal Darkness buries All."

"You were quite elevated," the confessor commented drily. "Did you realize that you were in the act of summoning someone, perhaps something?"

"I have no idea. Then, having sung that as though it were a canticle, I danced, not very well, with the whole party; we all danced, manifest in the music of the spheres. As my wife and I were leaving I hugged Nicholas's cute wife and she leaned down—oh, oh, she kissed my hand, the index finger of my left hand. Where the spot appeared, if it hadn't already appeared."

"Did she blush?"

"Did she blush?" he chuckled. "No. A virtue but at second hand; They blush because they understand."

"But you don't really understand yet. What is her name?"

"I don't remember."

"Think about it, babble, associate freely."

"Nicholas was an adjunct for one semester. I'm surprised I know that much about him. The only time I ever met his wife was at the party, and I never saw her since."

"She was cute, you said, so you must retain some memory of her face. Please describe her."

"Well, I was drunk, as I said, but that was so strange, a woman you hardly knew kissing your hand. Her face was cute despite itself, for it was hardly of a piece. Her mouth was small but smiling, a cupid's bow, and her eyes were small too, almost too close to each other but that didn't matter since she was short. Her head didn't reach my chin. But out of the space between her eyes sprang the most remarkable nose, imperious and long. Her hair was short, dyed a wet-brown and scarlet, and added to the impression of power."

"Very good. She did make an impression despite your condition. And what did Nicholas look like?"

"He was short too, coming up to my eyes, with a long nose also and a small mouth. One would think . . ."

"Yes?"

"How did you know?"

"Let's just say that in cases of this sort it is not uncommon to meet incest. The power is all the greater."

"Cases of this sort?"

"Yes."

"Well, that's a relief."

"No, this is no relief at all. He is a warlock and shape-changer, and she is a witch. They are like a battery, negative and positive ends, generating a new power. It's not good for you."

Both men were then quiet for a long time before the confessor spoke. No doubt it was a weakness, but Andrew imagined the small mouth of the witch passing across his body as the spot had done, pressing here and there like the hot poker that the dermatologist had used; but her kiss was not futile. He saw a glint in the confessor's eye also and knew that the man had neither dealt with these powers nor with their temptations. This was all book-learning, out of which nothing could come. These were powers: nothing human about them. At last the confessor said, "The only solution I see is exorcism."

"Isn't that . . . ?"

"Rather extreme? Of course, but the church does allow it and trains a cadre of men to perform exorcisms. They are not ordained priests. They belong to a lower order." He said this with some disdain. "It depends upon the calling and of course the discernment. It is not simply a matter of that spiritual power we designate as Satan or of those diabolic powers that personality commands. It is not simply a sexual obsession, and not simply the realm of the uncanny, though it is uncanny, deeply so, and not simply a question of the archetypes—Jung, wrong so often, was often so right. Yet all these powers and their entanglements are the powers of darkness you need to defy with our help if you are to be free of the spot."

"I feel overwhelmed." He did not expect such a theologizing of his spot.

"Of course, but this is also very simple. Show me your hand again."

Andrew gave him his left hand, which the confessor held up to the light and began to peer at closely. Finally, done with his peering, he asked, "What's this?" pointing at the bit of lead in the palm.

So Andrew proceeded once more upon that story, and when he had finished he added that the confessor must not ask for the name of his friend or for the reason he stabbed. It was too long ago and just as well forgotten.

"Nothing is just as well forgotten. It renders us vulnerable to the powers, who do not forget. It is no accident that her kiss was planted upon that piece of lead, bringing it to life. You must not believe that you were chosen at random. You were chosen, no one else. If we cannot probe these powers any closer, we know nevertheless what we must do: save you, your individual soul against these machinations."

"Please," he murmured, "don't take such trouble with me."

But the confessor did take such trouble with him, consulting with his bishop that evening about the case and in the following week introducing Andrew to an exorcist who he hoped would be sympatico, not so much to Andrew as to the spot. The three of them sat in the pews of the cathedral, making small talk until the confessor took his farewell. The exorcist, Father Raul, during the day a greengrocer for his monastery, was an elderly man, his few white hairs quite a tussle. He shook Andrew's hand fervently and assured him that he would take his case as seriously as could be imagined, taking his hand to pat down Andrew's hair. No one had ever treated Andrew so intimately. He almost threw himself on Father Raul's breast.

The exorcist took his case on as honestly as he could expect. "This is not without risk," he said. "It is a battle between me and your spot and you are the battlefield. The situation is more complicated and more risky since that thing is embedded in you. Have you talked with it?"

"No!" The very idea horrified him. What was he to speak with? And if he spoke at all, what creature would insinuate itself into his voice and his mind? No one.

"That's good, that's very good, but I will have to speak with it, and the time may come when you will have to take up the conversation. If that happens speak truth with the creature, and speak truth with me at your side. Don't"—and here Father Raul hesitated and repeated himself—"don't betray me."

"How could I?"

"I can't tell you, truly I can't, how many ways you could betray me, but this is the burden I have taken upon myself to the Church and to Christ: I shall not betray you."

"When shall we begin?"

"We have already begun. Let us meet in a few days, at your convenience, perhaps at my apartment."

So in three days he found himself sitting in a heavily cushioned chair in Father Raul's apartment. Father Raul stood before him garbed in his robes and wearing a heavy, prominent cross.

"Where is your spot now?" he asked, and without speaking Andrew pointed at his upper left shoulder.

"Very well, then, to that we shall address ourselves."

And to that he did address himself, first calling upon the spot to reveal itself, uttering the various powerful names by which it might be named, of which Satan, the accuser, might be the least. At these names the room shook, its agitation reaching down to the building's foundations, but the spot did not budge an inch; it did not even quiver. Both men began to sweat.

Father Raul then commanded the spot to leave. He did not tell the spot how it was to leave; that was in the spot's domain, whether into the earth or into the upper air. He uttered his commands in various languages, more for the intensity of the act than from any belief in the spot's deficiency. After a half hour of these commands the sweat was profuse.

At last he gave up, served two cups of green tea, and asked Andrew to return in a week.

During that week Andrew paid particular attention to his spot, which began to move slowly onto his upper arm, as though it meant to find a diving board in his left hand, but it had not come to his wrist when Andrew returned to the exorcist. The room, which before had struck Andrew as no more than nondescript, now had one wall, that facing the heavy chair, draped in a copy of an infernal, broken landscape, something human torn in an abattoir, in the manner of Bosch or Goya or Bacon, horrors transcendental and horrors perverse, offering the spot any demonic self it might choose to accept.

Now Father Raul thundered the names and commands, one after another in no discernible order, interspersing these with threats that appealed to the authority of the church. Among the parade of saints whom he invoked, he appealed in particular to St. Michael, the chief of the heavenly host. Once more the room and the building shook, but the spot seemed to pay no heed to this barrage. Once more, when silence came upon the lips of the exorcist, he served two cups of green tea and made their next appointment for the following week.

During that week the spot seemed to speed toward the left hand, the place where it had first appeared and where it first embarked upon its general questing. Had Andrew thought of the matter at all, he would have realized that now that so many years had passed the spot had in fact almost completed its quest, having touched he was sure every square inch of his body, some 5150 square inches. It was exhausting to think of. And if Francine had looked at her husband more intently now than she had after the forty years of their marriage, she would have realized that his body had begun to glow.

His exhaustion, however, increased; his body lay slack on their teal couch. It was so bad that Francine drove him to the exorcist's apartment building. He kissed her as he stepped out of the car. She waited for him.

There was not much more Father Raul could make use of. Now he took up the drums and cymbals in the corner of the room, which Andrew had not noticed earlier, sunk as he was in the deep comforts of the obliging chair. Never as today had he felt so ashamed of the chair. As he sank into the cushions he was battered by Father Raul's names and commands, exhortations, and demands. The Father would never let loose, never, as he beat on the drums and the cymbals; and as he refused to let loose of Andrew the apartment rattled and crashed—it was rank in names.

Andrew's body glowed as though lit from within. The quest was accomplished. Every square inch that the spot had traversed glowed, he shone out, honed to a new brilliance, to a horrid extravagance of light.

He grappled with his body but could not save himself, not for long. The dark writhen light was erupting from his weak body. It could not be gainsaid.

He exploded. The explosion could not have been measured by the clock on the wall. The minor solar explosion left him no time, not at all a moment in which to realize his death.

The explosion left so little in the two blocks that the first responders had no idea what fragments, if any fragments at all existed, they were to look for. It is hard to imagine that nothing could be found. A blank space, nothing more than a spot can leave, and peculiar isotopes of lead.

No one asked for Andrew, for nothing of Andrew was left, nothing was left of Father Raul, and nothing was left of Francine either, waiting patiently in the car. Nothing was so beautiful as the fire leaning above the explosion.

Nicholas and his sister heard of the explosion some weeks later in Europe. By that time the short witch, with her inviting, small mouth, had kissed the hands of several men in various countries, leaving on their palms or on their fingers a small, dark, scarlet-brown, oval spot.

THE CHURCHES ON THE HILL

"Zeal for your house has eaten me up." If only Joseph had understood those words he might have come out of the horrors of Kingston sane and whole. But he did not, so this is not a pleasant story.

So! When we read H. P. Lovecraft's history of Rondout Harbor, what we now call the Strand, in his letter to Elizabeth Toldridge, we may notice one omission in his striking account: the number of churches that exist in such a small area, one mile wide by two miles long—at least ten churches, three Roman Catholic churches and cheek by jowl with those three the two Lutheran churches, in addition to a Baptist church, an Old Dutch church with a startling rose window on its facade, a Methodist church, and two Congregational churches, one with a spire made of weathered bands of red and green shingles and another with a spire that resembles a pile of raspberry and blue berry icecreams. Most of these churches border Wurts Street and Broadway as those streets climb a steep hill from the Rondout Creek. This is the oldest section of Kingston, founded before Kingston proper was ever imagined. The oak trees interspersed among the churches are older than the oldest, the Old Dutch church.

Lovecraft, of course, was not interested in a church unless it had some interesting historical background or a piquant architectural detail. So he saw no reason to mention in his letters the churches of the Strand, most of them heavy or fanciful expressions of the Victorian world. He did mention with a certain thrill the "slum," still as malodorous as ever off to the west, that constituted the area when he visited Kingston in 1929, long before the renovation of the Strand—the renovation that did not extend west. Still, he might have paused to consider why the people thought they needed to construct so many churches up that street, climbing the hill. So many churches . . .

Jane and Joseph Ranger knew nothing of Lovecraft when they decided to rent an extravagant gingerbread house, its porch painted a brilliant orange and blue, on one of the narrow streets parallel to Wurts, hardly a block from this conglomeration of churches. If you looked from a more distant perspective, the couple had decided to live in the center of the conglomeration. This was not because they believed in any religion. They most decidedly did not; Lovecraft would have regarded them as his kind of people, despite the fact that Joseph was interested in the churches from a purely architectural viewpoint, having no predilection for this or that style of church; and he had written a number of successful books about them, as well as making several contributions to the *Architectural Digest*. He had a tony reputation, but he had earned it. Every style was of interest to him as an expression of the evolution of styles. Why did some churches have steeples and some churches did not? Why were some churches neo-Gothic and some churches not at all; nay, why did some churches hold the Gothic in anathema? And why did most churches, even if they were quite Gothic in style, avoid any charming gargoyles? These were the sorts of questions that Joseph pursued.

For as long as they planned to stay, and it seemed to be some time, Jane took a job as a waitress in a restaurant, The Cob and Snail. Given Joseph's great success, she did not need the work, but she did need the human contact. The Cob and Snail was very successful, boasting that its menu represented the food in the area as it existed two hundred years ago. Happily, therefore, the restaurant could claim that most of its food came from purely local farms, and it thrived on the virtuous fad.

"The virtuous fad" was Joseph's phrase, and he chuckled at his joke as he twirled a clot of spaghetti around his fork. Jane had finished her meal and was peering at the close stitch she was occupied in. She did not respond to him, and he immediately felt that she had in some obscure way snubbed him.

"Joseph," she said softly. Most of the time Jane called him Joe, but when she called him by his formal name he knew that she loved him very much.

In truth Jane did love her husband very much, so she was quite complacent as he poured forth every night the wonderful insights in stone he was gaining. But rather than those stones she was more interested in the people she met in The Cob and Snail, some of them the political spill-overs from the County Hall, some of them the owners of the yachts that were tied up ostentatiously at the Strand, some of them rather low-life types attracted by the money passing back and forth from the river, some of them from the stubborn slum to the west, and some of them tourists—easy pickings. The Rondout has a risqué reputation that stretches back to its origins. In time she learned that many of her customers had such a reputation and also attended the churches, but they were hardly enough to sustain the churches. There were too many churches, filled more of the poor than of the rich, and the churches were dying.

"So tell me," Joseph asked, "who were the interesting people you met today?" This was a part of their ritual every night. She was fascinated by the various customers that came to The Cob and Snail and was eager to tell him about them.

"We had a witch today."

"No, you can't have."

"If she wasn't a witch she certainly looked the part. Red eyes, hooked nose, hunched back. No taller than five feet. And in place of the broom she has a ragged umbrella, though as you know very well there was no threat of rain."

"What did she have to eat?"

"The snails, of course," and they both laughed.

"Seriously, I believe she was Russian. She certainly had the accent."

"What was her name?"

"Now you mustn't laugh."

"I won't." But already he was holding his mouth. "Umph, umph!" he grunted.

"Baba-Yaga."

"You mean that creature out of Mussorgsky's *Pictures at an Exhibition?*"

"The very same," she said, and her habitual smile became broader. She was one of those women whose lips turned up in an enchanting smile. Physically and spiritually she could never frown. Early in their relationship Joseph felt that her smile was like nothing in our material world. It was a blessing from the universe. It was difficult to return to Baba-Yaga.

"A very wicked witch," he said, recollecting the blurb of the disc. "Her house has chicken legs, very spindly chicken legs, and she runs all about on them."

"Yes. The poor woman must be half mad." And with that she dismissed the witch for that night and told him of the other characters she had met that day.

Joseph could not expel Jane's witch from his mind, and a few days later he met her, but in very unpropitious circumstances. He had spoken with Father Michael, the priest of the Roman Catholic church nearest to Wurts Street, and to his surprise the priest was aware of his books, not only aware but favorably inclined. Though the priest believed that the stone churches were prayers to God, as Joseph did not believe, they both agreed on the integrity of the church. The more we knew of the church in which the liturgy took place, said the priest, its history and construction and aesthetic, the closer we should be to God, however you understand that Being.

"Very well," said Joseph, "let me dangle near the apex of the windows."

The priest gave his permission, so there was Joseph, dangling fifty feet above the ground and taking small chips from the wall, when the witch came by, stopped, and howled at him.

"You up there, what are you doing?"

"Hello!" he called back, twisting and risking his life in his rope. "I'm investigating the granite."

"It's black work, hss, hss!" She held up her two fists, making the horns, spitting and hissing.

"Father Michael has given me permission to proceed here."

"And what does Father Michael know of this place, hey?"

Joseph slipped in his harness. The adrenalin caught him in his throat as he almost fell. The witch laughed and cackled, and walked down Broadway laughing. Cursing her under his breath he steadied himself and returned to his work. That night, for no reason that he could account for, he did not tell Jane about his encounter, and he did not tell her in so much detail as he often did what he had discovered that day. She noticed his change of mood but did not question him about it.

"Poor Joseph," she thought, "he has his periods," and brightened the air with the people she had met that day. She smiled, and he felt better.

Three days later he was sitting in The Cob and Snail, drinking a hot tea that Jane had set before him when he heard "Hss, hss" behind him. "You don't mind, do you, sir, if I sit with you?" It did not matter what he thought; she had already slid into the small space in the booth opposite him.

"Please, not at all," he said, and gestured toward the seat she had already occupied. She looked very small, snuggling into the vinyl cushion.

Jane brought the woman a deep black tea. It was clear that she had often served the witch in the past few days. She kissed Joseph on the top of his head and left him to it.

"I didn't want you to have the wrong idea about me. I was perhaps too harsh when I saw you swinging on the church, but I do have my reasons." She had a thick accent, Russian as Jane had remarked, but she was not unintelligible. There she sat, a hooked nose and a hunchbacked spine, perfectly reasonable as she sat there, but she smelled like a fish gone bad.

"My name is Baba-Yaga. I was given that name long ago, but I am not a witch, leastways not that kind of witch. I am the guardian of the churches here about."

"You have to get around, don't you."

She said nothing, nothing at all, peering at him. Then she said, "You think I am just a mad old woman. That's true, isn't it?"

"Well, you're not a young one." The words were hardly out of his mouth when he regretted them.

She screamed. The scream did not last long, no more than ten seconds perhaps. But it soared into a high register where it was certain to pierce any eardrums within fifty feet. And when the scream ended, something large moved outside, something grinding like an earthquake.

"Now consider," she said quietly, "does just an old woman possess that power?"

He had no idea what she meant. It was a powerful scream, yes, but anyone can scream. What was remarkable about that?

She slurped the rest of her tea, laid down her teacup, and slid out of the booth. As she did so he realized that no one in the room seemed to have noticed her or her scream. The afternoon diners were eating calmly, sedately, exhibiting no disturbance at all. She opened the door to the sidewalk and was gone.

That night he very carefully examined his harness and ropes and crampons—he didn't want to use them but he couldn't be too ready—everything that he needed on the side of the church. It was not that he felt nervous; he had a long history of climbing mountains and churches successfully. Before he and Jane came to Kingston he had tested himself on the western ramparts of the rocky Shawangunk mountains, famous among rock climbers as intricate challenges. She had taken photographs of his ascent, photographs that he had examined carefully at the end of each day. Nothing was wrong, nothing deadly, about his work. His calm confidence gave no room to the paranoia which he had suffered in the past and which Jane had so sweetly cured him of.

The next day he spoke with the Lutheran minister and obtained his permission to climb the two churches he served—another sign of the slow death the churches were suffering—and for the next five days he devoted his attention to them. Then he approached the minister of the Old Dutch church, who also gave his permission. The local clerics had by that time talked among themselves with great excitement about Joseph and the book that he meant to devote to the churches of the Rondout.

The stained glass rose window that blossomed on the façade of the Old Dutch church was the target of Joseph's climb that day, going up the side and then moving over to examine the window in detail. It was slow work, but he had anticipated that and did not approach the side of the window until noon. The sun was bright that day, shining on his brows and in his eyes. Soon he was sweating and shaking the sweat out of his eyes.

It is perhaps no surprise then to admit that the iris of the window suddenly peered and winked at him.

He was an object of interest to the church. It was frightful.

Fortunately he had trained himself over the years not to move suddenly, in fact not to move at all, in a moment of terror. He stared at the window, this immense eye, and slowly drew back. He watched his hands and did not permit them to shake. He watched his right hand draw back to its former hold. His right foot drew back and found its former stand. He did not watch the window now. It was only a window, and in an hour he was standing in front of the façade on solid ground.

Leaving his gear at the foot of the façade he walked down the hill to The Cob and Snail. Unfortunately Jane was not working at the time, but he did not have the energy to walk home, near as it was.

He ordered a powerful mug of coffee and drank it black. He was in much better shape, convincing himself that the wink was a trick of the sun and his sweat, when the witch came into the room.

"I hope you don't mind my sitting with you," she said, taking the seat on the other side of the booth, just as she had before.

After a few minutes of silence, she kicked his shin and slyly whispered, "You look like you've seen a ghost. You can confide in me. Look." Reaching into a bag he had never noticed before, perhaps because it was the same indiscriminate color as her dress, she pulled out a crystal ball and set it on the table. "If you like I can read your fortune."

He began to laugh, but it was not a good laugh. It was more of a choking cackle. "Put away your witchery. I have no fortune, and I will not be a good conversationalist today."

"Very well. We do not need the ball to see into your future. You are going to die." She put up her hand as he half rose from his seat. "Not the physical death, no. Your mind will die, just like the clerics you have consulted, but worse."

Again he laughed, "My mind is in perfect order, perfect."

She shrugged. "Your wife thinks I am half mad, but she would do better if she looked closer to home. Think of you, hanging like a spider on the churches, weaving your web to make money off the book you will write, and since you believe in nothing you will not even tithe."

"Those are honest books I write."

"No." She rose from the booth. "It's time for you to go home."

"I will finish my coffee first." But his coffee was cold. Looking up from the mug he discovered the witch had disappeared, probably through the screen door that was swinging back and forth.

He rose, left a tip on the table, and went to the door. No, she was not on the sidewalk. He stepped out and began to walk up the hill. He had walked two blocks when he stopped to look at the churches, which were brilliantly clear in the late afternoon sunlight. His eyes picked out every significant detail on them.

He did not, however, walk any further.

A scream cut through the air, the scream of a long sharp knife, a scream that could not stop. And the churches began to move.

His hand was at his mouth. "Oh, oh, oh," he groaned.

The churches were heaving from their foundations, grinding and clashing. He felt the ground trembling beneath him, saw the ancient oak trees sway in the air. It was like an earthquake but worse because he could see what the churches had in mind. Him. He was more than an object of interest now. He was guilty.

Leading the churches was the Old Dutch church, because it was the eldest, its sides striding forward, the right side first, then the left side, its face and its single eye, not red now like a rose but blood-soaked and blaring heat like the eye of the giant Polyphemus, crinkling and crackling.

He turned, but there was no salvation at the bottom of the hill where the thick, nondescript body of the Methodist church was waiting for him and booming, full of Wesleyan enthusiasm. He could not go home; on his right hand the two Lutheran churches were intoning an enraged Bach. The three Roman Catholic churches were cheering their blasphemous, heretical progenies on from the sidelines, blocking another angle through which he could not escape. He turned again to confront the Old Dutch church that was hurtling down the hill, and now it was upon him. He had nothing to say or cry out as it stamped him into the concrete, slam, slam, and slam.

It left little of him, and the scream of the witch soared into the sun. It was over.

Joseph slowly stood up. "Did you see that?" he asked a passerby. "Did you see that?" And after he had stopped several people and a crowd had begun to gather, he lay down on the ground and curled up like a fetus, crying and crying.

He has been in an asylum for years now. In order to be near him Jane has worked hard to rise in The Cob and Snail until she became its manager; she is certain to become its owner in short order. Keeping in mind his joke about virtuous fads she has varied the menu. She visits him weekly, but he does not recognize her. If she smiles, as she still does though her smile has dimmed, he covers his face, turns away, and cries. When a priest comes to pray for him he screams.

The minister of the Old Dutch church blames Joseph for the crazed cracks on the stained glass rose window; the lines had never appeared until his unfortunate afternoon, and now its light has dimmed. The minister calculates the repairs to cost thousands of dollars.

The witch is undoubtedly the fortune-teller who has set up her practice near the Reformed church. She is doing a very good business, though she does smell of bad fish.

THE *NARCISSUS* ANCHORS IN THE CARIBEES

Belike we are not alive any longer. The worst is come to pass, worse than I or any man could have imagined, and we shall be picked to pieces in the next attack. The things that attack us wield their strength and our strength, and we can endure it no longer.

Under the skull and crossbones what more can we expect, captain and cockatoo and crew, than this death, but this shall be more than death, this base loss of utter being? We stand here, and some of us sit, beneath the rubbery leaves and unsupportable sun, waiting for the attack. It is the appointed dog-watch. What a shame we shall not see the surprise of these filthy wretches when they discover that no further attack will be called for. We have lived beyond our means, so now we die.

Argh I say, it's a great shame! I feel so troubled and undone that I am compelled to lop off the head of my amiable third mate, Matt Lewis. Blood follows my cutlass, the head goes bouncy-bounce, and we huddle, me and the crew, a little closer. A captain of this sort of crew rules best by dread, but the death of Matt is a waste among us seven. I could use the merriment of my cockatoo at this moment, but she's fried. "Good day," she would chuckle and, "Who are you?" Clever bird.

"Who are you?" Since, then, introductions are in order, allow me to say that I am Captain Peter Montrail of the good ship *Narcissus*, a privateer of his beneficent majesty (whom I have never seen). This is the conventional, polite, and politic language. The name of my ship I did not choose, and I would give anything to change it now—if it would help at all. When the ship was hammered together several years ago it tickled the fancy of her first master to name it for the young wooden face at the bow that looked down speechless at its reflection in the water. When we're at sea I sometimes lean over the bow to see our faces shattered in the foam, tangled in the martingale and the dolphin striker. It's so difficult putting these shrouds in order, and our selves!

The *Narcissus* was a sweet boat, heavy in its hull but with a jib and two masts, one of them, the foremast, bearing three sails, and the midmast bearing two sails and a mainsail. It was not a large ship, but it was satisfactory to our needs. Four cannon, and a good store of powder safe in the roundhouse. Just bring us keel by keel with another ship and our ferocity would do the rest.

I was the third or fourth captain of the ship, coming by it through violent means which I need not specify and finding aboard it the golden-red cockatoo that I named Echo—for obvious reasons. But besides the obvious reasons, it does a captain like me good to have a mate who will talk back to him. "The baboon's rectum, squawk!"

It was late in August when we spied this island dead ahead, and with no sign of it on the charts we thought it a blessing. It was the very place, unbeknownst to the world, to stow a bit of the treasure we'd gleaned on this voyage, beating up and down the coasts of the Caribees. This treasure was the usual trash, necklaces that had once circled pretty necks that had since dropped off the plank, sacks of doubloons, guineas, escudos, and thalers and so much else, crucifixes, pearl-encrusted, that marked and regarded us out of their agony. We needed to find a trusty exchequer for these, and the island was just the place. The treasure would accrue no interest in its chest, safe in the roundhouse, but it is dreadfully hard to come by interest in our work.

So we came up on the leeward side, discovered a creek that had worn out of the beach a natural port, set the anchor, the next morning let down the long boat, and hove to. Both the twelve men in the long boat and the fifteen men on board seemed to think it a holiday, bedizened in every gorgeous stone or fabric they had filched from the storms they rode through. We were a wondrous sight.

I and the twelve men shortly landed next to the creek. Two men carried the chest, and I kept a sharp eye on them, you may be sure. Two other men carried the various bottles and provender that I had the cook provide. So we plunged into the underbrush of azalea and broom, causing a great noise, with snorts and squeals on our right hand giving evidence of wild pigs that would glut the crew that night, making our way to a hill that stood on the north head of the island, which I had estimated at some two miles in length. The isle was puny, undetectable to scopes and sextants, so we understood why it did not appear on the charts. I wished now to find a space easy to find again where I could with some precision find the treasure when I wanted it. And as we hacked our way through the thick brush I bethought me whether I should kill these men and pull back to the *Narcissus* on my lonesome, happy in my secret treasure. It is a custom more honored in the breach, you may say, for honest buccaneers such as ourselves. Ha! It's exclamation points in our ledgers! Flint, it is said, killed six men at one stroke. But I could not hold out against twelve men, the more fool I when we embarked in the long boat. Look at the broadsides that depict me, and you will see my embonpoint and my spacious belly that render me rather useless in such quick dammee gotchas. A pretty idea, nevertheless, to dream of as we trudged along.

Before we came to the hill, however, we found a place much more to my liking, a small valley at the hill's base, open to the sky and surrounded by three pine trees that would last an age. I brought forth my compass and instruments and soon had calculated a cozy spot, eccentric from the center of the valley, at the focus of the three pines, which no one would take note of except myself. It was the perfect out-of-the-way spot, far from the pines so that the roots would not reach for the shovels but not so far that it would be hard to reckon the distance from the three trunks, and it was I thought all mine.

"Here," I directed my crew, drawing an easy X in the ground, "dig away. The sooner done, the sooner you suck up the rum we have brought for your reward." The two men with the chest lumped it on the ground and took up the shovels they had carried tied to their belts, as had they all, and began to dig with a will.

Grunt and heave, grunt and heave, you may well believe they dug with a will, working out a space some six feet in diameter and four feet deep. But not far had they dug when they cut into the first body and a stench puffed into our faces. It was a surprise, yes, but only a sign that someone with no good purpose had been here before us. Well and good, I thought, and what else lies here? "Dig on, my hearties," I said. "The spirits will taste all the better." And they dug with a will, turning up three more bodies, then five more. We began to sweat then, a chilly, unwonted sweat, laboring at a work that was no amusement I must say, turning up twenty-eight bodies at last, twenty-eight bodies that had been laid across one another in the pit like logs, as though to balance the thirteen men in the long boat and the fifteen men we had left on board the *Narcissus*. But that was chancy, of course. The crew sweating over their shovels paid no attention to that. Ten fingers were all that most of them could count to.

The sun was high in the sky now, close on six bells, but the sun was not the reason for the chill sweat that I was rubbing from my eyes. I took the count once more, and I knew that the great horror was that the bodies lay there, in the very spot I had chosen, a spot that no one would notice. But there was nothing to do but to treat it as a perfectly natural occurrence. Don't let the crew think anything other, don't spook 'em.

"Carve 'em up," I said, meaning no more than that the crew should pilfer what was by our custom rightfully theirs. But they took out their knives and carved. Without being aware that something was wrong, they knew—they knew, I'm sure—and they took out their fear on the rotten bodies. They saw no difference between ripping up the pockets that clung to the corpses and ripping up the helpless corpses. No blood spat from the moss-green corpses, but it was not a pretty sight.

It's the shuddery work that's hard, even under that heathen, stainless sun. Slim pickings and stinking hands that not even the creek would clean. I stepped back from the pit and let them do as they wished.

But as the crew came to an end of their carving, lying in the middle of their carnage, gnawing at the bread, dropping coins into their pockets, taking long draughts of water from their goat-hide bottles, and swigging the rum I did not gainsay them from the thick, green bottles I had brought, I realized something else, something worse.

Those corpses were us.

I mean, each of the faces, rotten in corruption as they were, looked like someone in the long boat or someone we had left on the *Narcissus*. And yes, one of them looked like me, such as I see in my glass on a very bad morning.

Then he did the unspeakable, you know, opened his eyes to stare me down and spoke deep in his rotten chest, "A cat may look at a king," and he laughed softly.

My crew, satiated with their carving and digging, lying in the hot sun, paid him no heed, but I did. "You look all of a cat," I said.

"What is the name of your cockatoo?"

"Echo."

"Does she burn from any unfulfilled desires?"

"She doesn't confide in me."

This creature that looks like me scrabbled up in the sand and knelt there. He stared at the cockatoo, held out his right hand as though in supplication, and held it out in silence for five seconds.

Echo burst into flames, flinging her red wings up for a moment, her golden head staring through the flames. When I jumped back from the fire she fell from my shoulder to the sand, and as though at a signal the other corpses began to stir and rise.

My crew was now alert—how could they not be, drunk as they were?—and drew back from the lively dead men. My quartermaster Red Jerkin raised the shovel in his hands as though to attack them, but with the shovel over his head grimaced and dropped it, clutching at his belly.

Like my cockatoo he also burst into flames. As he dropped to his knees I realized that he was facing the man that was his double. Though the man's hand had been cut off in the earlier carnage, he held the stump of his arm out toward Red Jerkin as if in supplication. He looked much better when the flames died down, more alive. But he still lacked for a hand.

For a short time it was difficult to see which way my crew might turn. Would they bolt or see it through? I said nothing, feeling that words were useless for us now. Then slowly they drew themselves up and stepped behind me, as though there were anything I could do to save them. But that decision was better I felt than funking.

"I am in perplexity," the man said who faced me, holding up his two hands, palms outward in the sign of peace that we recognize throughout these two continents, if we wish to recognize them. We were not in a strong position, my crew and I, so I nodded.

"I allow, as you must also, that we have a series of remarkable connections between us. I have never seen you, much less myself, dead in this heap for God knows how long, but we do look alike, don't we not? Just as our comrades do."

At those words, having jaws and gnawed jaws, both sides of the pit groaned.

"So who shall outlive the other? I should tell you—for I am not a pirate, not yet—that fifteen of my comrades have taken your long boat and are on their way to the *Narcissus* where they will do all that is needful to take command of the ship. Honesty in dealing!"

He paused. I said nothing. I could not imagine what to say. Our lookalikes it seemed had all to say, and it all had to do with corruption assuming our roles. I could imagine them, loose jaws half eaten away, cutlasses in their left hands because the right hands had been severed, fighting to show they could fight, it is such a merriment, before reducing us to dust.

Where they would exchange their diamonds, pearls, and doubloons, I had no idea. Perhaps that would be no worry to them. Corruption enjoys nothing more than more corruption.

I thought of the last lady I dropped from the plank, naked, while I held her clothes over my head, and I groaned.

"If you will permit us," I said, "we will withdraw southwards to the source of the creek."

"We will talk tomorrow."

I turned around to walk south, gesturing to my crew to follow me. It cut me to the heart to abandon the chest, but there was no mistaking the gesture of the creature. It was the same gesture as I would have made, and as I walked through the late afternoon light I wondered, if he was me, did he know not only my hands and fingers and bowels but also my mind? Did his mind march in rank and file with mine or, shall we say, run parallel to it? Then I was dead, I was already dead. The eleven men around me also, I had no need to question them. Their minds marched to the other minds, and they were as dead as I.

As I continued to consider these matters we arrived at the source of the creek, a pretty spring that gushed from five stones at the base of a small hill where it formed a shallow pond before skittering its way into its course to the ocean.

My crew, what was left of it, for I assumed that the fifteen men aboard the good ship *Narcissus* were dead now. Let it all burn. Cleanse it. My crew that remained at this late hour, seven bells as the sun touched the western horizon, wanted to collapse, but I couldn't have that. I needed a redoubt, because our lookalikes at any moment would come screaming and maiming through the thick green world, and there was nothing but sand and the great green rubbery leaves to build with. Our blunt cutlasses could not bring down a young palm.

And so it happened. We had no food left, and they gave us precious little time to suck water from the spring when they came screaming and ululating from every side. It's amazing how high and fierce a body can scream after the Adam's apple and lungs have suffered just a touch of death. Just a touch. Fortunately, as we discovered frantically clapping our hands to our sides to discover whether we had any weapons that would help, we remembered our flintlocks. *Ping-ping-ping* they fired, and three horrors that looked like Matt Driver, Fishy Flint, and the Dutchman dropped and cuddled their escaping lives.

But four of our men were incinerated, their lives vanishing before us in a puff of gray dust, pillars of ash at our left and right hands.

They withdrew. The man who looked like me called out of the thick dark green, "We will wait for the morning in the dog-watch, then we will need no more than two attacks to take off all the life that breathes in the sign of the *Narcissus*." He laughed, choking, and we heard his laughter dying away in the distance. Was he returning to the pit, their only home?

He will take off this life. I do not appreciate this life any longer. I appreciate nothing about it. So at that moment I decided to write this account, the last moral work a pirate could write (who mourns for his cockatoo deeply), and with the account I will note the longitude and latitude of the island [the editor has decided to delete this part of the manuscript]. At the last moment, when it comes, I will throw the account into the creek in a strong, green bottle, well corked, trusting our fate to the complex currents of the Caribees.

So that is my story, quick and dire. Many authorities will recall the veracity of Peter Montrail, the privateer—his only virtue.

But before I cork it, consider what has happened, which was too tidy to happen by chance. Anyone who discovered the island would have been drawn to that little valley and discovered their likes, and I believe that the original captain of the *Narcissus* may well have discovered that island and fled to tell his cryptic story in the face of the young wooden face staring into the ocean. What was his crew like then? Missing their fingers, holes in their cheeks, green moss dripping off their shoulders?

Every one of us finds himself at some time staring into the ocean and finds himself given back in thousands upon thousands of selves. The power of that return is concentrated in that island just as elsewhere in the new land you will find belike gold, belike silver, belike dust.

Belike, ho ho, belike yourself.

What in the name of damnation are they? Psychotropic truffles, fattening in the earth until a ship approaches? Then they grow to look like us at the same time that they send out solicitous words, begging us to approach. And we do, digging them up and dying. Then, if they are lucky and careful, they sail off to conquer some decadent land and rule, but always as death at last approaches returning to the island to fatten once more and wait.

I am sorry to conclude in a philosophic mood. This is a pirate tale, and as such should conclude in blood and mayhem. And so it shall, oh yes, in cut and parry and lunge, in flintlock and flames, but outside the abilities of this poor account. It's time to throw it into the waves. I kiss it goodbye.

THE PUZZLE IN THE CELLAR PANTRY

"I don't finish jigsaw puzzles," my uncle said.

We were sitting on his back porch. Below us, gray behind the screens and the rainy afternoon, the vegetables sprawled going to seed, the cucumbers too fat turning yellow, the tomatoes pulling over the stakes, thick beans dangling on wet strings, and beyond that fecund garden a pond at the bottom of it all; the cicadas had given up but a cricket chirped.

The puzzle on the card table showed a courthouse commons. The courthouse was an ornate affair, all brick and sandstone and marble, Vitruvius gone to seed, presiding over a green lawn where a bandstand echoed to invisible horns and loud invisible marches. It was a Sunday morning; no one was out on the lawn. Old Glory hung at ease on a flagpole, raised by invisible hands.

"I don't need to fit that last prim piece of cardboard into its place," he said. The gray stubble at his mouth twitched. "It's obvious. The blue line, the white blur, the lobe which is that little bit larger than normal with the star in the corner, I don't need to prove that it fits." He shoved his chair back.

"Well, the fact is I can't finish. I'm too old not to say it. The truth is the pantry."

After a pause he said: "Maybe the truth is the cellar, I'm not sure which. All children are afraid of the dark. I was. Aren't you?" Yes, I nodded, I was.

"But when I was five or six I did play in the cellar during the day. I could handle my fear. When I walk into a dark room now, prodding my cane ahead of me to chase off goblins, the shiver is familiar; it's been a friend all my life. Ask your parents if that doesn't happen to them.

"Down in my cellar my collections of buttons, bottle caps, birds' nests, and ship models sat on the shelves to the left at the bottom of the stairs, or they lay about on the cool rough smell of the concrete floor. To the right was the coal-furnace that I would tend—at night, mind you—with my father, fascinated by the red roar as he pulled out the clinkers with clumsy big tongs; and to the right of that in the far wall hunched the coal-bin that always stank of darkness. But without my father at night I couldn't bear to walk down those cellar stairs.

"Beyond my collections, in the corner straight behind the furnace my mother's pantry stood built out from the wall, five feet deep and some ten feet long, if I can now compare the size of that tepid space to my child's body. So small the pantry seemed next to the bulk of the furnace when I put my hand up to the wooden handle, but so large it seemed inside. Six, perhaps seven shelves stretched above me on the left hand, full of mason jars of tomatoes, beans, sauerkraut, dainty bread-'n'-butter pickles and sweet pickles and gherkins that the Midwest loves to display in its linen dining rooms for Sunday dinner, cans of mushy green peas and corn, red labels, yellow labels lighting up the room above me, and the keg and the bottles of catawba wine at the far end. Every smell in the jars and cans found its delicate, dusty way into the room and jellied and aged in the cool air. It was a room for old people; the generations of our family albums kept watch. Dry geraniums swung in the air. It was my mother's pantry, despite the pale catawba, sealed off in the corner of the cellar in its own privacy, miles from the cellar that belonged to my father; in the midst of his work she had established the separate pleasures of her work, and I felt in place there. Beneath the shelves stood her stepmother's deep chest filled with puzzles.

"I don't understand why those cardboard puzzles were stored in that narrow space, fitted into a chest on the concrete floor that though it was always dry still persisted in an odor of soft brown mold. But I can't see the right-hand wall of the pantry; some details of our lives become lost, like a puzzle piece, and all that remains is the shape of the loss. But I don't think knowing what hung on the right wall would ever answer why the puzzles were there, or why I loved them, or what happened that day.

"The jigsaw puzzles were the old sort, like this one, the five-hundred-piece puzzles favored for long days in February or for the longer days of rain coming down in April before it's warm enough for you to run out and splash along the curbs. Or in August, like now. The jigsaw puzzles I labored over in the safety of my mother's pantry were all photographs of landscapes, American landscapes, seen from a great distance, selected according to an arcane code of etiquettes and common laws. The matted colors challenged and soothed America long before computers demanded our hands. Colors rode a long slope of mesas and arroyos, a few strings of cirrus, and lots of sky. Colors climbed muted mountains somewhere in the Alleghenies, stretching above new wheat fields, clear, with a lot of sky. Colors walked through villages on hills, a dense home front of clapboard and Chinese elms, fluted clouds with a lot of sky. Colors browsed in flower-gardens, hollyhocks and roses and dusty azaleas, arboretums, a lot of sky. Colors splashed in fishing-ports, dull-green boats nestled next to piers, rigging, masts, and nets tangled together, cormorants sluggish and tipsy on buoys, and, yes, a lot of sky. Sky poured above all those worlds, blue skies or skies heaped in a white orchestration of clouds or stacked up black for a storm."

As my uncle spoke his hand made odd gestures across the puzzle in front of us, gestures I can never forget.

"But no people enjoyed those pastoral dreams. Those puzzles had no people in them, no men or women walking beside those meadows or under those trees, no fishermen with their long stiff aprons soaked in fish-guts, no children cartwheeling down those Sunday streets or staring from those porches. Animals and birds moved through them. Bears ambled, gulls squawled, dogs leapt, cats slunk or assumed an attitude, but for no people, for no one's delight. The America that I took up between my index finger and thumb was unencumbered of human effort, pristine. Five years old, ex-hausted after the struggle with kindergarten and school-buses, I pre-ferred that freedom as, I am sure, did all America.

"Every person working on a puzzle has a favorite way to go about it. Some start at the edges, just the way you did, some do the sky. Some people study the copy of the picture on the cover to begin with the choicest corner. I group all the pieces into plausible piles and begin with the four corners, fill in the bottom and edges because those flat sides always promise to be easy, work a bit on the edge of the sky—though by that time I've usually begun to fill in an image that's caught my attention more than that boring sameness—and finish with the sky. And I always use the picture on the box. The picture I worked on that day looked like this one that you and I have almost finished.

"But now that I'm at the nub of my story, now that I have to tell you what happened that day, I'm not sure that I know what to tell you. I have a qualm, Puzzle-solving was not such a special treat for me; I played my own games in the pantry, constructed boulevards and bridges out of my mother's canning to run my toy cars through, or I played solitaire on that flat, wide concrete. This puzzle was not special either. I don't think, as I try hard this afternoon to see and feel the pieces and rub them through the fingers of my mind, that they were new. I must have put that puzzle together before, and my mother, and her stepmother before her. The day was not special. When the rain began that August morning my mother let me sleep late till I came down stairs for breakfast, cereal and milk, and moped about before coming down to the pantry and the puzzle. It was three weeks yet before school started and already the school-buses were lining up in front of my eyes in a wall of yellow confusion.

"The picture looked like this. On the left, the porch of a weath-ered log-cabin faced slantwise toward a small sloop riding self-possessed in the small bay of a lake, only its bowsprit curtained by a proscenium of low underbrush and evergreens growing on the hill to the right. Where mist was rising and becoming clouds, mountains swept from the far side of the lake; and it all rode, as though at an-chor, under the candid light of a morning sun, with none of the shadows revealing where the east lay. I have no idea where the sun was rising. After I had the smudges of flowers and unmown grass in place at the bottom of the picture and dealt with the topsy-turvy problems of the pieces for the sturdy evergreens at the sides, I turned my attention to the boat, wonderfully alien to a child in the land-locked heart of the continent—but now I think that lake must have been a river like the Hudson or the Columbia, harboring such a boat. It seemed like a lake to me.

"Working on the prow I encountered the first oddity. You know how it is with puzzles: certain pieces that must belong in one corner turn out to belong to a totally different zone of that world. The street sign is a curtain in the upper window; the garden-gate is a knob of cloud; the cormorant is a fish, slick on the planks of the pier. The more I concentrated on the boat, scrunched over the red line of its hull or the small port-hole near its prow, or laid myself flat on my side on the concrete and dreamed with a two-in, two-out piece in my hand, the more those bits of the boat began to suggest the log cabin. It wasn't right to begin afloat; I had to earn the sloop. The blue-dark, water-dark piece in my hand was the shadow of the evergreen brushing the tiles of the roof. When I rolled over and stared at the empty shape of the floor that the log cabin should fill, I had to give up for the moment on the large space that was the water of the lake where no water yet lay and pull myself back to the land and the home.

"But my change of purpose is no oddity that startles anyone who works jigsaw puzzles; if you depend upon the copy on the box you always meet discrepancies between its colors and the colors of the hundreds of pieces scattered around you. There is no full match be-tween the brick-red of the box and the fuchsia of the piece, the na-vy-blue and the night-wet turquoise, the dandelion and the sunset-softer yellow. It lightens, it darkens; the changing shape on the floor pulses in hidden tones that the copy on the box had never promised, though it always promised something brighter. Your disappointment and failure turn elsewhere. It's more than you ever imagined.

"One thing never changes. Turning each piece in your fingers, trying to make sense of up and down and red and amber, you're also staring at your own fingers and your own hand. It's yours, it's new, it's a comfort.

"By this time I had almost finished the cabin, and the light of the shy morning began to subside into the chinks of the logs and the not quite, never quite perfect fit of the pieces. The porch was ajar from an ice-heave of the past winter that the copy had not completely caught. The curtains were thicker but hung looser; the lace was tattered and rosy, whether from the stove inside, from age, or from the original pattern—you couldn't say. A wisp of wood smoke fell from the chimney-pipe, mixed in the mist that was almost gone. The boat was ready to sail.

"It is so hard to make sense of an individual piece of the puzzle. Each cuts out a random part of the world. The jigsaw-cutter is indiscriminate; and the shapes, colors, lines, whiffs of nothing, pressures call them, that move in that inch of space move according to laws that no abstract expressionism can discover. There is no accounting for the odd, white trembling of the piece that fits in the lower left of the sail. Each piece brings you closer to the patterned chaos that breeds in the heart of matter. The shapes in a photograph of galaxies, spinning away at the edge of the universe, make more sense than these gestures of dismissal and abnegation stirring beneath the skin of the emptied landscapes we pick at on rainy afternoons on the cold concrete floors of our cellars. I lay next to the puzzle, holding a piece of matte orange and apricot bark pregnant against the light-bulb floating across the ceiling. The pantry breathed me.

"But if you give up on the coherence inside each piece, the pieces taken all together, without content, are perfectly predictable because their shapes, the curving lines that the jigsaw-cutter makes sawing back and forth through the mechanics of manufacture, never vary. Everyone who works a puzzle gives the pieces private, typical names. This is the turtle, five nodules peeking out from the shell. The black-widow spider has a narrow waist, its two pincers grappling forward. This is the lake, surrounded by its bays, the in-cuts on each of its four sides. The fog-bank is one of the rare large pieces, swelling on one corner as though it were rolling across a road at night and your father slows down, cursing in a minor key the blur and the car lights. You don't tell your closest friend these private names; sometimes going to sleep you tell your mother how hard it was to find the blue turtle today."

As he described the turtle and the spider and the lake my uncle pointed them out in the puzzle that lay before us, his hand gesturing across it as though his hand were gliding across a Ouija board; and I guess now, looking back at that day, that it did have something to do with truth.

"But anyone who works a puzzle," he continued, "is also aware of a more public aspect of the pieces; they are the mass of people that those depopulated landscapes attempt to deny. They fling their arms out in appeal; their arms hug their starved bodies. Some have legs missing, cut off at the knee; some lean away, running for their lives. The faces are in profile, or they face forward, always staring; no one closes an eye. Every posture, every gesture, every eye expresses a wrongness that can only be healed by a fitting together that is all the more terrible because it represents an emptied earth and an emptied sky into which all those lost souls vanish. Then no one is nowhere. The puzzle is finished.

"But my boat was ready to sail now as I put its last piece into the notch where the roof-edge of the cabin hung under the boom; and clicking it into place and turning to pick up another piece I saw a hand slip off the gunwale. A small hand. The boat rode slow to the swell of the lake as the noon-light brightened; a cloud passed. I could hear the rain outside pick up. August was thickening in tomatoes that my mother would soon can in her mason jars, screwing them tight between her hands. I hate August.

"The sloop had changed. The sail was taut, not slack like the gray cloth on the mast in the copy. The sporting, brick-red line above the water was an intense orange, the taffrail more tilted, the stern turned more to land; and the bowsprit pointed to the far shore. I started the lake. But I could no longer avoid, as I had been avoiding all morning, as I'm avoiding telling you now, the small apprehension that comes in waves like the first slight waves, not quite in the tongue, of seasickness, of dismay, of something empty, that a change was upon me, lay before me.

"At first it was only that a trace of change flitted across a piece like a blue film on an andiron, flapping through fire. Though nothing moved on any individual piece, a few objects, from the corner of the eye, fluttered. A red was wrong, an oblique line not true; the shore was more pebbled, the water deeper. A hand shone in the window where no window ought to be set. But it wasn't a window, not yet, and not the port-hole; it was a fire-red lily in the garden behind the house, the hand was a petal. Or the hand pressed itself behind the tattered lace where the casement didn't fit right; but it might as well have been a hand that was tending a shy fire in the stove. But when each section of the puzzle was complete and the last piece inserted—because all these pictures have discrete zones carefully composed by their makers not for the sake of the composition but to emphasize the varied apartnesses that preoccupy all our landscape—my conviction that the hand was no longer in the cabin of the sloop, no longer at the stove in the deserted log cabin, no longer behind the evergreens or swimming across the lake, that bit of splash in the afternoon sun, no longer picking its way through a clutter of underbrush growing on a mountain path, my conviction weakened. The hand was everywhere, nowhere. It was not that it was no longer; the hand was prior.

"And at one point that rainy morning as I was working on that jigsaw puzzle, perhaps at that ephemeral moment of triumph as I clicked into place the final piece of muddy mauve and sepia that marked the shore on the other side of the lake and the late afternoon

air darkened, the most imperceptible pressure began bubbling behind me in that wall to the right of the pantry door, that wall I can
never picture. Did it hold brooms, calendars, burlap sacks? The pantry coughed, weighed down on one side, unbalanced. And far off, on
the other side of the wall that wasn't there and on the other side of
the cellar, my stomach heard a dry sift of dust in the coal-bin. The
air hung in hands. A turtle splashed.

"You know and I know that other people prowled America before the Aleut and before the Apache, before the Inca and Clovis,
before the continent slid off to its own emptiness. Others. The people who are prior. Their anonymous hands stirred mud for roots and
slugs: flat-footed, leaf-handed, feral, reptilian, left out of time, filled
with an innocence beside which our childhoods make gestures of
hopeless corruption. Small birds sighed in their shadow. I set the
last piece into its spot of deep-blue sky and blotted out the concrete.

"Then she looked at me.

"Twisting her face and body out of the sky and holding out a
hand, she swam up out of the sky, looking up.

"In that half-light that has no direction and isn't sunset or
morning I still cannot say whether her hair was dark or light. And
she has no one face, even now. Sometimes in my dreams she still
looks at me from the same angle but never as though she were in the
same room; if I am on the porch of the log cabin, she is in the entrance hall, or at the head of the stairs, or sitting at the mirror next
to the closet. She's at the stove, she's stooping in the cabin of the
boat, she's in the pantry. I don't believe she's ever in the coal-bin.
But however she looks in all those hidden rooms, her countenance
spreads out miles beyond her high temple and wide cheekbones, her
face suddenly dropping back, her thin embracing face. And her hand
is that hand.

"You know I don't have any children. You have no cousins."

"Yes, uncle."

"We don't need to set that piece into the puzzle; we don't need
to finish."

He tossed the last piece that I couldn't see back into the box and swept up a handful of the courthouse on top of it, mixing the pieces of the puzzle together.

THE BLACK PLASTIC RAG

It's nothing but a black plastic bag. No, it's a bastard nephew of plastic. It's nothing more than a shred of plastic and it's considerably less than plastic, blowing across the street. It's a bastard nephew of plastics or a bastard polyvinyl chloride. Something irrational has happened to it after so many recyclings and recyclings. It's been shredded and shredded again. It's ripped and torn and filthy. The traffic's not bad here on Main Street in the center of the city at this hour, but the cars are fast enough to disturb this ripped plastic rag— it is so light—that rushes across the street, dances and leaps in the air. It makes a dash at a Jeep and hops off. For a moment it's far away and can skittle no further.

It is nothing but a black plastic thing, recycled and recycled, not a voice of its own but a jumble of voices. Every voice has been baffled. It looks around for areas in which its recycled trash can play out its horrible malice. It's a bastard hybrid of plastics. Or it's nothing at all.

It is nothing at all but a rag of black plastic trash that settles for a moment on the face of a baby in a magnificent stroller, a gaudy mansion of strollers. The black rag hates it. Before the woman pushing the stroller has reached down to shake the thin plastic loose it has nearly strangled the child. It wants to strangle the child, to strangle it deathly and blue, but alas the woman shakes the rag loose and it dances away. Who would not want to strangle the child, strangle it pallid and blue? It is such a jolly piece of plastic.

It's nothing but a torn piece of plastic. Before it was ripped and torn it could have contained a gallon and a half of trash. Now it is trash itself and contains nothing, not a drop, in its rattling, ripped sheets. It is so malicious and red-eyed that it still wants to strangle the child; but the woman, nodding her head amid the oceanic splendor of her hat, is keeping a sharp eye on the child and the black rag. It is sucked into the traffic again. Out of spite it claps itself flat on the left of the front window of an unwashed Hyundai. The driver swerves and strikes another car sideways, but both cars gradually slow to a safe stop. The drivers exchange insurance forms. *Tant pis.* The perverse wind blows the ragged black piece of plastic to the other side of the street and into the oncoming traffic.

It is nothing but a black scrap of plastic, but it is home to a million, quadrillion dust mites. Between the numinous wind of the evening sunset and the profane wind of the commuter traffic, the black plastic rag is blown onto the T-shirt of a jogger, onto which another million dust mites skip ship. They are not to be counted. In a few days the jogger will unaccountably—for he is so careful— break out into hives, and he will find it difficult to breathe. All sorts of allergenic symptoms will assault him. His lover will find him disgusting. On this day, however, the black plastic rag knows nothing of the horrors that shall come to pass. The rag is still searching, blown on the winds, for a timely, gratifying, gratuitous mayhem.

It is nothing but a shred of plastic, black and filthy. As a motorcycle comes roaring past, the black rag is torn into the spokes of its front wheel, and rackety-rackety-rackety it whirls around, an iron shaft caught in its folds, knocking at the armature of the wheel. The rider spins to a stop and steps down from his machine gently. He takes off his helmet that is dense in signs of death. So few cyclists wear helmets, but he does. You take one look at his face; he will not explain himself, never. He has a gray, filthy beard that would have put Blackbeard to shame and a sweaty red bandanna bound round his head, his gray hair escaping it into the staring sun. His massive tattoos curse all that is good in life and in hell. He pulls the shaft and rag out of the spokes. He does this in an utterly casual manner, as though this happened often. He does not curse the shaft or the rag, but settles into his seat and roars away. If the black plastic rag had a mouth, only half a torn mouth, it would have snarled at the man's presumption and cursed him to hell.

It is nothing but a black scrap of plastic. It is nothing but a shred of nothing that twirls down the street again. It plasters itself for a moment against an old brick building, the least and the last that is left of the old city. In a week the great iron ball will come swinging against it. You have to say this about the black plastic scrap. It sets itself against time.

Murry and Renée notice the black scrap as he turns right off Main Street, and they leave the scrap bouncing behind. He says, "Yes, it pretends to be beautiful, shuddering up and down and free of gravity, but it means nothing, it really means nothing." She reserves her judgment but he proceeds, at length. Beauty only exists, he argues, in a purposive act, but the plastic trash, the sort of thing you see in the streets and the grocery store parking lots, has no purpose at all.

The black scrap is in a fury. Once more it snarls, mouthless and tongueless, and its fury hurls a truck of double-decker cars and a propane tank to clamber up the trunk of Murry's car, bursting into flames, into happy flames. This will give Murry something to think about, for an instant. It spits, but it has no water in its sinus chambers to spit with.

It is nothing but a black plastic rag. Nothing to spit with, nothing to speel with or speak with. It was once a sizable bag, blown hither and thither and yon, so it could not have known that the greatest success of its existence is in preparation. Someone will speak for it, but that will take some time. For now, it feels useless, as indeed it is. The wind blows it over a filthy, greasy pond, into which it flops. This is its death.

But that afternoon, as we have said, the greatest assertion of its existence is about to step forth. Daniel Cummings is in a rush. He is the first violinist in the County Orchestra, and he ought to have placed his violin with his customary reverence into its case; but he is in a rush, as we have said. He and his lover have been busy that afternoon, his young body to her young body. He makes love to the rhythm of a Mozart piece he will lead that afternoon. His lover Jean is ecstatic, and he is too, as the forgotten minutes tick away until he thinks, in the middle of their love, *"The Performance! O my God, The Performance!"* leaping from the bed and scrabbling his clothes on as best he can. He kisses Jean, one long kiss on her lips, her dear lips, picks up his violin, and is off to the theater where the performance will shortly take place.

Meanwhile the plastic black rag that is nothing is stirring in the filthy puddle. The wind picks up and dries a part of the sheet, enough to allow the wind to lift off the whole plastic rag, such as it is, if it wishes.

And yes, as Daniel comes rushing by the puddle, his violin defenseless in his arms, the wet plastic black rag billows out of the fetid puddle and flies smack into the belly of the sweet instrument, soaking it in its wet horror. No varnish protects its innards. It all soaks in.

Daniel has no time. It would have taken hours to heal the violin. He has no time to restore the instrument to its purity. So when he bows his violin in front of the expectant audience and the commanding conductor it gives forth not music but *blah*. He tries to brush the bow ever so delicately, so lightly, but it razzes nothing but *blah*.

He flees. He clutches his wounded violin to his breast, perhaps wounded to death. The violin he loves perhaps more deeply than woman. It was never less than the dramatic word, whether harsh or sweet or tragic. He remembers now his hours with Jean with shame as his violin lay in the corner.

Not long after this performance that came to nothing, Daniel's body was found in Jean's garden, his body dangling on a sour apple tree, his violin in its case, clutched to his stiff body.

It is nothing but a black plastic rag.

ALICE BY THE BEAUTIFUL SEA

I

Walking away from the Walrus and the Carpenter, a much more puzzled little girl than she had ever been except when talking with her elder sister, Alice met a Pelican waddling on the beach, looking out to the Ocean with dark and wishful looks.

"How do you do?" Alice said, for she always did her best to be a polite little girl.

"I do not do very well, if that's what you mean," said the Pelican.

"My, but this is a petulant bird," she thought; but she said, "I am very sorry to hear it."

"I'm more than half blind, as you should be able to see at a glance, and horribly hungry!" the Pelican sputtered.

"Please forgive me. I must be blind myself, because I don't see what you creatures behind the Mirror can see."

"What Mirror is that?"

"It's in the parlor?"

"What's the parlor?"

Simple as that question was, Alice did not know how to address it, not standing here by the Ocean where parlors seemed ridiculous. So she came back to where they had begun. "Why are you blind?" she asked in her most ingratiating voice.

"Watch!"

With that the Pelican loped down the beach flapping its tattered wings. After several false starts it leaped into the air and soared so high that Alice thought the Pelican was very handsome. At its peak, however, the ungainly bird plummeted into the Ocean, where it wobbled, ducking its head into this wave and that. At last, after several useless stabs with its beak, the bird flew to the beach, skidding into the sand next to Alice.

"There, you see?" it asked.

"What?" she said despite herself.

"Haddocks! I fall among them, almost breaking my neck, and every time I hit the Ocean the more it breaks in my eyeballs, I can't find my way through that weighty darkness—and the hungrier I become."

"But I saw nothing of the sort," the little girl said. "Can you do it again?"

But the Pelican chirred, dropping the accustomed solemnity of its kind, turned its back on her, and stalked away.

"Well, the Ocean will win," said Alice to herself, "if the creature will take that attitude." So she turned her back on the Pelican and left it to its distress. Soon it was no more than a spot on the beach, and soon she could not see it at all.

II

As Alice walked beside the Ocean the heat of the sand became unbearable. The sun hung at noon, and she feared it would never move. As she climbed a dune she heard on the other side a hammering that was as blunt and chaotic as the hammering of the breakers, and from the top of the dune she saw a crowd of people very like pawns at work on a pier stretching far out into the waves and next to the pier rose a tower.

"Good work, isn't it?" a quiet, oily voice asked her, a voice possessed of authority. Looking up she saw a great, green-spotted Lizard lying on a long rock.

"Yes," she agreed. "What is it for?"

"Look out, far out, and tell me what you see."

So she looked far out, and hovering above the horizon of the Ocean she thought she saw land.

"Is that land I see?" she asked.

"Yes, it is land, the end of the ocean," the Lizard said in great satisfaction.

Alice was prepared to agree, for she had been well educated and knew about the pirate lands and the convict lands, all very exciting; but nevertheless something stubborn in her did not like the Lizard, so she said, "Perhaps it's an island, or perhaps a mirage!"

The Lizard was a lazy creature, slow to anger, with a very low metabolism. "If you climbed my tower," it drawled, "you would see the ocean come to an end."

"Have you climbed your tower?"

"No."

"Then how can you trust someone's account at second hand?"

The Lizard winked at her. "They can't help but tell me true."

Unwilling to yield her point but seeing that the Lizard was devoted to an ocean that was not *her* Ocean, Alice said, "It is very hot today."

"But I," the Lizard winked once more, "am a rain-maker."

"I can hardly believe that," she said, and added, "My sister would not allow me to believe such a thing."

"Stand back!" The Lizard stood high on its two front legs, raised its head, and stuck out its forked tongue. It rattled its tongue, a challenge and a command to the sky, and as the tongue rattled and a crack of lightning shook the shore, a sudden torrent of rain spilled from the clouds and drenched them.

When it stopped, the Lizard was no larger than her forefinger, and Alice was a little girl. The tower had cracked in two, and the pier was washed on the shore.

"Oh dear," said Alice, soaked to the skin.

She sat down on the long rock until her clothes had dried in the high sun. Unable to find the Lizard, she left with no word of Goodbye.

III

She walked down the beach until the sun began to set. The heat of the day was considerably more bearable, and soon she met a Crab, sidling down the shoreline with a great rake in his claws, combing and raking the Ocean.

"Why are you raking the Ocean?" she asked the Crab.

"Because it is so large!" he replied.

"But your raking does no good," she said. "The Ocean is still as large as it ever was."

"That goes to show. I need to rake faster."

"But," she replied once more, being now in a contentious mood, "whether the prongs of the rake are thicker or thinner, whether the distance between them is larger or smaller, the Ocean will still escape every effort you make."

"There you go!" shrieked the Crab. "You do always make things so difficult!"

At his words she looked out on the Ocean, and she had to agree. It was more than large, it was huge. She had not known what she was saying when she argued with the Lizard. Alice wondered for a moment how the Crab knew so precisely what her sister would say in this situation, though her sister would never lose her temper as the Crab did. She then knew what she should say, and she said it very softly.

"You are nothing," she said, "but a Crabapple."

The Crab turned red as though it had been caught in a grievous error, flung the rake onto the sand, and shrank and shrank until—

—it *was* a Crabapple.

It was a red, knotty Crabapple, as wrinkled as an old man, sitting upon a dune and facing the measureless Ocean. It looked like a Crabapple.

Alice walked away satisfied, for nothing more was to be said.

MR. HOFFMANN'S CAT

Mr. Hoffmann's Cat was a cat of ill omen. It was no mere habit of the dogs to bark furiously, hopelessly, mindlessly to indicate the silky presence of the nasty ill omen, a rage that never put the cat out of countenance. It was not as though dogs had to bark at cats, and it was not as though the dogs had no reason to bark. No, it was the beast's slinky arrogance, its death-gray ambience, both rich in emotionless gray fur and in the impressive rich fluff of the gray air around it that drove the dogs insane. A fatal abundance of iron-gray absence. It performed a slinky and lively death, and of that there was no doubt. How could the dogs not know it? How could we not know it? Dogs and masters were in perfect accord in the matter of this cat.

A part of this ill omen resided of course in the fact that Mr. Hoffmann's Cat ran free. The dogs on their leashes in our modest development of townhouses surely realized that the cat was free, able to go wherever it had a mind to, but I do not believe that they barked from envy. They did not wish to climb a tree or the roof of a house or to crawl for shelter under a car. They wished and desired desperately to tear the ill omen to shreds, and we were apologetic in preventing them. "I'm sorry, Rufus or Patches or Sophy," we said. Like them we did not like the cat, but we did not understand how justified they were in their blind fury.

There is the question whether the ill omen of Mr. Hoffmann's Cat had descended upon it, as it were, from the fact that it belonged to Mr. Hoffmann. But he was, we had to admit, in his quiet way one of the most polite and courteous of men when we met him at the mailboxes and discussed the weather. Though he was not forthcoming, his long lean body and long narrow head, the entire set of the man, was not sullen or repressed. He had no secret agenda; he was no more than we saw on his surface. He was not an ill omen and had never been an ill omen; that is to say, no one believed that three gallons of ill omen had once sloshed from the man into his cat and left him the affable gentleman he had always been. And lest you imagine that he was an SS officer who had fled the atrocities he had committed, you need to know that he descended from three generations of German-Americans. Neither more nor less, he was a sweet, elderly gentleman.

But how then was this cat ominous? It sat there, poised on the slope of wild grass, thistles, slate and dangling flowers as though poised to pounce, looking down on us as we passed its purview. Whether man or beast, its look exerted a pressure on us all. But ominous as the look was, we did not truly understand it, not until the shroud of fur and flesh passed away.

I say "it" because we never did know what its sex was. Its gray fur was so massive that it hid, in post-Edenic shame, the significant organs. One day Mr. Granger tried to brush away the mystery by confronting Mr. Hoffmann.

"Have you had your damned cat neutered or spayed?" he asked, shaking in his hand the contract of the association.

"Oh yes, very early, barely no more than a kitty-cat—puss was puss and puss is puss. It's all been seen to. All the forms are safe with the veterinarian. You were asking?"

Puss was rubbing Mr. Granger's leg and looking up at his groin, looking up and showing its pearly teeth.

"Good," he said, "good," and stalked back to his patio. As he closed the door he looked back at Mr. Hoffmann and Mr. Hoffmann's Cat. It deigned him a distant notice and yawned.

After this encounter we did not know what to think. Was the cat of this sex or that, neutered or spayed or never seen to, for who would trust Mr. Hoffmann, innocent as he was, in matters like these since he never seemed very bright? Hereafter the androgyne cat, more ominous than ever, strode in our nightmares.

Incidentally, the cat in its droopy mustaches had no other name than Mr. Hoffmann's Cat, though the man never called it anything else than puss or pussy, and on one disgusting occasion referred to his kitty. We called the cat Mr. Hoffmann's Cat.

Mr. Granger had once asked Mr. Hoffmann why he could not keep his damned cat penned, but Mr. Hoffmann only smiled and said he simply did not have the heart to do such a thing. To pen the puss, no! it would have been a crime. The association of townhouses had the right to fine Mr. Hoffmann for his refusal, but he was too sweet a man to treat so—at least, that was the excuse several members of the board advanced when Mr. Granger, seconded by his friend, the impressive, tall, bearded Mr. Slingsby, raised the issue at the quarterly meeting; but no one believed it, no matter how far Mr. Granger or Mr. Slingsby could press the point. It was the fear that the cat roused in us, and not only the fear that the dogs felt. We all feared Mr. Hoffmann's Cat. It was the way its head darted quick and accurate as the head of a white owl. It was the way when it came upon a chipmunk that it gloated and purred and whispered its madness in its whiskers. It was the way—you can't understand.

And so things went until the day when Mr. Hoffmann's Cat died.

I must insist upon this point. There is no reason not to believe that Mr. Hoffmann's Cat died, although we had no first-hand evidence to the fact; nevertheless, the several rumors that served us as obits in the association all seemed to agree. Someone, perhaps Mr. Granger, perhaps the elderly dachshund Max, perhaps the sportsman Mr. Harper, one of them according to the rumors found the gray, deflated body on the steep slope that looks down upon all the townhouses, the back of its neck worried by the fangs of some fearless beast, perhaps a badger. None of the leash dogs ever confessed to the deed. For days they were more spooked than ever; for days they never barked or yelped, and Max meticulously avoided the slope. He felt it was best not to piss his elderly signature there, though it had been his favorite place in days gone by; elderly dachs-hunds may be sentimental, but that does not impair their rationality.

But a few weeks later the actual reason we had for believing in the death of Mr. Hoffmann's Cat came upon the death of Mr. Hoffmann. He had not shown any emotion earlier, no tears at the mailbox, no attempt to engage anyone for any casual reason. He remained the quiet gentleman he had always been. But one day his neighbor mentioned that Mr. Hoffmann had not been out in his car on errands for days, and he was certainly fond of his car. We rang at his bell and knocked. With no answer we consulted the police about the matter, who broke down the door and found him dead in front of his television watching the animal channel, holding a photo of his gray beast.

Some things you cannot believe. The Germanic essence of the lean Mr. Hoffmann was not given to tears. But he and his spooky cat were dead—and as far as the cat was concerned, that brimmed over in ill omen, good riddance!

That's what we thought for some weeks until we began to forget them, both the man and his cat. Then one day the Chihuahua Zoe had a bad experience. Her mistress was walking her out in the bright sunshine—it was late spring—when Zoe leapt forward at some invisible something, tottered back, lifted a paw as if to say, "Slap me five," or "Mistress, farewell," and keeled over dead, her throat ripped out.

We were all impressed, but we knew what Chihuahuas are like, and we had no sympathy with the hysterics of her mistress. We were fools.

Soon it was worth the life of your dog to take it out on a leash. We appealed to the board of the association, which was unmoving. All pets on leashes—that was the regulation. "What about the gold-fish?" someone jeered. They began to give way when Miss Muhlenberg's Great Dane Floribunda had a bad experience that left it gasping and bloody and dead on the pavement. Worse was when the flaccid body of a badger was found, dragged from its lair on the slope, beneath its habitual wide grin a triangular napkin of blood, its blunt eyes gray in the sunshine.

But that was not quite the worst. We became truly scared when Mr. Granger told his wife he would walk up the slope on the elegant wooden stairs that crisscross it to fetch the mail, as he told her without fail every Tuesday, but this Tuesday we found him sprawled next to the mailboxes, his throat maimed with great verve leaving a jagged edge of flesh and a nasty little scrawl on his forehead that might as well have read, "Mr. Hoffmann's Cat, His Mark." A careful anatomy revealed that the muscular hind legs of the beast, which we had no doubt now was Mr. Hoffmann's Cat, had removed Mr. Granger's testicles, to Mrs. Granger's sorrow until she married the chief gardener of the association two months thereafter and removed to South Carolina. She was lucky.

Do I sound put out perhaps? Yes, but it is not simply that my wife and I own a dog. For all his loud blather I did genuinely appreciate Mr. Granger and mourned his death.

And what do you think the police, called in multiple times, made of the terror in the townhouses? What were they to make of this case, besotted as they are, as we all are, by the worship of the pussycat, dedicated to its sharp pearl teeth and its uncut claws? But they knew nothing of the nature of Mr. Hoffmann's Cat. In truth none of us did.

Mr. Granger was the first human prey the phantom cat killed, but he was not the last the cat had set its sights on. Every owner of a dog feared going out. Those residents with jobs you could see at seven in the morning skittling from their front doors to their Hondas and Subarus, clicking the door of the driver's seat open and leaping in. Slam went the doors and off dashed the cars, happy to leave the townhouses overlooked by the slope for the safer prairies of corporate life.

Those at home plowed the growing piles of dogshit that gathered day by day on their wall-to-wall carpets and tossed the bags from the windows. At night no dog could be persuaded to go outside, whether on a leash or not, and it was striking that our cats shared the same aversion.

But it was no good to flee from the compound. When we learned of the fate of young Ms. Lily, crashing through the kiosk that stood by the entrance of her business, her cheeks scarred by claws and her throat sheered away by the thing's ritual aggression, we realized we were not safe. We were none of us safe, nowhere. We suspected that even if we sold our townhouses at a low price and fled the city we were not safe. Because we had scorned Mr. Hoffmann's Cat. We were one and all of us dead.

For this was the nature of Mr. Hoffmann's Cat. It was fatal and deadly, an ill omen we could not overcome, something bred horrendous. The optimistic Mr. Hoffmann had never understood these matters. Those of us left alive came to readjust our estimate of the man. He was sweet and gentle, yes, but he was also stupid, radically stupid to have never understood the nature of his cat, draped in its gray ill omen that was still potent despite its death. More potent. Released from its veil of flesh, it was now invisible. How else could it have succeeded in its attacks? And thinking that, we became more terrified.

We hung bags of catnip on our door knobs in hopeless appeasement. The catnip disappeared, but vital parts of Mr. Hawkes, the chairman of the board—his testicles, kidneys, and liver—also disappeared in the following week.

For three weeks we cowered. Mr. Hoffmann's Cat, as we imagined it watching us from the top of the slope, its paws set in the careful pose of the Sphinx, had assumed the status of an *éminence gris*, with all the rights and appurtenances the phrase implies. The right to kill, the right to play with its prey, and such appurtenances as claws and polished fangs. What more does an *éminence gris* require?

Well, of course, it required us, and it required of us all, body and soul. At the beginning Mr. Hoffmann's Cat did not demand that much of its prey—a bit of cheek, the Adam's apple, and certainly the testicles. But weeks passed before the cat grew, invisible though it was, to the next stage when Mrs. Gershwin was found one morning eviscerated, a few feet of her intestines trailing from her body. Had

we any doubt earlier about the nature of the beast that was persecut-
ing us, we had no such doubts any longer; for at the end of the trailing eviscera was the dainty mark of a large cat, its paws written in
blood as large as salad platters. The cat was not quite as large as we
had expected, perhaps the size of an ocelot, but that was sufficient.

I have said that Mr. Hoffmann's Cat played with us. A few days
after the death of Mrs. Gershwin a resident called Mr. Harper began to sport a revolver, but it did no good. Hardly had he begun to
boast of the gun and of his expertise with it but we found him dead,
not only his throat removed (as had become de rigueur), but the five
fingers of his right hand, the revolver hand, toothsomely gnawed to
the bone. That of course constituted the *hors d'oeuvre;* in the feast
that followed most of the sportsman was consumed. Ten feet away
the revolver lay in a puddle.

The victim I am most loth to speak of is Mr. Slingsby. He had
been with Mr. Granger the most vociferous member of the association, demanding that the fearful puss should be leashed, so the delay
of his death became increasingly curious. But our attempts to read
the mind of the *éminence gris* were never successful.

One afternoon we were fetched to our windows by screams, Mr.
Slingsby's screams. It was very peculiar. He stood six and a half feet
high, muscular and ponderous and, as I have said, heavily bearded,
but his screams were falsetto, shattering the blue sky. Black scars in
the sky peered down on the parking lot.

At one point the granite slope forms a narrow corner, and there
ran Mr. Slingsby, back and forth between the granite walls, horrified
by something we could not see. But then we understood. Mr. Slingsby was not simply running; he was being batted back and forth by
large, heavy paws. Mr. Hoffmann's Cat was at play. Its claws, extrud-
ed from those paws with great restraint, were ripping off the man's
clothes, nip by nip, leaving behind bloody gashes. For the first time I
realized how much Mr. Slingsby himself resembled an *éminence gris*.
Something gray, profoundly gray, dripped from his moustaches. It
was not a pretty sight, but we could not help but watch; no one

thought of bringing help. I mean, it was a naked, guilty pleasure, to see his six and a half feet batted about helplessly, and you who are reading this account should keep in mind your own guilty pleasures.

At last Mr. Slingsby, exhausted, almost naked, fell to his knees, and the cat, now the size of a lion if we could only see it, bit his head off. The head of the man on his knees disappeared in a fountain of blood, and slowly parts of his body joined the head, dispatched to the hell in the stomach of Mr. Hoffmann's Cat.

Rhetoric is hell. We were more terrified than I can tell you.

And then the slaughter ceased. For some time, terrorized as we were, we did not dare to believe our good fortune. For months in fact after the death of Mr. Slingsby it was almost impossible to leave home unless famine drove us to dare it—and several of those who could not set a foot outside the door, if they were fortunate enough to have a pet, like a sizable dog perhaps, found they could hold out. And we seldom spoke or tweeted or emailed each other, probably from the shame of our cowardice. At last, however, we began to realize that no one had died since Mr. Slingsby. The tics that several of us had betrayed during the siege—winking the eye, rubbing the chin, or drooling—did not stop; in some cases they worsened. Half a year after Mr. Slingsby's death most of us admitted and agreed that Mr. Hoffmann's Cat was gone. We stepped outside to greet the beginning of spring. Some of us found stepping outside impossible and still cower at home; we bring them food.

We have no idea why Mr. Hoffmann's Cat went away. Perhaps it had grown too large for us, or we had become too few to sustain it. Perhaps it had tired of the stray man or woman—or the child waiting for the school bus . . . as though we had staked out a sacrifice. Yum, yum. The cat could no longer trust us any longer to be so stupid as to leave the house. We don't know.

But you out in the populated worlds, be careful when you hear a low, guttural purr of ill omen behind you, such as an *éminence gris* would utter, its soft breath on your cheek. Run.

PLAYING WITH FIRE

A boy once held a magnifying glass in his hand. And the sun shone bright. He held it over the pile of leaves he had raked that afternoon with his father. It was mid-November. He had learned something interesting in *The Boy's Book of Science*. He held the glass in such a way that a bright, round spot darkening to a brown spot appeared in one of the withered maple leaves. It browned and darkened and smoked. It was a mystery and it wasn't. He held the sun in his hand.

He held the magnifying glass in his hand steady. The leaf took fire. When the leaf took fire the pile of leaves took fire also. He stepped back. The fire rippled through the pile of leaves and the gray smoke piled up in the sky. The boy's father, who had been sitting on the porch, came down and told him that he must be careful with fire. It could be dangerous.

Later it was summer. He sat on his heels in front of his family's porch and held the magnifying glass in his hand to look at the maple and oak leaves, to inspect their veins. He was the sun, he remembered that. An ant skittered across the concrete. It had business to do. He was the sun. He held the glass in such a way that the focus fastened on the ant. The ant paused, shriveled, and popped. Pop, pop. A small spire of swift smoke rose. Without curiosity another ant looked over the edge of the concrete and followed its fellow, but the focus fastened on it too. It ran here and there, butting its nose against the circumference of the focused light, but at last it stopped as though it had stumbled, popped, shriveled, and burned. Caw, caw, the black birds cackled, whether in approval or disapproval the boy did not know. He looked up at the porch, but his father was not there.

His parents had given him a microscope. Through it he examined butterfly wings, moth wings, maple leaves, and mayfly wings. He looked at monstrous potato leaf-hoppers and he looked at ants. He looked at flakes of his own skin. He felt shame.

He had a new book, and in it he could trace the mathematics of the magnifying glasses as they were set, one against the other, the discrete narrow triangles as they formed the different foci. The mathematics of course was simple: the division of the focal length of the objective lens, that which gathered the rays of a star or planet or moon, by the focal length of the eye lens, that which steadied the rays introduced to it by the objective. It was a dance and a game, how to gather the most knowledge by the least and the most taught matter at hand. He could see now how magnification came into being. Godhead on godhead, light upon light. He bothered the adults ceaselessly about these matters. He was still young, and he would be young till the day he died. If it weren't for the ants.

It was too bad that the house did not have a fireplace. He would have argued with his father about that, but his father was dead now, long time dead and gone. Instead, he could build fires in Cub Scout camps out in the fields, sometimes with matches if the Cub Scout master was standing over him, sometimes with his new, small magnifying glass. Everyone approved of his magnifying glass, so he made many fires every summer, watching the odd dance of the flames, darting between the twigs and dry sticks. Needless to say, he received a firemanship badge for these activities. He did not receive many badges, but he was proud of that one, though he took no pleasure in extinguishing fires.

In college he discovered the new delights of fire in the dormitory. He sprinkled oil from his cigarette lighter inside an empty wine bottle and snapped the lighter at the opening. A blue fire went *phutt*, a calm swift *phutt*, and shot into the bottle where the blue fire, like a spirit, hung inside, breathing up and down like a living creature, shuddering, yes, shuddering, alive in its own demonstration of life. He was entranced.

This moment as he watched the spirit of the fire rise and fall inside the wine bottle should have revealed to anyone else if it did not reveal to him that he was an artist of fire. It was not the death or the pain—he still remembered the ants, well, no—that sang to him when the individual ant burned and sizzled, the moment that now caused him such shame; it was the deep peculiar nature of that pain. For no one other than he could have created it, child though he was. Nothing of which removes any of the shame.

Also in college he arranged matches in various designs, having in mind a domino effect, one domino striking another; this was the time of the Vietnam War, so such language was in the air, the conviction that the world was about to go up into flames because of the domino effect. Instead, he lit his matches and watched them burst into flame, some slow and some ping, ping, pong, ping. It was not as exciting as the blue spirit in the bottle, and it did crack the glass plate he had arranged them on. He did not pursue his domino fires after that third trial.

When he was married he lit candles on his wedding night. He had caught white moths that day and now unscrewed the jar and released them. "Look," he said to his bride Jacqueline, "look," as the moths began their dance, circling the flames and circling until one by one by one each moth went *phutt* at its consummation in its flame. When every moth one by one had gone *phutt* he and his bride made love. She meant to ask him about the moths and the flame later in their marriage, but the topic never arose. She felt shame.

He was never aware that one reason he desired Jacqueline so profoundly was his love for her name, jagged like a flame and syllables that resembled when they were on his lips the varied colors of flame, dark-red, green-gold, and blue-white in a strong wind. His name was Donald, a dull, extinguished name. He was no one special except for his unaccountable dread of ants, scrabbling ants.

For a short time this dull Donald took a job as a fireman. Once he and his partners were called out for a fire in a large five-story building. It was a thrilling event in which thank God nobody died, but he had to extinguish the fire, not feed it. He really preferred to feed the fire, slowly, with care. He felt like a hypocrite in the station, called out day after day to extinguish fires, not to feed them, and though his friends at the station urged him to stay he felt at last that it was impossible for him. Besides, putting fire out was no art. It was only bravery and technology, but neither bravery nor technology was an art. And Jacqueline insisted that he come home, as was only right.

He could not, however, forget that building. A few acts of arson in which no one died—thank goodness—did not satisfy him, for what is a house after all? It is always and only a small, circumscribed space, and buildings of some considerable space enjoy guards.

He was never certain how he came upon a new, beautiful idea, but he bought some origami papers in a toy store and spent some time trying to represent flames with the fragile paper. Jacqueline sniffed. But then he realized what the papers were truly about. After some experimentation he folded sixteen of the papers into the shapes of kites, inserted small birthday candles into each one, and drove them outside of the city to a small, bare hill. He persuaded Jacqueline to come along, but that may not have been necessary to his project.

"This shall be," he said, "something very special, believe me." She had been very tired for some months, but now she brightened up. She needed an adventure.

On the hill he waited until the sun had set. Then he lit one candle and lifted its kite into the air. A small breezed carried it ten feet to his right hand and lifted it higher. He lit three more and released them, then another three. By this time six candles at different heights surrounded him and Jacqueline. She picked up two, lit them, and released them. They now were lighting and releasing the kites in a rhythm they seemed to have created between the two of them. Kites were shining and beginning to dip down while some were bouncing up. At last the sixteenth kite, glowing in the darkness, left her hand, soaring and dipping, and then they could not see it. He drove the two of them slowly back into the city. He was dreaming of larger kites and candles.

The magic, however, between them could not last much longer. Shortly after his divorce from Jacqueline on grounds of incompatibility, a divorce that he saw no reason to contest, he visited Providence, Rhode Island, to see the Waterfire event. The great spurts of flame in the middle of the oily river and their leaping reflections satisfied him very much, but he could not afford the event for very long though he rented a cheap room. After all that glory he returned to his small, rather drab apartment where he now worked as a night watchman.

This, then, was a life of no great achievement, a life of dreams in which things burst into flames, in which flames circled each other, and hot, bright cinders burned for eternity. He was drinking too much. Only a great desire would redeem him from his life, and only a great desire would save his world from combustion.

An artist aches for these things and thus transforms the world, transforms it with no idea how it has happened. So that is what happened.

On the Web he stumbled upon an historical event, a great fire that he wished he had seen. The films that had been taken were in black and white. More than seven million cubic feet of hydrogen! The construction, more than three hundred feet long plunging down, and the fire plunging up! It had thousands of tons of water as ballast and sported a smoking lounge, no doubt in defiance of the odds, which had nothing to do with the disaster. Oh, he wished so much he had been in New Jersey to see it! He wished so much he had not been born out of time.

As he read the details on the site something began to go wrong with his eyes. Often when he spent too many hours at the laptop he would begin to see double, but this was different. The space between him and the screen began to scrabble, scribbling and scrabbling, trying to write a message on the screen, or was that his fingers darting across the keyboard, or was that a creature attempting against all odds to appear? Was that an ant? Yes?

He knew perfectly well what it was, and could not say no to it. It was the ghost of the first ant he had ever killed, bright in the focus of the glass. No spotlight ever shone with such brilliance. Spurts of smoke rose from the creature as though it still burned. One of its two jaws was burned away, so it could not eat well, but that could not matter very much to a ghost. And two of its legs that would saw-saw its words at a high pitch were burned off. He had no doubt as he looked at this ghost that he knew this ant very well, just as it knew him. Nevertheless, despite its ancient injuries, this ant rattled out the crucial question whether he would like to go back in time and across in space to this event. Yes, he said in silence, in full humility.

And as he wished it so fiercely he was there, no longer sitting in front of his laptop but raised to his feet, walking into that space beneath an enormous airship, the swastika on its bulging side, as the sun was setting in the west and the last of the lightning was rattling off to the east. All the harm he had caused would be purged. Yes, he was walking into the space beneath the *Hindenburg* in the full and cheerful knowledge of the imminent expanse of fire that would soon engulf him. He was so moved by the fire and its heat that he hardly heard the glory of the long explosion when it fell upon him.

After a day on the pleas of his neighbors the police found his black, charred body in his apartment, still smoking. Spontaneous combustion they agreed, scratching their heads. What else could they say?

PUNCH STANDS ALONE

We do not know why it happened. She was a bright, balanced graduate student in sociology, living upon a sizable grant, but one night something went wrong and the whole tenor of her life changed. But do such crimes cause this? Or was it the newspapers she used, full of more atrocities than usual, horrors that wrench the beams of the world apart?

So one night—on a dark day in her life, when passing clouds were full of gross thunder and lightning and other clouds released sheets of rain, whatever the bad weather had in mind, this young woman decided to make hand puppets. No one but herself would produce her plays; she knew that very well. So she decided to be her own creator, director, and author. She would be in control. Her belated childhood struck with irresistible power.

First she tore up newspapers full of horrible things—so much for the *New York Times*—and made a great primordial pile of papier-mâché and scooped out of it an amount sufficient to form the head of a Cute Young Thing—that was her, of course. Crack said the thunder as she carved away the first strips from the puppet's cheeks, while above her cheeks rolled her large, yearning eyes. A toilet paper tube served as the neck in which the operator's forefinger would be inserted, as five other tubes would serve as the necks of the puppets to come. When she had finished with her beauty she set her erect and delightful on the radiator that was warming and drying her world as the temperature outside dropped.

Next she created St. Peter with puffy cheeks. His sanctity would also serve as an irate father or as a public man; he was the bourgeois as no one ever was. As the young woman splattered the papier-mâché around the forefinger neck and his thick jowls, St. Peter nodded and the black heavens rumbled and crackled. The young woman laughed.

Next in swift order she created God the Almighty, white-haired, aged, and angry, and the thin, red-faced devil fluttering in flames, his horns supported by paper clips embedded in the papier-mâché. This devil must have pointed out to the young woman that the devil and God were made out of the same papier-mâché, so divinity and deviltry shared the same being, and the young woman laughed again and nodded her head at the infernal theology. Barely had the two puppets left her two fingers to sit on the radiator next to each other when crack, crack, crack, full of a lightning not to be withstood the young woman turned from them in supreme indifference. It was time to make Punch and Judy.

Judy, of course, she made in a subtle contrast to the Cute Young Thing. Squalling and cursing, she whom in the depths of her being the young woman wished to love, a worthless mother, she labored over Judy, tough and procreative and monstrous. She set her on the radiator apart from the Cute Young Thing, half fearing that they would fight, as in the nature of things they would have. She kissed her heavy nose and turned to Punch.

Punch was set against all. That was the tradition, and the young woman meant to follow the tradition to the last drop of her being. Crack, crack, crack thundered the black heaven, rippling in thunder and lightning. The young woman dropped to her knees, holding up the rapist Punch as her only defense against other men, her right forefinger waggling the frightful, hawk-nosed, grinning face. This was Punch, murderous and victorious over all.

With that at last the young woman went to bed. It was late, very late, and she had two complex classes in the morning. But it didn't matter. She had her cast of gray mash, ready to assume and fight through any role.

But as she turned off the lights, took off the rags she had dedicated to the mess of making a papier-mâché troupe, slipped into bed and turned over, something happened, horror and acceptance! She had made them, but it was more than that because the blank, papier-mâché faces staring at her were more than Godhead, and they were staring at her. She was horrified and accepting. They were all of what she could give them, and she could give them so little, since they were divine. Many years and in another country she realized that she had learned that first night how easy it was for us to learn to worship the works of our hands. We had put ourselves into idols, and the idols, the gods that is to say, would not let us forget it.

For her, however, the gods bestowed power.

She turned the light on, and all was as it had been. The great nose of Punch, however, seemed to twitch in contempt. Once more she turned off the light.

She fell asleep at last, and she fell asleep more easily as the nights passed. Five days later the glossy paint helped; you wouldn't think it, but it did. By that time she had begun to write her first crude "Punch and Judy" shows, little plays in which every one of her characters played a part, but there was no doubt that it was anarchic, sprightly Punch who led the pack and who lived through the moral chaos.

One year passed, a year and three months, before Claire—for that was the name of the faceless young woman who had labored over her hand puppets and evoked the spirits that night—decided to start from the beginning as a theater student, despite the bad reputation she had in the major as a puppeteer. All the worse since Claire had never touched a marionette or a shadow puppet, which are the aristocrats of the puppet world. Everyone in the major knew that she had given performances in kindergartens, Montessori schools, and the parish halls of a few churches, where her God the Father had been received as a bit chancy. For the majors it was not so much the violence of the performances as their childishness. Nevertheless, she was a student in good standing, eagerly learning about the gear, such as the flats and drops, and the tradition of the stage that would stand her in good stead, even when her theatrical world, having no legs or feet, did away with the need of the stage completely.

She learned you must never name the Scotch play. But she fancied Punch as the leading man and Judy as his wicked Missus.

It was in this time that she met Nate. He was the handsome young man, with more than a touch of Punch, that she had made along with other characters on another, stormy night. She hadn't realized how real those characters could be. She and Nate had already slept together for more than a month and hardly regarded those nights as a wooing, quite the contrary, when one morning, the two of them happening to be at his apartment, he stood up from breakfast and said, "I'd like to show you something."

Nate was often of a comic turn, but not always. She would have said, "You've shown me about all you can," but something in his look forbade it. She decided to save the quip for another occasion.

"All right," she said, following him to his large chest of drawers. Bending down, he pulled out the bottom drawer and there they lay, Punch and Judy and the whole ménage, bodiless and naked. His mother had bought them at Macy's, as Claire realized at once, but she never let on that she knew.

"I've only performed with them a few times." She had heard enough rumors at the school to suspect this was modesty.

"I'm not a bad seamstress," she said.

"Would you?" And that was their wooing. They were married six months later, and better than her word she sewed the shirts and frocks quite elegantly. Soon she discovered ways to incorporate his consumer troupe in plays with her grotesque troupe, but it was noticeable that his characters were the villains.

And not long after their marriage, now that the family was so large, she at last constructed a stage. No more flicking her dramatis personae atop the chairs where she sat backwards and crouched down. No one knew that she had help that night as she clobbered her stage together. God the Almighty on his forefinger sweated out the world, in much the same way as Claire had sweated out her actors, and God the Almighty had help in Punch and his club. The effect was quite scurrilous when the red velvet curtain rose on these particular shows. Nate did not much care for her "Punch and Judy" shows that she presented at the college.

One of the performances had an odd moment that we should mention, though we cannot explain it. Punch squawked to Judy, "I'll show you what for!" and she screamed back words that were not a part of the play, "You've shown me about all you can!" Nate was quite embarrassed, but the audience loved it, and Claire collapsed, laughing and laughing, not so much out of control that she still kept her hand in Judy.

There was no great surprise that Claire left the college ABD. Nate worked otherwise, receiving his doctorate six years after their marriage. She and he had already spread their performances more broadly, moving to New Hampshire where they scrounged various volunteer jobs. Now besides the puppets they produced plays with live actors. By this time she had broadened her ensemble even further for a wide variety of adult performances, often without any intent still featuring the irrepressible Punch. They never made so little money as would sink them into poverty. God bear us into the great telling, she whispered, and may the great telling bear us through.

One of the would-be immortals whom Claire discovered was Maxwell—that was not his actual name of course, but Claire never learned that name nor did she care. She was only interested in Maxwell's biceps.

"You see," she explained, "we are not simply a company devoted to live theater. We are also devoted to puppet theater, and you will need to aid me with the hand puppets as we expand the performances."

"I have never done such a thing," Maxwell protested, jealous of his reputation, such as it was.

"Not to worry! I'll give you the training you need. The trick is always to move the puppet before it speaks."

Unfortunately, Maxwell let himself be persuaded. The play which they presented in the Town Hall had puppets that represented local as well as national figures. Shadows of Old Death. Shadows of Ibsen and Strindberg—shadows of Punch and Judy were there of course, as well as St. Peter, the owner of the local cheap rentals. It went along very well until Maxwell began to speak behind his characters. There he was behind the curtains, madly taking up one puppet after another; and to move him along, Punch belabored him with his club, hitting the Muscle Man adroitly at the base of the palm that supported the head. Maxwell screamed, and his wrenched head appeared at the proscenium.

The audience roared. They roared and slapped their legs, taking bloody Maxwell for a part of the play. Never again could Claire or Punch persuade him to take part in one of the plays. This was very odd, because Claire as Punch, screaming in a low key through his whistle, could be very persuasive. The difficulty lay in what happened to Maxwell as he walked home. The pain that had so quickly become as nothing returned sharply, doubling him up and knocking him flat on the sidewalk where he screamed his heart out as best he could. We need more Maxwells.

Not long after that performance Maxwell persuaded Nate to leave New Hampshire for the sweeter climes of California. Claire did not miss Nate greatly, and neither did she miss his bland puppets. The air was freer for the mayhem she was creating through Punch.

Still, she missed him.

Her productions with the hand puppets were very popular, but they began to tire on her, on her hands and on her spirit. So it is not surprising that with time she began to take interest in the history of the puppets, slowly taking up the tradition of the shadow puppets. She read much, with Punch squalling over her shoulder, and at last traveled to Thailand. Then slowly she began to design her own grotesque shadows for her own plays, stately plays in which Krishna and Arjuna and Draupadi spoke in long, stately lines. And even though she had put Punch in the old chest with the other puppets, he could be heard screaming backstage, his scream cutting through the leather and the wood of the old chest. "I'll kill you, I'll kill you, I'll eviscerate you!" he gasped and other such raw oaths. "I'll gasp on your guts, whatever!" The crisis was not long in coming. Despite the news of bad weather she staged once more a Punch and Judy show, one of the old-fashioned shows in which Punch slaughtered one victim after another, dancing around the stage and screeching his victory as a thunderstorm also echoed his triumph, and then to a great crack of black lightning meeting his scrawny fate in a bony, calcareous Death. But then, as he began to cavort in triumph once more, Judy rose up behind him. "No, Punch, no, Punch," her heavy voice rang out, and behind her the other characters ran onto the stage in a great babel of "No, Punch, no!"

But he could not be stopped. He swung his club, and at each swing the electric lightning swung through the hall. He flung himself upon Judy, and at one more swing of the club her head went flying off Claire's finger, and at the next swing Claire's head went flying also, the two heads bouncing through the security gate. And did he dance then! Did he dance!

He clambered to the top of the proscenium; escaping the hands of the terrified puppets and walloping the faces of Tragedy and Comedy, he screamed three times, fierce and long.

For five minutes the audience did not know what to make of his screams. Then he slunk off over the body of Claire and arranged himself carefully in the chest, his club at his side.

Nate returned from California for the burial. Then, hurling containers of propane upon the chest he burned the puppets. Watching the flames, he felt his own hands burn.

THE BROKER AND HIS PET

"Well, yes," he drawled, "you might think it's a bit over your price point, just a bit, but it's a central location, just as you asked, and the commute is less than half of what you expected, and the kitchen—well, you'll have to see."

That was the broker talking. And he giggled. Every broker talks that way. It's a generic occupation, and the clients discover that theirs is a generic occupation too. As soon as they engage a broker they are each and every one transformed from their individual lives and become clients. Every client assumes a particular language. "Ooh, ah, omigod," they enthuse, and then ask anxiously, "What about the grout?" Every client asks for an apartment in a central location, as near to the famous fountain as they can come—for every city has a famous fountain. They believe in history, they say. But they also want a modern kitchen clad in granite, and a master bedroom with a walk-in closet, and a space for Fru-Fru, their Great Dane. They want an apartment within history that has banished history.

They did not say so much that the residence, for so they called it, should be posh and tony—keep in mind they were Americans, democratic and class-free—but it should encourage their individualism and be nice. They were Midwestern with all that that implies; they have principles, but they do not go so far as to say, "Live Free or Die." This couple was certainly no more articulate than we were ever to expect of them. The broker was there to interpret for the young couple and for the other broker. And for himself.

This apartment, you understand, is in Prague or Lisbon or Trieste. The broker wishes to find the young couple an apartment that is in high demand. Or perhaps the apartment is in Naples or Amsterdam or Madrid. In Paris or in London, you understand, the broker would have been forced to fling the young couple into the outskirts where his commission would have not been so great. Our broker works as a matter of fact in Munich.

Our broker is also fond of asking, as are all brokers, "How much do you think this one will go for?" He is such a tease, after the other two apartments he had shown them. The broker, incidentally, might as well be a woman or a man, because the job erases sexuality, though of course the broker is a flirt and is manly; but in the case of this story, this peculiar case, the broker is, as I let slip, a man. He lifts his hand and begins the dance of the euros. His name is Zhuvazhki; many years ago he had arrived as a child with his White Russian parents. Very soon Munich had erased what little Russian the child knew. It is a remarkable fact, borne out by this story, that so many brokers are ex-pats, uprooted souls who are often themselves on the move.

The young couple are Keith Barns, a lieutenant in NATO, and his wife Sandy; but they do not have a pet called Fru-Fru, which is a good thing all round. They will have to contend with a very different sort of pet.

They have arrived for their appointment with Zhuvazhki on the third floor of the property they hope to rent, panting deeply. He is particularly eager to rent them this third-floor property, for reasons that shall only be clear later in this narrative, so he cheers them up on the exercise they will have. "This is the way that only true Europeans live," he says. "This is how they keep slim and can indulge in our famous pastries. Notice the bakery around the corner, very important." He has spoken only this side of insult, but they are laughing. He shows them the austere living room and points out the narrow balcony. Then he takes them through the hall to the bedroom and waits for the moment when the wife sings out, "Oh, Keith, look, a walk-in closet!" Sandy's joy is unaccountable to Zhuvazhki, but he does count on this reaction from every American wife. Omigod yes! Who knows what the walk-in closet means? Sing to me, you depth-psychologist, the song of the sexual symbols.

In this case, however, Zhuvazhki has more to show them. "Look in that back corner," he says with an air of mystery. "That knob."

"Yes?"

"That is the black hole. No, no," he rushes on, "don't misunderstand me. It's an empty space under the eaves, good for storage." That is a magical word in these times: "storage." And Keith and Sandy, who are so often on the move, are easily touched by it.

"Let me have a look," Keith says, lowering himself on his knees and taking hold of the knob. If he had paused at that moment he might have heard something snuffle and shuffle on the other side of the wall. But he did not pause. It was not his business to pause, since NATO had moved the young couple to Munich barely two weeks earlier. Keith is a fine exemplar of a man, one who seldom pauses.

He moved the knob back to his chest and peered into the darkness, and the darkness peered back at him.

"That's sizable," he said, rising and dusting off his knees.

"It's perfect," Sandy exclaimed, "don't you think?"

"How much do you think it will go for?" Zhuvazhki asked, uttering the words that he considered his slam dunk. Once more a generic moment has arrived. The guesswork immediately implied that they would rent and also implied that the price would be more than they had expected in their heart of hearts. Ah well, for such a wonderful apartment as this! In a half-hour Keith and Sandy will sign the papers for the rental.

"Oh," she said, stepping out on the balcony and looking out at the fountain that spouted with historical regularity two blocks down from their apartment. Around its rim cherubim that looked very like cupids strove with dragonets. An historical tram rattled between the cobblestones and beneath her window. Every hour the wooden warriors swing out above the plaza, twirling beneath the clock of the

Rathaus. All this is reconstructed, minutely reconstructed, after the mass destruction of the Second World War.

Zhuvazhki now leads them through the business of dickering with the corporation that owns the apartment, but he has worked with its broker before. They understand each other perfectly. And then comes the business of arranging the mortgage, but Keith would not have approached the broker if he were not well paid by the powers of NATO.

Therefore at this point in the story we would have said farewell to the broker Zhuvazhki. The truth of the matter is, however, that we never say farewell to brokers. They are ever with us. Like ticks they stick to our raiment and find their way into our flesh and pubic hairs. There's no escape from them. Nor should there be. They are your first friends in a new city. To find your dream space they must become your intimates. They know how swift the turnover is in rentals and every other financial engine that the banks have invented in this latter part of the second decade of the twenty-first century of the Common Era. Formal times oppress us. The turnovers are immense, and it is upon these turnovers that the broker waits; but not for long.

Zhuvazhki, of course, was waiting for something more than a mere turnover.

Five years earlier he had undertaken a vacation to the American Southwest, on the search for the big space and the great heat. Adieu to the snows of Bavaria! He was on a tour of course, being himself as much a slave of the tourist world as everyone else. But even for him the polite discourse of Arizona and New Mexico, their cities a/c, that artificial inexhaustible breath, it was too much. So not quite knowing what he was about, he wandered off into the high desert, entranced by the marvelous mauves and pastels that the desert showed at five in the morning. The emergency squads did not find him for two days, and when they did find him he was no longer speaking English or German. Just as in his childhood his first languages had been wiped from his lips.

He was speaking something else. It is difficult to say what he was speaking of. "Oi conon quertz," his cracked lips uttered, with great urgency. "Oi toron quartz." He clutched to his chest the water bottle he had taken on his adventure. It was empty now, but he clutched it to his chest in the emergency room. Even when he was fully recovered he would not let the water bottle out of his sight. This was no doubt understandable. The water in the bottle had saved his life, though that does not seem possible—two days in 120-degree heat that sucks the life out of you as fast as an oven sucks moisture from a crouton.

The truth of the matter is that Zhuvazhki had discovered a pet. Or perhaps it is more true to say that the creature in the bottle had discovered its own pet, one that it would never let go. "Oi conon quertz," it says, and Zhuvazhki will not be allowed to forget it.

Zhuvazhki brought his pet home, back to Europe; he had been anxious that the pet might set off dozens of sensors as he navigated customs, but the creature was immune to them, slinking off into other dimensions of the universe when the sensors of the nasty folk approached it. Zhuvazhki soon discovered that his pet could be very useful to him as a broker. In most of the apartments that the broker was selling or renting it discovered a black hole. Oh, the bliss of utter darkness! Zhuvazhki could not comprehend, and no human being can comprehend, the life that this alien being had led out in the great desert. Its senses, which had for millions of years endured the cold and darkness of interstellar space, now—and what a peculiar word "now" is—discovered the bright heat of the desert. Things do change. The desert died under the seas and in time returned. And Zhuvazhki, poor, pitiable ex-pat, pisser that he was, brought the creature to a space that reminded it of its interstellar life, cold—but not that cold—and dark.

The earth is good. The creature spoke, in words few could hear, "Oi conon rod maskan," words that probably meant "I'm hungry." This is a very rough translation, but we know what happened later.

So what is the scam our broker Zhuvazhki ran? It was very simple. The innocent young couple, Keith and Sandy, rented the apartment and moved in. Keith gathered together all their goods that needed to go into storage and opened the dark hole. He peered into the darkness, and the darkness peered back; eyes and noses and tongues said, "Hello." Keith paid no attention to the regard. He shoved into the black hole the boxes he and Sandy had agreed upon—that took some time—and retired to the kitchen where he clicked open a Löwenbräu while the creature wiped a small scrap of his brain.

In time Keith no longer felt that he was Keith, and Sandy, who had imagined her culinary inventions, dawdled over a ham omelet in the granite kitchen. Their minds were wiped. In two months, out of a deep despair, they decided that they needed to offer the apartment through the good graces of Zhuvazhki once more.

And this was the way he and his pet had bought and sold the apartment since the five years that the two of them had returned from the Southwest desert. A young couple bought or rented the apartment, lost the brilliance of their minds, and called on Zhuvazhki to sell the apartment again. He did, several times over, often month by month, and never bought at a loss.

Until Keith went into the black hole again.

It was Oktoberfest, and the masterful pet slowly extended its magical senses to discover that most of the minds in the city were wiped. Even the great statue of Germania seemed to wobble above the city, her mind wiped, nothing but a brazen metal left. Keith and Sandy had moved out almost all their belongings to their new apartment in the outskirts of the city and Keith had returned for a last review, room by room, to be sure that they had not left anything.

Later that evening he and Sandy were hosting a party to celebrate their freedom from the dark apartment and to celebrate Oktoberfest. Keith had already drunk two bottles in celebration of their new rental. It was easy, room by room, to see that they had done a good job in cleaning the old property. So at last Keith came to the walk-in closet and the dark hole.

He dropped to his knees and twisted the knob. He peered into the darkness, and a hundred horrendous eyes in the darkness peered at him. It was an easy habit to wipe a man's mind, the way a man in a restaurant wipes the dishes that come out hot from the dishwasher. Keith had once been a dish wiper in a restaurant; it was a bitch.

What was left of Keith came out of the walk-in closet slowly. In the living room he looked out the window and his eyes settled upon the fountain. Around its rim the cupids fought with the dragonets, but the rabid battle was now in earnest. Just as the statue of Germania was wobbling on its pedestal, threatening any moment to come down on the city, striding to the determined oompah band playing, "Bier hier, Bier hier, oder ich fall um, fall um!" so the figures on the rim of the fountain were transfigured.

"Put my money on the stony dragons," whispered Keith.

There was a knock at the door. He slowly walked over, dragging his feet, and knocked on the door and giggled.

"Keith, is that you, still there?"

"Yes, Zhuvazhki, just a moment," and with that he opened the door. "I've cleaned out the apartment, no worry about that, but come and see what's happening at the fountain."

Gripping the lapel of the broker he jerked the man over to the window.

"So?"

"Don't you see how the dragonets have almost conquered the cupids? The cosmic principle of Satan shall bring God down in a tremendous crash." And once more Keith giggled.

The broker was perplexed. To his eyes the fountain and its cosmic battle were still as much a parody as ever; God had lost long ago. What was the news? The battle on the rim of the fountain had never taken itself seriously, and it still did not. But then, he had not taken part in the Oktoberfest; and his pet, out of some respect for its pet, had only wiped his mind ever so slightly.

"Well, you have to see it from the veranda," said the ecstatic Keith, opening the door to the balcony and pulling on the broker's lapel again. "You have to see it," and on the next jerk of the lapel he sent Zhuvazhki toppling over the railing and screaming to the cobblestones below. He had been so eager to sell this third-floor apartment, and now he had the third floor in spades.

Keith looked down, tiptoeing off the balcony and out of the room. That night he said no more to Sandy than to praise her cleanly work. A week later he shot her dead and shot himself dead also. Who does not have a black hole?

The pet had felt the horrible rip tearing through his being as the broker struck the stones and his red blood spilled through the cracks in his skull. The pet shuddered, and its shudder rattled everyone that day of the Oktoberfest. For three minutes the people in the tents and booths and the people on the streets were struck blind, groping to find their lost sight again. It did not take long, however, before the corporation had found another broker to pass on the apartment and to give the creature another pet.

Down by the Alyscamps, Up on the Hill

I

If he didn't know any better, a careless ghost would walk right through you on Christmas Eve. Five inches off the ground.

On any night you hear things, if you ignore the steaming neons, the oranges and lurid blues, the torrid greens and reds, the hurting, aching golds. At night the voices begin to speak. Hard times they say, hard times.

On Christmas Eve it's ten times worse. The endless chains of stars down the streets, looped in light-bulbs from streetlight to streetlight, don't hush the voices; the broad gold bows don't tie the voices off; the intimidating shop windows don't hinder the squalling voices. Hard times.

On Christmas Eve there's every kind of voice because there's every kind of ghost, worse than Halloween. On Halloween it's the frights that come out, the licensed terrors, but for Christmas God lets loose the voices of extermination as well as the voices of love. And we can't tell which is which.

On Christmas Eve John Frederick Mason was walking the streets of Arles. Once more he had left Janette in their loft on the lower edge of Soho, Janette and her cat Carrington. She had urged him to go, the cat also, because they had no doubt, she and the cat, that this exhibit was the break he needed. He was not so sure, just as he was seldom sure of anything but his art; he was not sure of the blandishments of Madame Quindonc, but there was no doubt that this dubious break came through the good offices of her bunched black brow.

He had enjoyed other European exhibits, though he had not been invited to attend them in person. The problem with the one in Avignon had been its size, where he was certain his work had been lost in the press. Nevertheless, it was that exhibit, as she later intimated, that interested Madame Quindonc in his work. So here he was, but the problem with Arles was van Gogh. An artist must not think of the past, but how, walking these streets, could he not think of the Dutchman? His presence troubled Mason in ways the American could not divine. He had been uneasy during his visit in August, and he was uneasy now.

The lights of the town seized him now as he walked, as though he were walking through a Christmas tree. Christmas trees lined the curbs or leaned inebriated from the stores, cross-eyed, strung with red bags of gifts and pastries and the guardian-crosses of the Camargue. Fetishes against the mistral. And stars, garlands of stars, shone unabashed through the Christmas lights.

But also in his head moved the lights of the industrial complexes and refineries of Fos sur mer, jittering through irregular geometrical gestures that have the most hypothetical connections with human needs and desires, the sort of complexes that during the day seem void of human intervention. No one walked there; and if any workers in truth walked there, they were absent nevertheless. Those lights were the sort that served as models for Hollywood spaceships; a monster swung its jaw through those spaces. In Fos sur mer the spaceships had landed, hurtling from the activity of their own occluded spaces. The lights reminded Mason of the card he had prepared for his View-Master when he was eight years old. Carefully he had aligned the two frames and punched holes in them with a needle, little pinpricks that had glittered raggedly in the contraption like stars seen through the wide eyes of a god. The immense space his stars had formed blotted out his mother's kitchen. He remembered that now. His experiment, one of his first works of art, might as well have dreamed Fos sur mer into existence.

That morning, when he had driven through Martiques in the Renault that waited for him near the station of Marseilles, where the train from Paris had deposited him, he saw the immense siloes, runways, girders, and pipes of Fos sur mer for the first time. Now, walking the streets of Arles, Mason imagined that the alien lights of the complex lay congruent against the Christmas tree he was walking through. The dark, inhuman swell of the Mediterranean laid itself against the human murmur of the Rhone as it found its way to its extinction. What was better then, an art of the future or an art of the familiar? The juxtapositions of the photograph and the atrocity, of the indecent and the indifferent, or the comfort of the old oils that trailed their old-fashioned love through the vanishing fields and clouds? Of course he hankered back to the oils; one must, with a small part of yourself still human. But, in addition, more than you can bear, you have to be faithful to the world that opens itself up. "Il faut d'être absolument moderne," he whispered with satisfaction, licking his lips.

That afternoon in the Place du Forum he had sat in the café. Where van Gogh had painted and stewed with the growing susurration of wind and despair and bad blood in his ear, Mason stared at photographs of scarecrows and punk goddesses getting it on. The ambiguous Arletty, swathed in black crape, did her imitation of Mona Lisa, Princess Grace and Princess Di leered upon him, Brigitte Bardot conspired, and Jane Fonda as Barbarella stripped. Meanwhile the impertinence of the voices had begun to push itself across the edge of his attention; he couldn't make them out, but the words were, he was sure, beginning to dissociate from the rhythm of the sentences—soon they would stand forth.

Tonight he could feel the stones of the Arena hanging above his shoulders as he turned onto the Alyscamps, the avenue of Roman sarcophagi lined by cypress. Once the Arena had the sense of a structure built for human needs; as the years pass and the stones fall, it comes more and more to resemble the ruinous, alien lights of Fos sur mer. Not so long ago they cut off your ear inside that arena.

Voices mewed in his head.

Janette struck out, in the dark corner of his mother's kitchen, with the bright kitchen knife like a comet in the Book of Hours, cutting a white, cold streak in the yeasty air. After some years the knife remained bright in his mind. Like a comet, like a star. It was wonderful what Christmas brought you, gifts from the mines, gifts from the trees, gifts from the deep past still growing larger, more spacious, in the backward depths of the mind. He had kept the View-Master in the kitchen, in a tin pail of toys beneath the peeling paint next to the sink. The rotting boards sagged when he rummaged in the pail. And Janette had visited there only once. And then two years ago, as he was reading in the late afternoon with snow sprinkled against the red brick across from their loft, as the chair sank beneath him, Janette's hand had blazed through the darkness with the knife. Carrington jumped from his lap. Now, bright as the knife remained, it was hard to remember whether it had been real or a dream.

Walking down the Alyscamp with the canal on his left hand, the sluggish water lapping against the stone, he pulled a small sausage from the side pocket of his windbreaker. He walked, slicing slivers of sausage with his penknife; piece by piece the slivers peeled away from the red face of the meat. Bull of the Camargue.

The problem is how to make an art you can believe in. You can't believe in the landscapes; and you can't believe in the flares and unwinking otherness of Fos sur mer, even though you believed in it enough to create something that resembled it and brought it to life when you were only a child.

A View-Master, for Christ's sake! Soho wouldn't believe it, but that's the only way, though what that would mean he couldn't imagine, not with the mistral picking up and hanging over his head like a headache you can't put your finger on, not with the voices. The mistral is a heavy, yellow splotch of your hungry flesh. And he left it behind as he entered the line of cypress. Black flames lit up his left and right hand.

He couldn't see her at first. She was only a brown mass, smaller than a human body, larger than the potato it might otherwise have resembled, that poured from the slab of a sarcophagus as though an impoverished figure of riot on an Etruscan tomb. But when the brown mass came erect it bore a head that stood out from its gray shawl, a big-boned woman who peered from an earth-smudged, scooped-out face, bending up from the slab on the side of the tomb.

"Wiltu etwat, aliquantulu', quelque?" She was one of the voices, but she was hard to hear. It was not that she whispered; overtones in her voice overlapped, echoes shook in the stones and in the rock-hard frost crystallized in the air. At her voice any moisture left in the air leached away. The flakes of salt in her breath snowed.

He fished in his pocket for coins. A few euros jangled against his penknife.

"Stellje vor, I'm not that sort of woman."

"Of course not."

"It's my man here. He can only sleep so long."

"Your man, here?" He stood back from her to have a better view of the tomb.

"Here," she said, leading him to the head of the stony box. She pointed down at a man curled in blue and yellow rags, snoring against the white blank stone.

"Look at him there," she said fondly. "Watch."

Out of the rags that hung on her breasts she drew a baby, its gray face gasping for the dark air. It couldn't have been more than two weeks old. Quicker than a brush stroke she whipped the infant up by a leg, dangling it over the man, at the same instant that a knife streamed out of her other hand across the child's neck and its blood spurted across the face of the man.

"Vois, vois, vois," she whispered, and John Frederick Mason stared as the man stood up. He stank. His blue jerkin, wet in the blood of the baby, stank from his unwashed skin. "Vois."

"Waarom weck jij mi? Nee," the man snorted. "Jij weck mi?"

Mason startled awake. The lights of the café blurred as he lifted his head from his hand. Princess Di lifted her eyelids fondly, her blond eyes looking down at him from the poster, leading off her square blond jaw. He sipped his cold coffee and decided to walk back to his hotel. Now that she is dead, he thought in the twinkling streets, she is more than alive. Her icon invites everyone to use her; it's obscene. Perhaps she had a place in his new canvas, the one that he was slowly conceiving, a montage of photographs, shapes in oil, and odd lights descending upon a rocky landscape. Odd lights fit for her death. He could occupy his hands in those three days before the exhibit.

She died in Alphaville, in the Paris that is the itch of the future. Godard's cheesy images, living among us now, even in Arles, took on a gloss into which she was being assumed. A divine assumption. He laughed. There is a seismic event outside this world, shaking together the photographs of her, vague shapes of masks and goats, and the odd lights descending. The stink of absinthe and oils.

II

The previous summer in the restaurant of his hotel John Frederick Mason had picked a small roll from his plate to nibble on over his café au lait, rising early to attend the convention where his few canvases were to be hung. He had spent the previous day recuperating from the flight. In that visit, routed through Frankfurt, he had landed at the Marseilles airport, so he arrived in the early morning daylight that poured across the shoulders of Mont Victoire. Sparkling in the August sun, the golden Virgin of Marseilles had greeted the airplane from her precipitous chapel that overlooks the bay in which the hopeless Edmond Dantes lay in chains. Full of that light in Arles, thinking it was possible that like van Gogh he could never have enough of that light, Mason walked through the early morning of the rue de Grilles. At the office he asked for Madame Quindonc, the assistant caretaker of the exhibits, and a tall woman strode out, thick eyebrows bunched at him before she smiled.

"How good of you to arrive early," she beamed. "So much needs to be done before the convention. And then it opens on the twelfth." She shook his hand with a firm downward stroke and kissed him on both cheeks.

"So come along now," she said, turning briskly to lead him down the stairs to the hall before she could see the blush that burned his cheek. But Carrington would have seen it.

His seven canvases had arrived a week before, works he had culled from the last three years, and now they had to be set in order and hung. Madame Quindonc had her own very definite ideas of the order, the height, and the illumination, minutiae that flattered his sense that she was looking at his work with care. Every time he tried to place the origin of her attention to this or that work, this corner, this line, those lights leering out of the darkness, she would turn the argument to the canvases that adjoined his concern. At eleven-thirty she stepped back at last, with five of the works hung, and gestured to the sixth.

"Now that," she said—"how ever did you come to paint that?" The picture that leaned in front of them was recent, a combination of fantasy and fact that still made him ashamed—the reason itself that forced him to paint it. A wooden door stood ajar, too heavily scored in oil for a trompe l'oeil, its hinges lifted off the lintel; and next to it three figures stood, swathed in dark-green cloth. It was cloth in fact, chicken-cloth, that merged into the paint surrounding the door, paint that brushed lightly and thickly across a montage of enlargements showing this and that angle of a cabin and shed, a cubist cabin, one house no doubt but a house taken apart. In the angles where the enlargement didn't meet there were doodles, some of them obscene but the obscenity of a child, some of the doodles cups and wands, a travesty of the tarot suit.

"Hard Times? That's a song." Mason began to intone heavily in a minor key, "Many days you have lingered about my cabin door, O hard times, come again no more."

"You had hard times?"

"We all do. That's how the painting has to work, because we all have had hard times and don't want to open the door on them. I don't. And my hard times were never as bad as other people's."

"But you seem to have found something here you might not have known." She pointed to one of the doodles that seemed to show a monolith, or a small stone, that a pottery pitcher sat upon, brimming in something red. A crescent moon hung like a slanted horn from the lip.

"It seemed right, that's all."

"Let's make a picnic—I really have something to show you. And we'll finish this this afternoon."

Yes, he was famished, hungrier than he remembered being for a long time. That's what comes of a continental breakfast. Mason had been totally honest; his hard times had never involved hunger, and he had never lived in a cabin. That was a symbol, probably inept—it was the paint, the technique that counted, never the subject. But he was so famished he could hardly follow anything Madame Quindonc did in the next quarter-hour to throw together a picnic that only the French would have dreamed of. Into a basket that came out of nowhere went pheasant paté, brie, a warm baguette, two wine glasses, a wine bottle, fruits, napkins, linen, *mais oui,* and they were in her car speeding down a road that curved in so many directions he would have felt utterly lost if it were not for the sun. Then some ten miles out of town—or was it ten kilometers?—she turned right onto a small road and began climbing a hill that shot out of the ground before them, cutting off the sky. Mason yawned.

"This is St. Blaise, one of the earliest archeological sites we know of in the Provence," Madame Quindonc was saying. She had been talking for the last few minutes before he woke up to follow her subject. "The Greeks arrived here before they founded Marseilles. It was a defensive post, as you see. The Gauls were not good neighbors."

He stuffed into the pocket of his jacket a pamphlet she pressed upon him. Tourists were strolling across the hard ground, but not many. The area had achieved none of the popularity that his guidebook had warned him against. This was not Vaucluse or the Roman aqueduct; he didn't think, in fact, that it had achieved any mention in the book at all. The grounds were closed, a great metal fence surrounding the various diggings, but she took him to a hole dug behind a bush, an entrance that only the locals would know, and led him through.

Stones stood out of the ground, and over them the pine-trees swayed in the mounting wind. She settled the linen on the ground behind a stone wall that protected it from the mistral, placed each in its place according to some internal sense of placement that picnics demand, and pointed to the spot where he was to sit. They began to eat, but still she prattled on.

"What must it have been like, do you think, those Greek merchants with their belief in Hermes who would conduct every bit of the business through their lips? Hermes would speak for them, translate for them, pull the scam for them." She tittered at the slang. "But this was far from the polis that had sent them forth; they were west of nowhere. The Greeks believed that the river of the dead lay westward, and so Hermes awaited them as the psychopomp. Do you think one of them saw Hermes one late evening, standing on that hillock, ready to conduct him across the valley to the hands of the Gauls, ready to place him in the wicker beast? And so," she said, wiping her lips and leaning to take his hand, "they brought their other gods here," tugging him up to follow her across the path.

The wine had dazed him, and now the sun was shining overhead, heavy and hot. The scream of the cigales deafened him.

"Look."

He saw at once what she meant. The stone that stood waist-high in front of him might have been the stone he had doodled in that spare space of his painting "Hard Times," the same proportions, the same indentation on the upper surface that would have held the pitcher, if there had been such a pitcher here. And a crescent moon, thin as an infant's fingernail and curved like horns or antlers, carved in the side.

"You see who the god was, the god they brought?"

"No."

"It's hard to imagine now. Despite the environmental vanities we attempt to legislate, the smoke rising from Fos sur mer still smothers the earth. But when the Greeks arrived the land was wooded up and down the hills. Probably the mistral did not blow then, who knows? Woods and boar and deer and hounds, the hunt was rich here. They brought Artemis, the goddess of the hunt, the moon. So when the Romans arrived they found that Diana had been here before them, and was still here."

"That must have been very gratifying."

"Don't mock the goddess. The Greeks called Arles Théline, the breasts, which the Romans translated more fulsomely as Mamellaria. All in honor of the goddess." Mason found that he was staring in the depths of Madame Quindonc's cleavage.

Unperturbed she continued, "And when the three Marys came sailing into the Camargue the great goddess was still here. Bumptious parvenus, they magnified her glory. When the Albigenses were being hunted down by the Inquisition she was still here. Some say that in their hard times they died for her sake. The papacy could not squeeze her out."

"Goddesses are very stubborn." For a moment he saw the knife in Janette's hand streaking through the sky.

"Twenty years ago the government finally turned its attention here—the Provence has never loomed large in the minds of the centrists in Paris—and fenced off the area as a national park. It is for tourists, of course, but the fence is there to prevent harm."

Mason leaned back on his hands, his legs stretched out in the grass as he looked up at the lean evergreens that the mistral had screwed into the most impossible shapes.

"It's beautiful. And how did they conduct the worship?"

"Do you know the story of Actaeon?"

Mason reached back to school, when he had memorized snippets of Ovid. "He saw Diana in her bath. She splashed water in his face and changed him into a deer."

"Complete with antlers," Madame Quindonc murmured.

"And his dogs tore him to pieces."

"Voilà."

"Human sacrifice."

"Mais oui."

John Frederick Mason shrugged and laughed.

"No, you are an artist, you must not laugh. This is the place of sacrifice. Where the church over there stands was the temple to Diana. Near it the archeologists discovered a decapitated statue of Saturn, scarred with the signs of the zodiac and wrapped in a snake. Deballed. I like to think that he is van Gogh, struggling against the course of the year. This is the place where van Gogh's spirit passed incarnate into the landscape, because he had the spirit of sacrifice upon him when he lopped of his ear and gave it to the prostitute Rachel."

"Yes, his Christmas present."

"You need to think about his work more deeply, and his hard times. He is always at the door with the hard times. The place of sacrifice."

Madame Quindonc took his hand more urgently. Near the stone a small, grassy depression seemed to open itself as she lay down in it and pulled him to her. Janette and Carrington would surely disapprove he thought as he shrugged his pants off, but they had insisted he make this journey. He had made many sacrifices to come to this point.

III

And now that it was Christmas, back in Arles once more, he still stood astounded by his luck. The people at the August convention had not simply admired his work; they insisted that he return for his own exhibit, to open three days after Christmas, the Feast of the Holy Innocents Madame Quindonc had reminded him pointedly, "Another human sacrifice one might think, n'est pas?"

And so in three days his exhibit opened, his exhibit, and there would be no more hard times to look back on. At the reception he moved among the French and Italian and German voices like a Neanderthal lost among the more gracious *Homo sapiens,* gawking at the floor through the rosé in his glass, studying the deformations of the spotlights sliding off the rubber boundary that presumably concealed the security sensors. Bowls of peanuts sprinkled in thyme lounged upon two tables in the center of the room, placed there earlier by the careful attention of Madame Quindonc. At the door she was speaking rapidly in French with a middle-aged, leather-loined man whose pince-nez clambered adroitly up his nose. He seemed to require convincing, because Madame Quindonc was becoming quite heated. Her black brows bunched and leaped above her acute eyes. A woman in a chinchilla muff joined the argument as the three moved into the gallery and stood in front of his monolith. Madame Quindonc pointed her left forefinger at the crescent, and the pince-nez and the muff nodded violently. John Frederick Mason nodded to the Rhone wine in his glass and disappeared once more into the swirl of continental Babel.

That night he returned to van Gogh's café. The clock above the door as he peered up at it showed twenty-one o'clock. How odd, he thought. It was hard times again, though the reception had been an obvious success. Hard times, to be twenty-one o'clock—that seems so much worse than nine o'clock and suffering from jet lag. What were his hard times then? Despite the success of the reception and the sums that people were beginning to quote for the paintings, he felt something weary, an impermissible failure, tugging at his heels.

He was sipping an eau de vie, something fiery brewed from pears. Despite its incongruous source every sip bore a wake-up call to oblivion.

His mother had gone through the depression, and from her he learned before he was of an age to consider it the necessity of repression and rectitude. From his great-grandmother, who had endured the War of Northern Aggression, he had learned the necessity of hatred. And from a great-great-grandmother, so ancient he could not find her, a Choctaw from Alabama, he had learned dispossession. The hard times of America burned in his bones.

"May I sit with you, Monsieur Mason?"

The man standing next to him he had met at the gallery. With some effort he remembered. Monsieur Paz, an acquaintance of the leather-loined pince-nez and the chinchilla muff, an executive at the jittery geometries of Fos sur mer.

He wore a face hard to read, whether to say that he smiled or sneered, like a slap or a caress from the finely tapered fingers. Then for a moment the face melted. Its Vandyke became the pointed chin of a devil. Draped between its horns like a snake's head, a speculation ceaseless in its penetration, angular and oblique in the art that it pursued, a russet face peered out at him. John Frederick Mason should not have ordered the eau de vie that swirled in the small glass his hand gripped.

"Your work was very persuasive, you see," Monsieur Paz said, sitting down without waiting for the bemused Mason to reply. "I was moved by it, and startled by it. You work through those different objects as though their configurations were something you had seen in a different life, or a different place. I do not speak English very well, you see, so I need to speak as simply as possible."

John Frederick Mason praised the Vandyke's command of the language.

"I was wondering, you see, whether it ever happens to you that the things you imagine or the things you dream take shape, take . . ."—he paused to find the phrase—"they take reality?"

Mason shook his head, trying to escape the effects of the wine and the eau de vie. "I couldn't say, I'm sure, Monsieur Paz. I do what I can."

"How do you, an avant-garde artiste today, feel about our Dutchman?"

Mason found himself once more at a loss.

"Vincent."

They have always pretended to an intimacy with the man, Mason thought, the intimacy the man had invited, but he replied, "He was a great painter, of course. What more is there to say?"

"His death was such a tragedy."

"Whose death is not?"

"But if you could bring him back, let him complete his work, you would?" The voices and the neon lights collided in the swirl of the eau de vie. Princess Di winked from the wall as he remembered the blood pouring over the stinking blue jerkin.

"Monsieur Paz, I do not know what to tell you, but I think I saw him three nights ago in the Alyscamps."

"Monsieur Mason, of course you did, we are so happy that you did." The Vandyke rose and stood behind Mason's chair. "If you would please finish your digestif now, oh yes, please, and come with us. Allow me." He paid the tab. "We will see whom we can find alive tonight. I know where Rachel is playing the role of the Widow of Ephesus." The pince-nez had entered the café with Madame Quindonc as the executive rested his hand on John Frederick Mason's shoulder.

IV

It might have been a cortège, so carefully the cars drove down the highway south through the night, a dingy Deux-cheveux, showing its ragged leather as a sign of integrity, a black Peugeot, a scarlet Lancia, a silver Lomborghetti, and a new, hunter-green Mercedes. Out in the cold Camargue and north to the fortress of Les Beaux that soughed under the mistral down to the salt fields, up the side of the cliffs and stone walls and stared across the rows of the crippled olives, the inwardness of rock groping through the foundations and oubliettes, across the slopes of the mountains, Mont Victoire's terra-cotta slabs blacking out the rush of the blue-black sky, the witches committed to our memory and fumbled through ancient sacrifice, hurried and measured, the terror for their bodies at war with the terror for their souls. Provence had absorbed the combat of the modern mind because generations ago the extermination of the Albigenses had made the rock fortresses sponges, deep homes for the heretics; and hard upon their heels the Papal armies had riddled it.

Turning off the highway, the cortège began to find its way upon a road shrouded by pine trees. The crescent moon had almost set, and in its absence of the Provençal sun John Frederick Mason meditated upon the other side of the Provençal sun, upon the darkness that demanded its sacrifice. The cars were nearing the top of St. Blaise before he realized where he was.

The Vandyke and the pince-nez helped him almost tenderly from the Des-cheveux that had led the cortège; some of the men in their cloaks bowed to him because he was the dreamer who could make his dreams take flesh. They cut a passage through the fence and brought him to the depression where the past summer, the mistral in their hair, he had lowered himself into Madame Quindonc. Monsieur Paz steadied him as he sat down heavily.

"Do not be concerned," the executive whispered. "You are priceless to us—simply concentrate, dream, listen to your voices, follow your brush strokes. Now think of the café, which belongs to the great painter and the great princess. Think of that."

"Los, los." Other people, faces that Mason recognized from the reception, were helping a man from the second car, and the reek of oil and alcohol and dirt billowing out of the door through the cold, clean air identified the man, the inarticulate drunkard whom he had seen three nights earlier in the Alyscamps. Gold and blue paint smeared his blouse. Mason didn't need to know what he was saying; the gestures were transparent. "Laat mig alleen," he muttered, but they led him to a large, shapeless stone and began to pull at his pants. When he struggled, one of the men held out a tray with a glass of absinthe, held it out like a magician who has just pulled a thin, green rabbit out of his top hat and raised it to the spotlight.

"Gaa," the man said. They raised him for a moment as he sipped at the glass, then shrugged down the green glow in one draught.

Again they lowered him and bumped the pants off his scrawny legs. He gurgled, but Mason could make out nothing he said.

Another car now appeared, Madame Quindonc's. She stepped out, satisfied, still very much the arranger of the gallery and the picnic, and withdrew to his side as the door of the back seat opened and the chinchilla muff helped another woman out of the car. First Mason saw her blond hair, then the blood that slobbered across her face from her brow to her loose, square jaw. She needed their help, almost slipping out of their hands as they held her upright in the poor light of the crescent moon, where she seemed to gather herself together, her jaw clacking against the prominence of her upper teeth and her shoulders and legs falling into place. The blood was wiped from her face.

Mason knew her. It didn't matter that his stomach churned; he had breathed her into being, just as he had van Gogh. The Dutchman was the god, and now the goddess had arrived.

She shook off their hands.

In the light of the stars, shivering through the sky swept clear by the wind, there was no mistake.

She was the princess, the goddess Diana—we knew that she would splatter the shifty streets of the city with her blood. At last her pursuit had rounded on her, Actaeon and the hounds had rounded on her and chased her to earth at a hundred and fifty kilometers an hour, roaring through the tunnels next to the Seine.

But no goddess dies, not when she occupies the dreams of an artist.

Now with a careful step she stepped across the uneven ground where generations of the dispossessed and outcast had knelt and knocked their heads on the rock, to find her place at the foot of the man on the stone. Slowly she undid her belt.

"Dream this," Monsieur Paz said. "'Le tournerol avec la lyonesse.' When our Provençal prophet Nostradamus wrote that line he could not have known the intricacy of his foresight. 'The sunflower shall lie down with the lioness.'"

But John Frederick Mason hardly needed to dream. The goddess seemed to incarnate every woman he had ever entered, whether those whose names he could no longer remember or the others, Rachel, Janette, or Madame Quindonc, who stood behind the goddess now, lowering her into the man in the blue blouse.

As she lowered herself fully and began to rock on him the audience murmured their approval.

"This is the conception," Madame Quindonc announced, her brisk attitude in the ascendency as she helped the goddess off the man and brought her back to the car where she leaned, exhausted and demure. She composed her blue dress. Blue for the Virgin Mary, our star of the discomposed sea.

"And this is the birth," Monsieur Paz chimed in on the beat. "Look," he commanded, lifting his head. And John Frederick Mason looked.

Overhead it was as though the lights that he had created in his View-Master or the lights he had seen in Fos sur mer had come to life. The starship was descending on St. Blaise, but it was no starship. The stars clamped themselves into a new form, the head of an immense snake, its nostrils flaring through Aldebaran and Capella, its jaws opening above the hill. On its fangs stars spiked. The dark matter of the universe, its swell as massive and slow as the tides of the Mediterranean, had discovered its form in the chaste womb of the goddess and was now opening its maw above the planet. The Midgard Serpent was the merest of intimations, the tiniest hint, of this compound monstrosity, which even as a little boy he had begun to dream into being. This is the result of hard times. It was a tunnel of teeth with no outside. It was a black Christmas, festooned through the boulevards and alleys of the universe in black lights.

But though this was the grandest of his visions, John Frederick Mason began to sing subvocally, "Though their spirits are silent, their pleading voices sing," and as he sang pale forms began to rise around the circle that surrounded the two somnambulists. Nondescript, blurred in the wind but stalwart, they had marched so many

stony roads and plowed so many furrows, figures breasted with lori-
cas and greaves, their helmets firm on their small heads; and beside
them, also rising from the earth, figures in tunics and reed-bound
sandals; and also rising, peasants, their faces avid for holiness, their
rags crawling with palaeolithic lice. Their fading forms still say, O
hard times, come again no more. They stand for the honor of the
earth, they will not allow it to be harmed.

He knew who they were, the Greeks, the Celts, the Phoenicians
that had once fortified themselves on the hill of St. Blaise, only to be
erased by newer powers. Even the Albigenses, perhaps the most
thoroughly expunged heretics in France, were holding out in the
midst of these other voices, all these the voices that had attempted
to speak to him on Christmas Eve.

Madame Quindonc hissed in his ear, "Whatever you are doing,
you must stop it now." At a swift gesture the pince-nez and Monsieur Paz hoisted him onto the sacrificial stone. In the stars above
his head she raised a knife that recalled Janette's. Perhaps this was
the knife itself, he thought with gratitude, and Janette had never at-
tacked him. He had predreamt it, that was all.

He smiled as the knife plunged into his breast. It didn't matter.
Those faint forms had already defeated the devourer. He would be
the sacrifice Madame Quindonc demanded, but no one could cap-
ture the soul of the artist that he and Vincent would bear away. The
goddess would allow that.

THE VIOLINIST

At the end of Anne Belford's performance the applause was immense, more than any that had ever been heard in the hall—so her mentor had assured her. But the audience was not without self-interest. Her friends were there, and Mark, a young man who might in time become her lover, her other mentors of course, several professors from the music school, and other people, eager to hear the piece they loved; it was for free of course. She did not trust them.

The lights flickered, and she stepped into the spotlight of her shame, bowing her head.

The event was not that important, only to her. It was her senior recital, her last performance as a student. She had no real reason to be ashamed. She could put her shame behind her as she stepped into her life beyond school and beyond all these people, none of whom she trusted.

But it was her shame, hers. It made no difference that her mentor could whisper that it could happen to anyone.

Anne had chosen her own disaster, playing the violin for that famously difficult piece, César Franck's Sonata in A Major. So much sadness and sweetness, so much ragged ferocity, so much acceptance as this world is given, so much contrition that joy it seems must follow, and it does follow. Doesn't it?

So she worked at it, playing through its tricky parts several times and trying to be worthy of its slippery minor splendors. Once she had chosen the piece, despite the advice of her mentor, she worked at it morning and night. Her left shoulder, which held her violin steady and straight as the bow raged across it, began to ache at the

193

rush of the work, especially its lengthy melodic demands. At night she dabbed at the small spots of blood on her shoulder; but she could do nothing to relieve her growing exhaustion.

Her shoulder ached past belief and her body sobbed for it.

So when Anne found herself in front of the audience, her body and soul sawing across the violin as it dug into its familiar ache, in the middle of the second movement she dropped the violin and the bow to her hip and rushed off the stage, holding back her tears. The shame had hardly begun; she was weeping from the pain at first. Then it was the shame she would never overcome. She had failed, failed in public and failed in her heart.

It did not matter that she came back to the stage and, striking up once more from the beginning of the second movement, finished the piece credibly. The shame stuck in her like a thick bracelet of brambles. Could they not stop clapping, she wondered? Stop clapping and let her step out of the spotlight? She had already made two clumsy curtseys, but they would not stop. They knew her of course. But now they saw someone they had not seen before, a slight woman, a glittering crown of black hair that shone in contrast to her pale olive skin. They could not realize that the crown was weighing her down, just like the shame. At last she left the stage, leaving their applause behind.

After she collapsed in the dressing room, lying on the floor and unable to rise, her close friends called 911 and she soon arrived in the emergency room at the local hospital. She was a medical accident as well as a medical anomaly. The nurses put her shoulder in an icepack and put her to sleep, afraid that she might be suffering from pneumonia. In four days, deciding that she would be all right, they took her to her small apartment, releasing her to her shame that awaited her. But she could stare it down now.

None of her doctors knew of the remarkable encounter which she experienced in and out of her waking and slumbering that first night. In retrospect it was not perhaps that remarkable. Many have had this encounter. Anxious that she might have pneumonia, given the pain in her side that she confessed to with every breath she took, the doctor had proscribed oxygen and several night pills. Shortly after midnight she woke to see a nurse leaning over her, a hypodermic in her hand.

"Ms. Belford," the nurse said clearly, calling her out of her half-sleep.

"You do me wrong to lift me off this wheel of fire," she whispered.

"Well, aren't we leery. It will hurt at first, but not for long."

"Oh, oh . . ." By this time the oxygen, which the nurse had turned up, had begun to work in her, and her shoulder hurt, and more than hurt. She screamed weakly, "Oh!" and the pain tore through her throat and shoulder. "Kill me, give me that hypodermic."

"I'll speak to you again in three hours," the nurse said. "Now," slipping the anaesthetic needle between Anne's shoulder muscles.

"But I don't care at all . . . My death is . . ."

"Ms. Belford."

"Yes?"

"I'm here again." It still seemed the deep of night.

"You are a spirit I know."

"You do have pneumonia. But you will not die."

"That's not much. Will I ever play Franck again?"

"Yes, but—only if you consent to a bargain."

"I can never play without this shoulder." Tears began to gather in her eyes.

"Well, there it is," the nurse giggled. "The bargain is that your shoulder will never hurt again. Never. You will play like an angel. I only ask for your soul."

Anne heaved herself up on the pillow, gasping at the pain in her side. Her shoulder clapped together, what remained of her upper arm and her clavicle, and her lung and rib scraped on each other horribly. "Who are you? What are you?" But she knew very well. The soft voice of the nurse began to change, modulated by the growth of fangs in her dirty yellow jaws, and smoke circled on incipient horns.

"You have heard bad things of me," the nurse grunted. "I have killed a few people in this hospital, and elsewhere—had to, hence this hypo. It's been in all the papers," she said with some self-satisfaction. "But I mean well by you."

"If you mean well by me, stick me with more anaesthesia."

"Of course." It was as if the needle flew into her shoulder on angel's wings.

"More oxygen. We need to talk."

"Of course." But as the nurse turned the oxygen further Anne lost sight of her. She lost sight of everything. Then it was dawn, and the dawn was real. The window, which Anne had not taken note of earlier, shown in the dawn light. The nurse was leaning over her, no fangs and no horns.

"You will play like an angel." she said. "No pain in your shoulder, none. For that, you give me your soul."

"How can I do that?"

"We (you understand whom I mean) have utter faith in you. Simply say, *Here is my soul,* and the bargain stands."

Anne had no idea what she could do. The shame of the evening rose up in her heart again, drowning her, beating at her ribs and lungs where the pneumonia had cut her apart. She had no alternative, no escape.

"Here is my soul."

As she said the words she collapsed, sinking down on the pillows painlessly. "Oh?"

The nurse said, "Hush," sinking one more hypodermic into her wrist, and she knew nothing more. Nothing.

In four days Anne was released from the hospital, but for some days more she did not feel healthy, truly healthy. The pain no longer rubbed at her side, forcing her not to breathe, and the bitter ache in her shoulder no longer existed; but she was exhausted, exhausted in mind and heart, and empty.

When Mark came by later—he was truly anxious for her—she made an omelet with some élan for the two of them. She tossed it with her right hand and realized that if she had tossed it with her left hand, the hand with which she held the violin, she would have had no problem. The ache was gone as though it had never existed.

Three weeks after her release from the hospital she took up the violin and struck the first bars of the Franck sonata. Perfect.

There was no feeling. It was not deadened, as though a hypodermic had slid into the joint. It was simply that there was no feeling, nothing human in the way the violin rested upon her shoulder. And the sound, the profound, quick vibrato, was perfect, yes, but not human. It had no soul.

She shivered and played to the triumphant conclusion. She looked forward to a well-received career. Shortly thereafter she departed for Europe.

Johnny's Tin Toy

His surprise was multiple. First, he had not thought of the toy for years, and here he was now thirty-seven years old, staid and married, everything in his life settled, settled like dumb dust, and he never thought of his childhood. Second, whenever his wife Susan insisted that they visit an antiques shop he always wandered the rows of dusty objects with less than his two eyes awake; it was simply not his thing to do unless in a grudging, uxorious way that never reached the level at which he congratulated himself for humoring the little lady. Susan would have objected to such language. And third, this shop was a wretched barn, almost hidden from the highway by a stand of locust trees and thick honeysuckle not far from Yarmouth where you would never have expected this, this! where instead you expected only marine trinkets.

So John was astounded—no, let's call him Johnny as all his friends did. We shall be more intimate with him than they ever were, perhaps more intimate than Susan.

Its faded red and yellow paint flashed at him. It was exactly the same toy that had entranced him for hours when he was four or five years old, a tin roller coaster with three tin cars that a child—he himself in fact—would wind to the summit where the first car, then the second and third, would slowly click on the track that dipped and swerved and dipped and swerved, the car at last rolling to the base where once more it found itself being cranked to the summit . . . It made him dizzy to think of it as he looked at the toy, dizzy and enchanted. The smell of the honeysuckle thickened the air inside the hot barn.

He looked at the price tag. Seventy dollars! Being not at all acquainted with the market in antiques, especially the market in old toys, he was outraged and gestured wildly to his wife's blond head.

She sauntered over slowly, her eyes assessing the objects in the rows that brought her to Johnny.

"Look at this," he said, barely containing his rage.

"You have a better eye than I thought. I've never seen a toy like this before."

"It's exactly like one I had as a child. The same toy exactly—it might even be the same toy itself. This scratch, it might be the scratch my index finger left when I was five. But look at the price."

"Seventy dollars," she murmured, fingering the price tag knotted on the key that wound up the toy. A tin banner was draped across the entrance to the bottom of the rise, and next to the entrance a tin ticket taker appeared in garish paint, wearing a striped shirt and tipping his boater. Across from him was a smiling, tin brunette, standing behind a banner that read "Five cents a Ride!" She had the bright, healthy, alert look of a whippet.

"It's outrageous."

"No, it's quite reasonable. If you like it, buy it. In ten years you can sell it for two or three times its price now."

"It's outrageous." He could not let go of his sense of outrage, but he stood in front of the toy for a long time as she went to the other side of the barn where paintings in ornate frames were hung. Susan had a thing for old frames.

Johnny called the owner of the barn and asked if the roller coaster still worked. The man shrugged and wound the key. The toy emitted a tinny clank, clank as the first car rose to the summit and began its swerving pitch downward.

Johnny stood enchanted but still outraged. Someone was trying to sell his childhood; and Susan's suggestion that he could make a profit on it, not a profit on the toy but a profit on his childhood, outraged him all the more. The childhood that he had forgotten became priceless as he looked at the tin roller coaster.

In the end he bought the toy for sixty-five dollars. He was happy, as though he had saved a maiden from the dragon; and the dragon, which is to say the owner of the barn, was happy too. Susan found nothing to her taste and bought nothing. But she was happy with the excursion.

At home he set the toy on the dining table, wound the key, and clank, clank, clank, the cars rose to their appointed run and swerved down, one after another, to the base of the rise where they clanked upward again. He watched it for two hours. The repetition was oddly soothing. He knew what Freud had to say about repetitious acts, but he didn't give a fig for Freud; and when Susan announced that supper would be ready in five minutes he lifted the toy with good humor and set it in the corner, without touching it once more that evening.

The next afternoon when he returned from work he first read the newspaper, as he always did; then he went into the dining room and set the toy on the table again, winked at the ticket taker and wound up the toy, watching the various swerves of this car and that car, his eye close to the dangerous curves. It reminded him of the Wild Mouse he and Susan once rode in England, and then she and he made wild love that night in the B&B. As well as he could remember he had never been phobic about roller coasters before that experience. Would one of the tin cars of his roller coaster ever jump the tracks or run up against the car ahead of it? Had he or she jumped the tracks? As they were now, he and Susan had a salad and meat loaf that night and he slept very well, waking up the next morning with no memory of any dream but with shoulders and legs aching. Most peculiar. True, this was a new mattress, but his lithe body usually slept well wherever they slept.

It was at this point that we began to take a special interest in Johnny and his childhood toy. For the next few weeks he fiddled with it no more than he had that first night. But though he had no memory of his dreams we inspected them and smiled.

He is at a fair, one of those small affairs that during the winter months travel through the South to play for two or three days before moving on. At this fair his roller coaster has a central place, now that it is a proper size, so in his dream he steps up, buys a ticket from a brunette huckster, and waits for the car to rattle into place. He sits down and hands his ticket to the dapper ticket taker. The car clunks forward, pressing his back against the seat cushion as he realizes he has made a bad mistake. The car is rising to the summit, and as it rises his heart begins to pound. It won't stop pounding.

"No, no," he mouths. He waves to the people below to save him, and they smile and wave back. "No, no." A calliope nearby, gawky and fat in old melodies such as you never hear any more, drowns out his voice, but he has no voice.

He rushes past the first curve, a line of faces beaming at him as he screams without a sound and heaves his back against the cushion as his body attempts to escape. At the next curve the faces are level with him and once more have no idea of his terror. The car slams into the track where it began, and the ticket taker, whom he tries to wave away, helps him out of the car. He almost falls.

For hours he rambles through the tattered midway, whistling "Johnny's So Long at the Fair"; but at long last he finds himself once more buying the ticket, stepping into the car, and asking the ticket taker, please, if he could strap him in as tightly as possible. The man says nothing and does not strap him in. He never says a word, and once more the car is bearing Johnny away, clunk, clunk to the summit of terror, and whoosh!

"No, no," he whimpers. His words might be audible if only the calliope did not swing into a buoyant tune in the light of which everything is ecstatic. He dies a hundred deaths.

The next morning his shoulders and legs ached so much that on Susan's advice he began to inquire among his friends about masseurs and chiropractors in the area. His insurance does not cover such an indulgence, but there is nothing else he can do. He had no idea what was wrong. Perhaps in the cubicle he was spending too much time at the terminal—he would have to speak with the manager about that. The masseur he found, however, Mr. Govinda, who did an excellent job at pressing the kinks and knots out of his body, felt that his trouble had nothing to do with the terminal. It was more, the masseur offered, as though Johnny had spent ten bruising rounds in a boxing ring. He was losing, but his opponent would not do him the grace of knocking him out. But no, Johnny protested to Mr. Govinda, that was ridiculous.

The next day the aches and sores had returned and his fingers could not unclench the fists they formed until he held them for five minutes in the shower. The hour under the pummeling of the masseur helped, but the man insisted he could do little more for Johnny than he had already done. He could not save Johnny from the basic cause, whatever that might be, of his pains. So Johnny began to attend a therapist weekly where he talked a good deal about his mother who lived three states away and about his relations with Susan, which had in fact only the frictions of any good marriage and nothing more. No, he told the man, he and Susan had no children; the various doctors they consulted were very good, but unfortunately they could not be helped. It was sad, but they had a good marriage nevertheless.

At this stage Susan stayed awake for two nights, watching over Johnny. She had become convinced that he was sleepwalking, his blind eyes guiding him to a horrible place where he suffered unspeakably. But she was wrong; he hardly moved throughout the night, and only once did he turn over. On the second morning she told him what she had done and he embraced her, carefully, in gratitude.

He said nothing about his dreams, which he still could not remember and which in those weeks began to change their tone. He is no longer in a cheap traveling fair but in a modern theme park where everything is so much more arranged and so much cleaner. Strolling about and quailing before the sturdy, submissive lines of people waiting for their rides, he sticks his hands in his pockets, not ready or willing to take part; and lo, in his pockets he discovers tickets for the roller coaster, The Consternation of Winds. He shrugs and steps up to that steep concession, which has no line in front of it. This is magic, but to him it is the matter-of-fact world in which he can do as he pleases. The ticket taker, no longer a middle-aged slick gent in a boater but a properly dressed young brunette, takes his ticket and leads him to the rocket in which he sits. No one sits with him. He sits, and she buckles him in, hips and ankles and shoulders, and taps his forehead. He looks up at her and she taps him between the eyes, but she says nothing.

The rocket rushes him off, twisting to his right side and then to his left. He has no time to breathe, but he gasps as he realizes that he is hanging suspended one hundred feet in the air. He has no time to distinguish a face, any face, in the terrifying drop beneath him, no time to gasp, "No, no," when the rocket whips down, once again to the left and once again to the right, before the rocket spins up, turning over once, twice, three times, while the buckles at his shoulders begin to loosen. He will die. He always knew he would die.

The rocket slides into its accustomed place silently. The ticket taker releases him and as he stands up kisses him once and twice between the eyes. He looks at her dumbfounded, speechless, and almost falls. She slips her hand into his pocket, finds the tickets and clips one off. There are so many more to go. He sits in the rocket, she buckles him in, and once more in a great whoosh he is off.

It is impossible to describe the ways in which this dream, its shocking curves and sudden flip-flops, changes from what it had been. It gives him no time and no warning. "No, no," in this world has no meaning as the track hurls him from one impossibility to another. Staggering from one rocket into another, wanting to step into the new car, abhorring and allowing it (he has vomited twice, but that offers no problem to the young people hired to clean the park), he spins through worlds upon worlds, hurled through those worlds.

He woke with no memory of the dream. The only relics of the dream were the aches and sores, the horrendous emptiness in his stomach, and the contradictory yearning that filled his whole body.

What did he yearn for? He had no idea. Was this the horror of love? No, he loved Susan greatly no doubt, but with none of the extraordinary passion that mortals find in fiction and puberty. They were adults, living in an adult world. It was in him, something aching in his mind, something errant.

As he fell asleep that night he rubbed her shoulder.

He falls asleep. The brunette ticket taker buckles him in and kisses him between his eyes. He is torn away and after many hours—it must be many hours—he comes back to her, she tips her boater and hugs him, slams down a lever, and the car rushes him off to his death. He cannot speak to his death or whisper it or say it, but it is as though he has died a ferocity of death. Ticket by ticket.

At this point images from his dreams began to leach into his daytime life, though it did not seem to him that he was remembering anything. These were, he felt, only disconnected images. He saw the concession with no idea what it was, looking up at the thirsty horror of it and feeling something horribly tight in his belly. As he stepped into the rocket he felt dead, and the brunette buckled him in, wrist and ankle and shoulder. They raced him away. Much thereafter he could not see, but he was dead.

Every morning that he woke up he felt worse. He now exercised on his own treadmill and lifted his own weights. It helped no doubt, and Mr. Govinda the masseur helped too, though he said once more that in his opinion Johnny needed a therapist. Johnny did not tell him that he had been seeing a therapist for some months. He settled beneath the man's fingers and the heels of his hands, bumpity bump, bumpity bump, as the edge of his palms cut into his shoulder blades. When Johnny slid off the table he felt fine, just fine. That afternoon as usual, after he read the newspaper, he took the key and wound up his own, private roller coaster once more, his father and mother looking down at him from their great height. Somehow the afternoon was so much more peaceful than he had imagined possible.

He called Susan over. "Don't laugh at me, but this really is a remarkable toy."

"Yes, as long as the three-year-old child doesn't choke on the tin car."

He laughed. "Why do they think they need those very small warnings?"

"Legal protection," she said solemnly.

He slapped her butt. She grabbed his ears, shaking his head. They wrestled and tumbled and enjoyed the afternoon very much, and he did not bother to wind the key any further that day. As they often did, they decided that evening to eat out.

That night the look of his dream changed once more, this perhaps the most radical of the changes. It is so strange and so out of context that at first he cannot say what it is. In bright, flat colors, red and yellow and blue, he faces a station. Its track glows. It might be the T in Boston, but that of course is rather dirty and this is inexpressibly clean, even cleaner than the midway of the theme park, which of course he does not remember. No, it is the cartoon the movie theater plays before the main attraction, urging the audience to rush for more popcorn, to turn off their cellphones, to prepare for adventure. The car, a large open wagon in which orderly seats are arranged, rests upon the glowing tracks that spiral into empty space. But before that he must hand his ticket to the ticket taker, a cartoon version of the young man in the boater who displays a huge grin, and receive three kisses between his eyes, bestowed by a sleek cartoon version of the young brunette. He fits in this cartoon because the scene is not flat. It is three-dimensional, but since he is in the scene he does not need glasses. The boater tilts above the heads of the audience, and every eye feels the breath of the woman's ritual kiss.

They lead him to the car and strap him in. Great bands of steel click over his legs and chest and across his forehead; no danger of whiplash here. As they step back the car begins to edge forward, gaining speed as it follows the spiral track into the void. Beneath him he senses rather than sees oceans, prairies, the escarpments of mountains, skyscrapers, twisty highways, and twisty bridges. He would have screamed, "No, no!" but what is the use? His scream, had it been articulated, would have been excised in the editing process. No corporate body would have allowed his scream to exist. These considerations save him for a short time, but when they cease he returns to the full horror of the scream beginning to tilt to the left and his inability of tilting his body to the right against the steel bands on his chest. He wails, and his wail is torn into an impassable face that broods on him like an unbroken god.

It is his father, the face of his father, and the face of his mother juts beyond it, as impassable as the face of her husband. The car twists three times and four times between them. He has no means of saving himself from the thick, heavy clouds, umber and rosé, that measure his speed through the immeasurable depths of this world.

His car glides into a station, slows and halts. Five feet beyond the hood of his car the track ends, the abyss abruptly beneath its nose. The brunette unbinds him, lifts him out by his armpits, and sets him on his unsteady feet, then shoos him away. But where to go? There is no midway here, only the lounge where the popcorn is sold and he can take a piss; but he senses that the lounge is forbidden him. He cannot step out of the film, and in any case he pissed himself in the ride. As he pauses the ticket seller hurries ahead of him. She looks like tin and film. He buys a ticket and steps up a short staircase where the ticket taker waits for him, a model of patience. He takes the ticket and leads Johnny to the car where he and the brunette, whose eyes have begun to darken and age, perform their accustomed rites. It is as though they were arranging him in his coffin or wrapping him in the shroud that will clothe his nakedness in the ocean of the ur-abyss.

This car does not accelerate slowly. It shoots forward. "Agh, agh, agh." He can no longer attempt an articulate word, and the sound in his throat rises, "Igh, igh," as the track races him down a vertical brow into a sudden turn that then flips into a manifold spiral that somehow enters the eternity of a Möbius strip. At last the tracks spit out the car that slides and jerks into its station, its nose hung over the abyss. He cannot believe that his life hangs on a shift of a dime; he does not dare to breathe.

The next day he could not roll out of bed until twenty minutes after he woke, muttering "Ugh, ugh," as he stood up from his invisible bruises. His muscles stretched painfully as he spread his legs and touched his right hand to his left foot and his left hand to his right foot. Later in the day he visited Mr. Govinda. Besides the usual work on his calves and back and shoulders the man spent much time clicking his tongue. No more could be said than had been said. At the end of the session he refused to be paid. He lifted his hands and shrugged. The case was hopeless.

That night Johnny stands once more in front of his toy, once more full size as it had been that first night. The ticket taker tips his hand, and when Johnny tries to buy a ticket for a dollar the brunette points at the sign on her banner, five cents a ride, and gives him a piece of paper. It proves to be a letter. "Dear Johnny," it begins to his surprise, "As you have noticed we cannot speak, but through the years we have learned to write. It has been a pleasure to know you. We—he who takes and I who give—are members of the Congress of Forgotten Toys. That may seem a small thing to you, but it is not so to us. Humans made us, pouring into us so much of their desire, humans played with us, playing out their desires, and forgot us, forgetting their desires. They had become adults. Excuse me if I sound bitter. You, however, have been a delight from the first moment you saw us since childhood, and we are grateful. We can now give you more of your desire if you wish it. Five cents a ride." He read the letter twice over, reached into his pocket and took out a nickel. He held it up and she nodded.

The ticket in his hand, he walked into the roller coaster and gave it to the man in the striped shirt and the boater, who despite his full, merry humanity still had something tinny about him, just as the brunette did also. Both of them, the tinny man and the tinny woman, strapped Johnny into the car with the old leather straps. He had barely noticed they did not do so good a job about it when the machinery clanged and the car began to rise.

What had he done? "No, no!" he screamed, a full-bodied protest that could be heard in the next county. From the summit looking down on the tracks he could see that they were rusty; nails were missing. "No!"

The tragedy of course was Susan's when she woke the next morning and discovered that he was dead. Bones were broken, his skull was crushed. In his hand he clutched a generic, cardboard, dirty blue ticket, worth five cents.

HER CROOKED MOUTH

"Sharrie! Sharrie!"

That was the boys calling her for a game of kickball. The children were lucky on their block to have a good number of boys and girls, all of about the same age, to play together after school and on Saturday afternoons. Saturday morning offered the ten-cent matinees, and Sunday was impossible—they kicked back their heels but nothing else and endured family talk.

"Sharrie! Sharrie!" they called louder. She was the prize tomboy on the block and much in demand. She could kick the ball, putting a spin on it that made it impossible to catch. And she ran fast between the bases, very fast. So she was often the first kid chosen. She was not the captain of a team, the one who chose the kids on the team, since she was only nine years old. Mike was fourteen and her most frequent captain; he was the special child because he had the basketball they played with. But she was the prize tomboy, and she might as well have been the prize boy too.

If any boy her age got out of line she put him back in his place, and his nose showed his place too for two weeks.

She ran out of her house and jumped from the porch, hitting the flagstones running. Mike, Diane, Missie (the youngest girl on the block), and Donald were waiting for her. They slapped hands, laughed, and followed her running to the field where they played. Soon the other team was rolling the ball to them. Donald and Missie were struck out, as everyone expected, and Sharrie stepped up, the first player of their powerhouse. It was a wonderful day.

Yes, it was a wonderful day, an early November in which the flaming maple leaves were still dangling on their trees and grasshoppers were skittling and soaring through the high grass. Sharrie kicked the ball over every head and the kids in the outfield chased madly after it.

It hit the ground and kept rolling straight up and against the porch of the old green house at the end of the field. Then the kids stopped running. They stood there, looking at one another. One of them, Tommy, stuck his thumb in his mouth and stared at the house and backed up. Missie, where she had been sitting in her shame of striking out, jumped up and ran home crying. Because they all knew about the green house, playing next to it all the years they had lived.

The house had a history, simply told. The house had a witch— so much better said than to whisper that in that house there lived a witch—the house was possessed by someone and possessed others. And they all knew the name of the witch, but they would not utter her name out of respect for Sharrie's feelings. Children can say almost anything. But certain things they will not say. Because children respect the honor of their friends.

Sharrie, who was rounding the bases full of rich jubilation, did not yet know that her mighty kick had come to rest against the porch of the great green house where the witch kept watch. "How's that?" she yelled?

"Yeah," the catcher Daisy said as Sharrie pounded across home base. "You've practically knocked on the door of the witch."

She looked off to where Daisy pointed, and she giggled. She knew much more about the witch than any of her friends. When she was barely five years old, looking in the mirror for not the first time, her crooked mouth that displayed a crooked smile was exactly the same crooked mouth that spoke to her from the ragged family album. The children who claimed to have seen the witch described her in the same words, staring at her when they realized that she looked like the witch. There was no way not to see it.

"Yeah," they said, catching themselves up. "Just as she pops you in the pot she gives you that nasty crooked smile, plastered across her crooked mouth." She did not bother to ask how they escaped from the witch if they knew so much about her.

"Yes, dear," her mother said, who didn't know that people were talking about a witch that lived directly across the street from their house, "that's your great-grandmother. Isn't she beautiful? And you have her name, a beautiful name, Sharon." Her mother had lips that always smiled in a Cupid's bow.

II

For years Sharon agreed with her mother: the crooked mouth and the name Sharon were beautiful. Then she turned against all that and wanted nothing to do with either the crooked mouth or name. Sharrie was the best name she could have. But after years of playing in the field she had come to accept the crooked mouth. It was neat.

So now, hearing that the basketball was practically inside the ghostly green house, she ran again.

"I'll fetch it, I'll fetch it!" she cried in defiance. She was no coward and would give no one the chance to think so. But as she ran the house loomed larger and larger.

It was late Queen Anne, no doubt, and something now of late Victorian. It had passed the gingerbread stage and amplified that look, and now Baroque crooked corners confronted a visitor from every direction. The façade began at the corner of the house, its two flanks of the porch draped in patriotic wood cuts. Above the porch the second floor carried forward the martial theme, a hypostasis of the Civil War, at least nine or ten gables peering down on the village, and two towers, one ten feet higher than the other, launched themselves against the astral and astronomical order. People in Massachusetts understood these matters, keeping in mind their difficulty with witches years before. If anyone came too close, a bit too near, the intruder could hear a humming or a buzzing or something like a gnawing. It was not a good place to be because the house was hungry and waiting for fulfillment. The witch was hungry too, the neighborhood supposed—not that any adult believed in witches. It was the children that sang, "Witch, witch, the hungry witch!" and did not approach that house on Halloween. But they never approached it.

The most obvious feature about the green house, however, was its color—a drab, old, nasty green, the sort of green you saw on Margaret Hamilton's face as she flashed and raged through *The Wizard of Oz*. A bad liver, maggots alive in it, would sport this green after it had been lifted from a corpse three days dead.

But Sharrie paid no heed to any of that. She picked up the ball and threw it back to her team, made a face, and marched up the porch to the main door. She knocked several times, paused, and knocked once more. And someone let her in—or she let herself in. Thereafter it is all speculation.

So let us imagine. Sharrie walks in, juggling an imaginary ball in her hands, still hopping right foot to left foot. She sees a parlor furnished in rich cushions and beyond that a dining room in which a wainscot balances a charming pastoral scene, a young man tootling a flute and a young lady rich in her bosom back and forth on a Watteau swing. On one side a convenience is in evidence. The basements that she now rummaged through were dry. The sump pumps were in good order, so she spent very little time there. The second floors invited guests into spaces that the first floor had already promised. And so it was as it had always been and as it had always promised, from the foundations to the roofs.

But other rooms, especially the pantries, were not what they promised. It was late morning according to her watch, and she was hungry. The pantries were empty except for three fly-swatters. Two cans of marinated mackerel also sat in an obvious possibility, but nothing succeeded as far as she was concerned, no crackers and no peanut butter, nothing that she considered a tasty comestible. What was she to do? She found a drawer of knives and forks and spoons, but she gave up on them once she discovered that there was nothing in the house to eat but an abundance of insects—and according to her sense of shadows it was now in the late afternoon—there was nothing ready to hand but to try out the grasshoppers. Easier to nab than you might think. But remember, we are only imagining this scene.

And the grasshoppers were tastier than she had imagined. She had taken a course in school that had tested the various cuisines of the Sub-Sahara world, all of them praising grasshoppers and other insects. That helped a bit as she crunched the flighty creatures between her teeth. No doubt our insects, crackly and rich in proteins, you might expect them as rich as any in this world. Absolutely.

By this time Sharrie had tried to go home, but the doors wouldn't open for her. When they did open, it was only so far. She pressed her thin face out of the door and no further. But she did not try very hard. It had been very strenuous, filled with more adventure than she could comprehend. It was a witch house, filled with magic in every room, and a magic meant for her. When she called for her friends her voice was weak and quavery. She gave it up, and before she realized what she was doing, she had fallen asleep in the profound couch of the first parlor. And she had fallen asleep many times. Every time she woke up her ears were blurry with the hum of the grasshoppers, and without thinking she captured them and crammed them, crickety-crack, in her crooked mouth. Beetles were good too, fatter, and she slurped them from her fingers. Some people might have thought she would have difficulties with the tough carapaces, but she had no problems had all.

At some point in that first year the dreams began. She was sitting in school, and a tall thin woman with a crooked mouth was the teacher. She learned that she would never leave the house, but she shouldn't be afraid. Everything was taken care of. The payments for the water, the electricity, and the gas were arranged to be paid *in perpetuum*, which meant forever. The teacher wrote the two words in capital letters on the blackboard.

In the second year of her life in the green house she was snatching up crickets and huge long cockroaches, testing how they would taste in an American cuisine. She went back to the basement and plucked some beautiful escargots from the sump pumps, which she fried in the olive oil from one of the jars in the pantry.

In the towers she discovered that two colonies of bees had taken up residence in the walls. On the golden side of the walls the golden honey was dripping down, rapt in the hum of the hive-world, more humming and honey than she could deal with. What a world it was, what a seemly world. The sun seemed brighter in these towers than anywhere else.

In time she plucked honey from the towers, and very seldom was she ever stung—very seldom did she ever have to pay for the honey that she lifted from the dripping walls. She never ate a bee of course, for some obscure reason she could not hold on to. She felt good, better than the house allowed her. But honey and beetles, crickets, cockroaches and termites—it was not a bad diet. And she had no other idea what she was to eat. There were the flies, but they were squishy and she only ate them in dire need. She remembered the fly swatters in the pantries and she made good use of them. The crickets and the beetles were so much better.

One night in a bedroom that she had often avoided because of the green light that shone through a green window, or at least so it seemed, she found a mirror in which she discovered her old crooked mouth glaring out at her. The glass was clouded over by the web a spider had woven across it, snaring flies and beetles. At first she thought the spider would be tasty, and she was probably right, but then she thought better of the notion. The spider created so much in the patterns of its web, the roach and the termite so little. In addition, perhaps more importantly, though she could not consider the concept very clearly, she and the spider sat down to the same commensal meal. She could not eat the spider, no.

III

Then she fell asleep again, and time passed. When she woke she was much thinner, but she had always been thin, and she was very hungry. All the rooms, upstairs and downstairs and in the towers, were loud with the insects' clicking, humming, and clacking. The roaches had taken possession of the air as they sailed from one shelf or drapery to another. Placing her ear to the walls on the first and second floors and to the base of the towers, she heard the termites gnawing and boring through the wood.

She was quick, snatching at the cockroaches in the air and at the termites when they scurried across the carpets, wet from the rains that came through the broken windows. She had more of a taste for them now, the crackling of the carapace and the thorax, the delicate snap of the antennae. Her tiny teeth had more work to do than they had when she first entered the house. She was not well fed perhaps, but the insects fed her thin figure well enough. And she liked the hunt.

Well, we must imagine that she liked the hunt, because she had now been in the green house for many years. Things had changed outside. Her parents had moved away, stricken with sorrow for the loss of their daughter, and her father had died. The children had been ashamed to tell the police what they knew, and they never came back to the field again to play—and they grew up and forgot what had happened, and could not believe what had happened. They told the police it was a man with candy. Wasn't that true? It was always a man in a car with candy, and the police went away. The story of the girl with the crooked mouth had blurred in their minds.

Other children had gradually moved into the block, and they knew that they had to avoid the great green house where a witch lived, even though they did accept the field, which looked innocent enough, where they played kickball and other games not so innocent. They were different from the children that had once played there.

One day Sharrie stood at the door, watching the children, thinking of the day when the basketball had hit the porch. You might think that she envied the children their youth and their strength, but that was not the instinct in her mind and heart as she watched them. She pitied them, knowing that they would grow up, and so much would happen. Thinking that, she forced her way through the door. She knew that she could not escape, and didn't want to. She wanted simply to see more. She had no idea of course what they saw in the doorway, an old, thin, haggard woman dressed in rags scratching her head for lice, her mouth smeared with something ugly, roaches and flies.

The children squealed and pointed at her, singing a song that they often sang in other games:

> "Witch, you witch,
> You hungry bitch,
> You won't get me,
> You can't get me!"

That was much more than she could bear. The old spirit of Sharrie rose up in her as she grasped the doorjamb of the formal entrance to the house and ripped it out, shaking it at them and screaming. She shook it like a mad woman.

The green house, devoured by generations of termites, could not bear it either, not having the jamb ripped out. It trembled and shook and slowly crumbled. The children turned and ran. They ran as the two towers tipped from their bases and collapsed, falling upon the porch that tore away from the main structure of the house.

Sharrie died, shaking the doorjamb, water pipes broke and water sprayed, and fires flared from the electric sparks. Gas exploded. But indomitably from the ruins of the house a great thick cloud of insects rose up, whirling away in the smoke and fire, termites and roaches whirling away. An old queen bee rose up also and all the bees behind her, leaving their pupas in the wax behind, an immense soughing in search of another home.

THE WIND OF HIS PASSING

This is the story they tell by the dull green light of the monitors, in the afterhours when only a few hackers and crackers lean back and close their eyes, when they breathe deep, when they rub their wrists to test for carpal tunnel syndrome, when they dream. The dull green light flickers and steadies across their washed-out faces.

Whiff, ff, ff. Do you hear it passing over your heads, insubstantial as the scythe that death forges out of the air?

It's not often that you hear it, and you hear it only in this one room, this enormous hall that was once a gymnasium when this building was the Normal School. Before it became the center of a teachers' college, before it became a state college, before it became a university college, before it became a second-rate industrial park. Above the floor where a basketball court and the various horses, trampolines, and mats were installed, an oval running-track was laid out on a sloping balcony. And that's still up there, a junk room, a storage area they call it; they didn't know what else to do with the space, and tearing it down was too much trouble. What's there to do with such a space? So it simply becomes a bit of space off by itself. You can see the railing from here and at seven-foot intervals the bronze balusters and the pineapple-shaped newels that head them, beneath the high windows that look down with the blind, vertical eyes of Easter Island stones. If you walked up the stairs (which have been sealed off), you could still see specks of the paint that outline the lanes and mark the slanted starting lines. Just as down here you can see the worn foul line at your foot.

Whiff.

219

It's not often you hear it. Sometimes the wind of his passing flutters against the mind as you sit at the cheap terminal, thinking about the terminals in airports, thinking about your terminal state. Sometimes the wind is a pressure of light that ruffles the dust in the windows. Sometimes the wind of his passing strokes your neck. But it's not often you hear it. Once in a blue moon. When hell freezes over. When the planets enter into significant houses, the neighborhood of the zodiac is rezoned for business, the bureaus of the universe merge. Something dark moves.

Less often you become aware in another fashion of his passing. A faint spray seems to be sifting down from the balcony, at that point, then at that point, and when the laps are run a soft gasp thickens into a shadow. It's a spray of dust possibly, but it seems liquid. Perhaps it's a settling of dew that's found its way through a crack in the high window that every year the janitors consider too high to repair. Maybe it's just the light; but it's red. You know very well it's a faint spray of blood, it's heart-blood thrown from the lungs.

Sit down closer to the light of your monitors; huddle in your workstations. We have a ghost.

His name has been lost. Some say it was Norm, some say it was Meade. The truth is it has been lost, but we have not lost his story.

He had been a graduate student in the biology department when this was a state college, but what he loved was running. His green eyes beneath a thick blond thatch looked at the world as one long track where he would never die. Not that he was very good as a runner, don't believe it. But you don't have to be a good runner to be caught up by the dedication, by the spring of its ascetic pulse. You don't have to be a good runner to achieve the brightness that descends on your head and your heart after so many miles, the brightness that descended upon the man who ran with the good news from Marathon. You don't have to be a good runner to be converted after a certain stage to the belief that the gods hover around you, touching your feet, your hands, your breast. And that's a brightness that remains in the air like the scent of a woman remarkably beauti-

ful walking across your path and you'll never see her again. You have
fallen in love with running and you'll never outrun it.

When he took his degree it had been easy, too fatally opportune,
to accept a job as a part of the staff and to continue running. Every
afternoon you could see him out on the fields and in bad weather on
the running track of the old gym, just above us. He was here when
the gym was converted to the partitioned rabbit-warren we're familiar with now, each workstation blocked into a plastic cuboid burrow
and bestowed with its own dull green window looking out into the
abstracted world of spreadsheets, hypertexts, muds and moos, and
games. He didn't like the conversion; no one liked it but the state
auditors and accountants who liked it very much. What can you do?
And in time he came to sit in his own burrow, the hidy-hole for
which he had trained himself.

When we bellyached at the coffee-machine about downsizing,
he would pull his head aslant, fiddle with his decaffeinated packet,
stare at his sneakers, sip three sips, and sit to his screen without
comment. He was perfect.

No doubt he felt painfully the transformation of his life. On the
other hand he was here, on the gym-floor, from eight in the morning
to four in the afternoon, and could look up when his back and neck
and wrists ached to see the railing and newels of the balcony shining
down on him like a promise of eternity and imagine the running-
lanes that lay beyond, loping and loping around his head, where that
afternoon and that evening he would be running over the dead glow
of the monitors. Sometimes, since he had a key to the room because
he had now sat at his monitor for several years, he would be jogging
at seven in the morning, sometimes at six, in the winter in the dead-
morning darkness, sometime before the nightshift rose from their
monitors, turning them off for a few minutes, and he would come
down, after a shower down the hall, to take his place at his station.
He would have done very well in a monastery.

And so now you sit here late at night, working at your station,
your fingers playing lightly over the keys, working no doubt, or sail-

ing out through the green window into the clarity circling the world through the optic fibers, chatting, smiling your smile-face; and above you the wind of his passing passes your heart.

Whiff pianissimo, ff.

The faint spray of his blood-tinged breath comes down like refreshing dew.

At this point as I tell this story some people look up from their terminals and ask why he's there. I don't see how he could not be there, circling the place hour after hour as he did, day after day. He no longer ran in the fields, no longer in the streets, no longer in the marathons. He belonged, the balcony belonged, they belonged to each other; no one else ran it. For a short time a young woman, whose name has been lost like his, ran it also, often at the same time as he did. They talked—he could not avoid talking—but in time she left our life here, moved to another city, and he never tried to persuade anyone to run the track. It was his track, his monk's cell, his refuge. He imprinted himself. But I suspect he's still running up there because of the hard-drives down here; they may be sustaining. Despite the transformation of the business to Quantobionics, Inc. after his death, his handiwork at the terminals and even his school records still remain imprinted on the hard-drives and may leave a trace in the electro-magnetic sculpture that shapes the air. Every time we upgrade or even fiddle a small detail the old files are transferred as a matter of course. So as we work his influence passes through us.

I know from your smirks you don't believe it. You have to sit in front of the screen long enough, you have to give yourself up to it, the terabytes humming at your feet. But you better believe it, or something like it. We work ourselves into the instruments of our work.

You can't live like that without getting sick. I'm not sure how sick he was. Maybe he didn't know either. The blond thatch had become thin and gray. By that time, when he was rising at five in the morning to start running at six, working his eight hours, and then running that night, sometimes until ten or eleven, he must have been running in a way that knew without really knowing that something was running after him, clicking away the laps implacably, snouting his heels and snuffling the sweat of his nascent anxiety. That's when he began to breathe blood and began to weaken, began to lose control.

Then he fell.

I was here that night. I saw it, I touched it, it touched me.

It was like that old line by Stephen Spender, the only line we remember. It applies to the runner. He left the vivid air signed with his honor.

Whiff whiff. We'll hear the wind of his passing, circling above us, going through us.

The planets that circle a black hole will move into their proper houses, quasars and moons will cooperate; a thousand miles away the tides will pause on a narrow, white beach. God will condescend, something dark move.

Whatever does the trick, it works.

The fine spray of the blood will start to film and settle.

At that moment that man upheld by eternity will stumble again on the sloping balcony. You can't see him, but he'll slide helpless onto the pineapple-headed newel.

I saw it then, you will see it again. Out of the air flies a rope of unknotting, muscular, tight intestines, the compact stomach and liver, a thick spout of blood, onto the workstations, monitors, terminals, us. The blood on the green face of the monitor drips down black and the room darkens and screams.

Work, work.

Nancy's Dreams

Nancy is dreaming, but her dreams are not happy. If she believed in ghosts, as she does not, she would understand why thousands of ghosts are scrabbling for room up and down the coasts of Cape Cod where so many ships, lawful and unlawful, have gone down. The wreckage of ages. No doubt these drowned souls are bewailing their fate, to wander upon those wet and treacherous shores, the sands slipping beneath their naked heels. So it would be if she believed in ghosts. She leaves them there, their jaws yawning and their hands clapping their ribs. It must be awful, clambering ashore out of your death to find that so many ghosts are here before you. You're cast on the rocks, the thud of the tides almost washing you out to the deep again, the same tides thudding you in. There's no joy here, no, my Billycock. It hurts, oh it hurts, even though you're nothing but a ghost.

At this point she snaps awake, out of her dream, the early morning sun peeping into her eyes, the church steeple tolling six bells, the tang of the ocean on her tongue though she lives some three miles from the ocean, and once more she cannot escape the fact that her Billy rolls up and down, drowned out there. She would pray for him or ask the minister to pray for him, but Billy was one of those unlawful bodies. And besides, when she dreams those dreams she never sees him in the crowds of naked, drowned bodies. What's the use!

She gets out of bed and makes herself ready for the day. This morning, as always, even upon the blessèd Sabbath, she tends her garden. It has a few beds of medicinal flowers—chervil, patience, and borage as well as mint and garlic. Great yellow gourds are beginning to swell, and next to them the orange pumpkins roll into one another as though they were bodies, cold—no, this was no time to think about that. And he'd promised her rings for her fingers and bells for her toes, long necklaces that would hang between her breasts, not that she could have worn such things except in private, and you never know when someone will be peeking through the window. So those pretty things he had promised were now clinking on the sea bottom, shivering with his bones. She sighs and pulls up a local weed, its stiff bristles clinging to the roots of the corn.

It was ten years now since the ship had cracked up on the sand-banks and weird currents; back in England the Pretender had come down from the North and retreated again. Because the handsome ones have no staying power. Billy was missing some teeth, but that mattered no count when he kissed her. And he's missing more than that now, she thinks, and catches herself between a frown and a laugh as she pulls at another weed.

"Witch, witch!" It's the boys coming home from school, stop-ping for a moment to bedevil her. She stands up wearily and makes a horrid face at them. Such satisfaction. They scream and run as though she really were a witch, as their grandmothers and their mothers swear she is. Some day she will catch a nice juicy boy and boil him in her cauldron, herbs and spices to taste. Some day they will pay for her torment. She shivers and licks her lips.

But what truly made her a witch and what truly made the tongues of the town hate her was her independence—she owed them nothing. They could go and hang. She and her husband, whom she can now scarcely remember, embarked for the colony, neither saints nor sinners, but untouchable under the aegis of the king. Her hus-band was an independent creature and made the room for her inde-pendence also. An independent and rational being. She truly rejoiced in their conversations; he listened so closely. But she could not remember a moment in their bed except that she slept very well.

She is tired, working the garden. Well, she is old, no mistake. She goes into her house, lies down in the horsehair bed, and falls asleep on the instant.

Under a leering quarter moon the ghosts are scrabbling onto the beach. She realizes it is their only safety from the pummeling breakers if they can only stand sturdy. They will only be allowed so far up the dunes. They are naked, and she is naked. She had never seen herself naked in a dream, but here she is, shivering, bowed down, bowed under the horrors of the cold beach. Every face she looks upon is hopeless.

She snaps awake.

The cries and accusations of the children are still in her ears.

She remembers how the banter of the children and of the adults began if they don't. It began in idle talk. Just talk. Talk across the well and the village green and the commons. No one would have said so to her face, but she heard the talk anyway, the gist of it, and learned that because of her black mouser Dalsie people were thinking her a witch. So she did what she had to do. She lured her little Dalsie into a burlap sack with a rotting fish, twisted the top shut and carried the sack through the locust trees to the great salt sea, waited for high tide and cast the sack with Dalsie into the gulf behind the breakers. It twisted and heaved for a short time before it went down. The talk subsided slowly but never quite came to an end.

The years passed. She muttered the name of Dalsie in her sleep.

When she entertained Billy that one night the talk began again. He appeared at her door, rapping loudly on a cold day in December. The saints did not celebrate Christmas as true Christians would, so he might as well have arrived with a sprig of mistletoe in his hand, which he did not. She knew the ship he had come from, as did everyone in the village; but if the pirates wanted to do business rather than pillage, she would as lief do business as anyone. She opened the door and there he stood, holding a large wicker basket. There was no doubt where he came from.

"Hello, my lass—that's a fine, deep dimple on your cheek," he said, and would have flattered her to the stars if she had not cut him off.

"I'm hardly a lass. You can see my white hairs."

"Yes, and if I could run my hands through your hair your hair would run like silver."

"Well, your business, sir?"

"Some cheese if you have any, some eggs. I see you have no cow shed, so I shan't ask after any milk. I can pay well."

"I can do cheese and eggs if you like."

"And can you let me in while we bargain? It's bitter cold out here."

And so it was. This cold day in December was packed in sleet. He would have a cold time, thrashing in his boat with his comrades back to the ship.

"Yes, you can come in," she said grudgingly.

"Oh, thank you, ma'am," he said, rubbing his hands. "I'm Billy Martin," he added, rubbing his hands more fiercely. He was missing teeth and saw not so well through a walleye, a strapping body though, stout shoulders and small hips. She did not dislike him.

"You can call me Nancy," she said. She was walking to the store room for the cheese and eggs, so she said those few words over her right shoulder. Her hair was a bit white as she had said. Yes. She was old. But her body was good. She worked every day, and the work showed.

"Would you like smoked ham and hamhocks?" she called out.

"Oh, yes, mistress," he called from the front room where he was standing.

"Then come and help me, but my name is Nancy—I told you so."

"Yes, Nancy." So he came into the storeroom, where after some argument they agreed on prices for the cheese and eggs and ham and agreed on their bodies.

"I'll see you tonight."

"Yes."

And that's how it came about. The weather worsened, but sleet and snow and hail did not hold back her Billycock, as she called him that night, from her door and storeroom and bed. It did not hold back the tongues of the town either. We have no idea how the people of the town peered through the horrid weather, but peer they did. Whatever the legs and arms and private parts were about, the peering eyes knew all. It would set tongues wagging for years. The witch offered herself to one of the pirates—that's what some of them would have said. She knew, as he entered her God knows, the good God knows how many times, she knew she would never outlive that night.

Billy paid for the eggs and cheese and ham in Spanish doubloons and carried the provender off in his wicker basket to wait for the boat. When it came he handed over the basket and shook his head. "No," he told the man at the helm, "I'll sleep on shore again."

The man at the helm, the second mate, laughed and wished him good hunting, but to be on the beach at eight bells. Captain Bellamy, nevertheless, had other notions. Known as Black Sam behind his back, he had captured the *Whydah* a year earlier—it was a slaver then—and he ran a tight ship. They hunted Billy down as he walked through the woods, knocked him about, and brought him back to the ship where he was put to work at the stench below decks. He did not greatly mourn his fate. She was good, but not that good, and old. To the young Billy Martin she was impossibly old. Nancy learned nothing of that, of course; she knew only that he had been carried back to the ship against his will. She saw the last of her youth going with him.

The *Whydah* survived the nor'easter the night they spent snug in bed, and the next day the sleet and snow melted away. It was two days later under a bright sun that the *Whydah* went down at a sudden wind and Nancy's Billycock with it. The village was divided about the event. Very little washed ashore, so no honest souls profited from the wreckage as they ought to have. Some, like Nancy, had met the crew and pitied them. But after the trial in which six of the eight men who remained alive were found guilty of piracy and hung as swiftly as was decent, no one pitied the two men who were found innocent. The saints bullied them out of town and everyone got on with their daily labor, so it was the malice of the wreckage that remained ingrained in the town tongues through the years. She talked with those two, but they were agreed that Billy Martin went down. He had no chance down below deck.

That night she stumbled ashore naked once more, floundering and slipping. She fought the breakers fiercely, and at last crawled onto the beach on her hands and knees, bruised, bloodless. She was more exhausted than she had ever been. She staggered upright, then put her hands to her neck where the deep wale of a rope circled it. She tried to speak and couldn't.

Her eyes snapped open. "The *Whydah* has made me a widow two times over," she thought, "ten times over." She had no escape, and her hair became white as snow.

She's thinking, maybe, there's something to her dreams. She's thinking, maybe, there's ghosts. The medicinal flowers at her feet these mornings are pale, dry pink, exhausted. There is no health in them, not any longer.

So one night she takes a boat, dumps its fishnets and rows out slowly into the ocean. It's rough tonight, but a full moon. She has no great need to know where she's going. She has always known, all the days of her life, where she was going, and it's an immense home. So now she's leaving the port and turning out to sea to find Billy, her long-lost Billycock.

When she has come out to the ocean, fully out, she pulls up the oars, listening and looking up at the moon. Then she takes one of the oars, lifts it high, and rams it down, hard and fierce, upon the bottom of the boat. At the third ramming the bottom cracks and the water begins to pour in. The owner will not be happy. She has left him a note that will more than pay for the boat. As she knows, he will still not be happy.

After some time the boat goes down and she is left in the steep waters, heaving and dipping beneath her. Her clothing is soaked, pulling her down. This is what she wanted, but nevertheless her arms beat at the water. She knows how to swim, and she heads herself toward the full moon, but very soon she is cold and dragged down. The horror of the water is already upon her as her dress drags her down. O, O, she is drowning. She cannot pull herself up. She is drinking despair.

And then something happens.

It is night. She is clambering naked out of the sea, bumping into a crowd of naked, cold bodies, her heels slipping in the wet sand. A quarter moon hangs in the east.

"When will it be day?" she asks the bearded man next to her. Most of the people in the crowd are men.

"No, missy," the man says, "it's never daytime for us. It's just night and a quarter moon. No more than that. No, no."

She looks up and down the shore, the tide rustling at it. The crowd under the poor light of the moon seems immense. "I'm looking for someone. Perhaps—"

The man shakes his finger. "Yes, we're all looking for someone, and we've never found him. I gave up on finding Tommy Bunsen years ago. Not that we count the years of course."

"Tide rising!" a man near the stones calls.

"It has been good to talk with you," the bearded man declared. "I won't see you again, but it's a blessing to talk with a good-looking woman. If just this short time."

She hardly hears him. She has turned to look at the breakers as the tide creeps up the shore. They have all turned to the breakers, which in a short time under the quarter moon smashes into them, sweeping them away and bearing their dead bodies out to the bottom of the sea.

We have been ghosts, and when the shore accepts us we will be ghosts again.

The Infected Land

A week after the disaster the field still smelled of mud, sawdust, elephant dung, and ashes. And of something else—the delicate odor of evil. It is hard, though, to recount that scent without admitting its entanglement in the mud, sawdust, and dung, through which in the following summer the fallow field would become so fertile. The farmer who had rented the field to the circus had struck a good bargain. But more of that later.

The morning before the disaster Arnold Johnson, a.k.a. Bufo, woke as usual at four in the morning when his railroad car bumped to a stop in the new town. Everyone the length of the train bumped, and everyone woke. He groaned, unable to remember the horrible, earthy events of his nightmare, and dropped his pillow on the toes of his wife Margery, a.k.a. the Princess Starlight, resolutely asleep in the bed beneath him. In disgust, the aimless disgust he always felt at this hour, he clambered down the ladder of the bunk bed. It was time to dress and set to work, arranging the two large tops in place for the elephants to raise.

"Look at this!" the men around the center pole shouted. "Drive it in! This ground is like putty! Is it a vampire laying down there? Down, down, my lads!" No, it wasn't a vampire—oh, if it only were! Soon the pole was erect, the flags flapping from the pinnacle of the world. Only then could Arnold—but we'll call him Bufo from here on—join his wife and friends in the makeshift cook top, slurp his black coffee, and pile his plate with slapjacks.

"Bufo!" his friends welcomed him. "Bufo!" He ate fast because the tops of the freaks and the menagerie needed to be seen to. He waved to his wife hard at work in the kitchen and rushed out. Sweating under the late July sun with the other men, he unrolled the canvases for the sideshow top and the animal top. He would eat lunch at twelve-thirty and join his colleagues in Clown Alley.

"Bufo!" they welcomed him—"you wrack of vices!" He waved to their acclaim and sat down next to his best friend, Matto, to paint his face lead white, examine it in the mirror, touch his lips a jolly red, and shed his denims for the white pantaloons that came directly out of the laundry that morning. The earth rumbled, but in the heat of that sun it was nothing to notice. Someone laughed, "The ground is sick!" Bufo paid no heed, crowning himself with a white sugar loaf hat and going out to meet the people from the town who were already arriving. Silly, silly. He was an old-fashioned clown, learned in silliness. He threatened no one. Matto applauded his look and followed him.

Margery in the meantime had worked in the cook top. There she was happy to be Margery and no one else. But after one o'clock she shed her everyday clothes and took on the garb of Princess Starlight. In a short time she found her partner, Signor Ventoso, who in one show after another pinned her arms and legs with long knives to the spinning wheel she had positioned herself upon. He was very good. Only once did one of his knives cut her flesh, and he did not forget what she said to him. Today, at the slow rumbling of the earth beneath them, he asked her to step down, and only later took up the knives again. Thump, thump, thump, he struck at her armpits and thighs, points in a private map that he never mislaid.

He was one of the few men in the circus who took the rumbling in the earth seriously. The circus had come to the Midwest, where the earth never rumbled or trembled, so few people in the circus paid any attention to those signs. Bufo and Princess Starlight had played to several towns in California, where these rumblings could not be compared to those quakes, which despite the deaths they left behind are a healthy readjustment of the earth. Margery, stepping out of her role, rubbed her hand across the ground. It was porous, soft, and inviting; and it leaked. She shrugged and stepped onto the wheel once more. This was a performance in which only practice made her and Ventoso beyond them fearless. Later in the evening Melippitur sawed her in half.

Like Ventoso the freaks were also uncomfortable with the mumbling of the ground. Tom Tom, the speaker for the little people, went to the boss, Mr. Chambers, and argued far beyond his height. But the sizable man on whom so much depended, biting down on his thick cigar, rebuffed him. That night the little people performed as usual, running up and down and between the two rings and kicking Bufo and the other clowns in their butts, but no one could ascertain whether it was silliness or terror that drove them.

That's what they do. That's what Bufo does, and his friend Matto.

By now the people thronged the midway as the calliope began to bubble such mellow tunes as "Up a Lazy River" and "Shine on Harvest Moon" or the more lively "Entrance of the Gladiators." That was a music that told you a circus would begin soon. In this noise no one took any notice of the bilious earth. Walking among them came the candy clown Puta, hawking her redhots and the spun sugar.

None of this comforted the little people; and another indication that something was wrong, which no one at the time noticed, occurred in the animal top. A five-year-old boy was feeding his redhots to an elephant nut by nut until the elephant, no doubt with some justice, swayed his trunk down and snatched up the boy's entire bag. The camels on the other side of the elephants spat beneath their elegant noses. At first the kid was shocked and speechless. Then he sobbed and sobbed, but that is not the true point of the story.

This elephant, Raja, had never exhibited such aggression. We, however, did not regard this as an important event except in retrospect. And in retrospect we could make almost nothing of it. Later that night, during his performance, Raja trumpeted his anxiety but went through it all as he was supposed to. But later—I'll tell you.

The gaudy procession at the beginning of the show went off without a hitch, the acrobats, jugglers, and camels stepping past the center pole sedately. But later, when the ponies and the bareback riders went whirling around the main ring, a pony tripped on misstep and its rider pitched to the pitted ground, rolling aside despite her broken arm, screaming not to be stopped. If she hadn't rolled aside she would have been trampled in an explosion of her blue tinsels. It took no more than a misstep.

Everyone now was anxious; the audience was, and we were. There is no doubt that the lions were anxious; and the tigers and mountain cats, waiting for their turn on the multi-colored drums under the lead of Signor Respicci, were more anxious than they could utter, perhaps anxious because Matto, the clown supporting the act, more silly than usual, failed to lock the door to the cage. Is that why the beasts needed to call our attention to them? Homeless, with no line between their cage and the great outdoors, they roared and snuffled and ripped the chair out of Respicci's hand. He fired three blanks from his gun, but they roared all the louder. We should have known they were not to be touched.

They were not to be touched. First they ripped off the head of Signor Respicci and tossed it through the open cage door into the crowd to follow it into more bloody mayhem. Poor Donny, thought Arnold, shocked into using Respicci's actual name. But there was no time to think any further as he tried to bring down a chair on the head of the mountain lion. Fortunately the mountain lion was preoccupied, wrenching its muzzle into the belly of a woman in the first row. He had to bring the chair down three times on the beast's head before it slumped over; and now there was no time to see to the woman, who was choking up blood for some three seconds before she died.

The noise was deafening and confusing. The sound of a rifle as it exploded once and twice and paused for the man slinging the rifle to reload punctuated the chaos but did not alleviate it. Now the beasts were dead, their lovely bodies draped across the chairs that the people had fled from, but the mayhem had not ceased. Outside in the animal tent the elephants shrieked. The acrobats who had been performing when the beasts leaped from the cage were now in trouble because the rumbling had increased. Soon they were dropping from the ropes like rotten fruit. The sight riveted some of the crowd, those convinced that this was a part of the show and those convinced of its horrible reality.

And here the inexplicable rose up, pulling its way out of the earth as it grappled for its existence on the central pole.

I can't tell you what it was because I am convinced that no one has ever seen such a thing until that night. It was larger than human, how much larger I can't say because some of it existed at the edge of the big top and may have existed outside; and if it was human it had more arms or legs or heads than we could count; and still more frightful than the arms and legs wrestling in it, the creature had layers upon which different ugly, ferocious humans seemed to be striving for supremacy and always failing. And the smell of it made many of us too near it gag and reel. It was the odor I have already written of, the odor of evil, which you could still smell a week later, even a year later I am told. If it was a horse—but it was not a horse—it whinnied for the day of battle, lunging forward and snatching up anything handy. One of the first men that it snatched was Tom Tom, who vanished into the creature's fangs as though it had popped a bit of candy—if it had fangs, which it did not.

It was at this moment that Ventoso stepped out, weighing his knives in his hands, and threw the first one straight at the breast of the creature. It sank in but not to the hilt. Ventoso then threw one after another, in the breast, in the breast, and in the breast, exhausting all his knives. By this time he had the creature's attention, but it did not seem at all affected by the breastplate of knives it sported. One swath of his hand took up Ventoso and engorged him, if that is at all the way to say it. Ventoso screamed, and it seemed as though his scream would never stop.

Princess Starlight was frozen at the wheel, unable to believe the horrendous death of the man with the knives. When Bufo grabbed her and bore her off to the exit she beat him around his shoulders and face as though she did not recognize him, the clown with the great smeared smile clutching her and running; but they made it out of the exit as it burst into flames. He stood there, wiping the white paint from his face, smiling in all reality despite his burns, then leading her further from the tent before it exploded in fire.

It was providential, if you believe in providence, or perhaps it was a stroke of good luck, that at this point the fire started—if you could call that good luck. Many people would speak later of the horror of the fire as the big top fell in flames upon the audience that was still alive, but they have forgotten, happily forgotten, the monster that had clambered up the center pole. But there it is—they could never believe in the twisty creature that they had seen, and few of us can. As the days pass we lose it. We lose it because we want to lose it, and it is impossible to hold on to the thing. It sinks into the ground, evading the flames, and we hope never to see it again. We will never return.

Everyone who was left wanted to take the train as soon as possible, but that was of course impossible. The local authorities and a few federal agents interrogated us, but they did not learn very much. We were too ashamed of what we had seen; or better put, we were too ashamed of seeing it. Hour by hour it presented itself to our eyes, the unbelievable, the incomprehensible. We told our interrogators only as much as we could—and any more than that they would have never believed. In that week we very much felt the loss of the big guy Mr. Chambers in the fire.

During that week we quietly conducted our own interrogations, trying to discover what that creature was in that peaceful field. And we learned this little bit.

Decades ago two brothers had argued over the possession of the field. Their father had left an ambiguous will, probably out of a mean humor, and they fought and fought for it, each of them as mean as their father. When the one brother died, never yielding an inch, his wife and son took up the battle; and late in this lawyerly struggle one of the children brought down his cousin with a bullet cunningly placed. After some years in prison he came out, meaner than ever. And at last they all died, none of them in possession, and were all shoveled under the field they had yearned for, none with a tombstone to grace him. These were people that the townsfolk wanted to forget.

The man who owned it now, from whom the circus had rented it, was a very distant cousin who was cautious to plow it. Well he might have been! Renting the field to the circus was the best bargain he ever struck. And the last I heard, he still owned it to rent it to any other fool who might come through.

So there the bodies lay in the earth, rotting and corrupting, the one laid fast on top of the other. It was a Potter's Field, yes, the emblem of family treachery and the family flesh determined on its suicide, a suicide in which they had all collaborated, and every now and then the creature that was them, empacted and enthroned, came out to range the countryside, gaining strength year by year; and woe to anyone who themselves greeted those spectral brothers, the horror of the bloodied family, shoveled under, not to return. Not that anyone believed these stories.

That's what we learned, and little enough it was. Desperately wounded, so many of our friends and lovers dead, we could not wait until the train pulled us away from this infected land.

Badly disfigured, Starlight and Bufo have left the circus. As for me, I'm the only one left of that clown alley, paying off my guilt. I'm Matto.

THE CREATURE FROM THE ZODIACAL CRAB

I

It was not an earthquake. I need to say this quite up front, no matter what the various seismographers across the country may indicate. The experience was very different from an earthquake. My wife Kirsten and I have wobbled through earthquakes, the several quakes you experience up and down the spine of California and the recent hefty surprise in Virginia, so we know what an earthquake is. But though this was not an earthquake, it was explicable. It is what happened later than that soi-disant earthquake that we still don't understand, despite the explanations that Eldritch offered. We don't want to understand it. But this is what happened.

Our friends had stayed in the cottage once more; it must have been the fourth or the fifth time, and the wife Eldritch called to describe their new triumphs in the lawn and garden. Kirsten took that call and enthused her thanks. At the end of the call, which seemed to last for all eternity, Eldritch told her what more was needed from the garden shop: more brown mulch, much more, more beeswax to burnish the stone tiles that led from the garden to the back porch and that led from the front porch to the stairs and the car lot, and more sulfur spray to buck up the roses. The woman was a titanic mistress.

Kirsten noted all this on her careful notepad and promised that it should all be as Eldritch ordered. Nevertheless, we received several other calls from the woman, one day after another. Eldritch fretted, she was vexed. Our lawn, barren and burned after the long droughts of the past three years, was still a scorched horror, a thorn in her

241

side, a prickly, nasty briar in her side that could not be screwed out. Even the weeds were pitiful. She worked in the gardens, the flowers and the dwarf trees and the fruits, and they were dazzling; but that was no comfort to her. Every blade of grass that had once existed did so no longer, and its non-existence galled her bitterly. It was painful work, I'm sure. Nevertheless, however she and Monmouth turned the trick, two weeks later when we drove out to the cottage we were stunned by the look of the place as we turned in on the driveway. It was elegant. That is to say, from our first look at the renovated cottage we knew it was not the style of life that we led, but from the front lawn to the back lawn and the garden we were overwhelmed by the grace of the house, so surrounded as it was by such a smooth, fresh treatment. Not that the lawns were in any way restored to their previous grass, but the weeds of its barren lot had been laid low. The witchery of the place was inescapable. We were seduced, yes, just as the couple had intended. We had utter confidence in Eldritch and Monmouth.

I had only one doubt in Eldritch. She was given to horoscopes. She did not, however, inscribe her horoscopes on yellow business paper; she wrote them large scale on papers draped down the walls of their bedroom, a guest bedroom which was rather large. Spacious in fact. The work did not absorb her day, but at least twice a day she scribbled a horoscope across the wall, ripped it down, and began to write and paint a new one. The detail was overwhelming. I suggested to Kirsten that this was more art than science and that Eldritch should save her work, words that Kirsten passed on to Eldritch, futilely; art, unless expended on lawns and gardens, played no interest in her life.

That afternoon on the back deck of the house we watched the sun decline as it tried to find its perfect house to home in. At six o'clock, when the sun was over the yard arm, that was all that concerned us: the proper tilt of the sun, mirrored in the proper tilt of the Manhattan, in that late summer day when the landscape seems to tilt. Sitting on the deck we watched the pines groan and rub in the late afternoon breeze. They have grown over the last few years. Now they and the pin oaks and a maple obstructed our view of the long Ruggers Pond, which was one of the reasons we bought the cottage, so we took that obstruction amiss; we took it ill. The foliage would not accept our proprietorial rights, magnified by the dollar, so it obstructed the view, that gorgeous expanse of water. Eldritch agreed with us, and in fact had already contacted various tree doctors who could radically prune it. She was swift to imagine what next should be done. Tomatoes and garlic and lettuce would soon find their proper place in the garden. It was impossible not to imagine the tight, constricted glory of the soil.

On the other hand, after tinkering with various spirits and sipping my second Manhattan, I pointed out to Kirsten that we had some reason to approve of this thick greenery. It dampened the sound of the trucks, roaring up and down the highway that separated us from the pond, and it also separated us from the incessant roar of the jet skis on the pond. And truth be told, we would not be sitting out on the deck at this time if the trees did not protect us from the sunset. It is beautiful, yes, dependably beautiful, just as the realtor had promised some ten years gone by; but the blare of the sunset was really not good on our eyes until last year, when the trees had grown fifteen feet more and fanned the western horizon.

It is all very well to discuss the pros and cons of having the trees pruned back, as Kirsten and I did that afternoon, but since Eldritch had already contacted some men with chainsaws who would descend upon us and the trees in a few days, after the operation of mulching the lawn the next day, there was nothing more to be said.

Eldritch and Monmouth arrived the next morning. They were a striking couple, let me tell you. Both were tall, each of them about six feet in height. Eldritch was a thorough New Englander, dour, practical, and eccentric. Eldritch, as you might guess, was not her real name, but she told no one what that real name might be; at the time I was not sure that Monmouth knew it. Dark in feature with a great spiky mop of black hair, dark as a gypsy, she presented a most commanding presence. Monmouth was of Chinese descent, tall and broad and sturdy. As I have already intimated, he was often silent, positively Confucian in his silence. In all weathers he wore a thick black sweater that sported over his heart a gold pin in the shape of a heavy iron chair; when asked he assured the curious that it was an electric chair. "To everything there is a season," he said sententiously. Monmouth was an accountant. We had met them in the local Rotary club where a common friend introduced us; after they listened to us complaining about our difficulties in finding help on the Cape, they intimated that they could act as help, and we made a bargain that they could enjoy the cottage at various times during the year. It turned out to be a good bargain, since they were in fact passionate gardeners. They paid attention to other problems inside the house, but it was the outside space that most truly fired their attention.

Eldritch and Monmouth had come up to the cottage a few weeks earlier when we were there, and we conferred about the mulch. We had agreed about the trees, more or less about how much of them, branch and foliage, had to go. The orphaned fireflies would mourn those empty spaces, but what were we to do for them? Their homes were gone, it was August, and the fireflies would soon be gone also. At the extinguishing of those frail, biological lights every summer we admitted we could do nothing for them. Yes, it's as true as you guess, that I grew up in an orphanage—me and the fireflies.

Our practical topic was mulch, the great obsession of Eldritch and, so we assumed, of her silent mate. Every time he spoke we listened. Earlier that year, when she demanded mulch, I had found myself in a quandary. Was it to be black mulch, red mulch, or brown mulch? Black mulch I thought must be composed of dung and other such rich materials as sustained fungi and mushrooms. Red mulch must be made of cedar, smelling like rich red trees, cedar and sequoia, as reached to the heavens. Brown mulch did not appeal to me at all, but as it turned out it was brown mulch that Eldritch in fact desired. I was disgraced. As Monmouth pronounced, in one of his few pronouncements, "The state of the earth enjoys brown mulch, the state enjoys much." The man was Confucian, and that was that.

Were they confidence artists? Read further to judge.

We decided that a few days before the trees were lopped we would have Mr. Cousins, the man who mowed the lawn, put down brown mulch across the front and back yards. I called him that afternoon and he agreed to the arrangement. It was often difficult to be in touch with him, but he was enthusiastic about our business and agreed readily. Brown mulch he thought was the stuff, brown and goopy and no other. My wife was happy that I had made the phone call rather than she, and we sank back to the pleasures of the late afternoon.

The next day I drove to the garden store to buy the mulch. Oh my, I can't say how heavy the thirty bags of brown mulch were! My back ached and my car squealed and complained as we pulled away. The next morning early Mr. Cousins arrived and began to put down the mulch. The sun had driven away the mist and a breeze began to blow from the pond—a good thing too because the smell of the mulch threatened to be overwhelming. It was not a bad smell; quite the contrary. It smelled healthy, overwhelmingly healthy, reeking of herbs and vitamins and moist vegetable stems and stalks and brown leaves. The kind of smell that was ready to rise and do somersaults and sweaty push-ups. The up-and-doing, beamish vitality of it all outdistanced any we would have had from the black mulch or the red mulch. This mulch roused you from your dogmatic slumbers. It simply flattened the weeds in the lawn. There was a touch of the outhouse about the smell—that's true. Eldritch sat on the porch and breathed it in with the vigor the mulch deserved. The local osprey screeched ominously.

Eldritch had reason to be satisfied. She had persuaded Mr. Cousins to lay down the mulch in three layers; she was not to give mercy to the weeds at all. It cost a rather fearful amount, but I had several months earlier decided to support Eldritch in all her endeavors. The cottage looked so much better now than it had for years, and I recognized that in fact I knew nothing of these matters. My business, from which I had recently retired, was carpentry, working wood for high-class furniture. Oak, ebony, mahogany—that was my business.

Mr. Cousins tried to argue the point with her. "This has never been tested," he said. "I can't really be responsible."

"Then now is the time to test it," Eldritch had retorted.

"One layer of brown mulch has always been sufficient." I did admire his determination that one layer and no more was all that I needed to pay. Not that that was a problem—brown mulch is cheap.

"This lawn has been desiccated by three years of drought. We have already decided that we must have three layers." In retrospect I do not know whether in that word "we" Eldritch was referring to our short conversation or whether it was the royal "we" she employed. She did exude royalty. Her statement was forceful enough to silence Mr. Cousins. Monmouth watched in silence, a strong presence standing behind his wife. So Mr. Cousins began to lay down the vital brown mulch.

In the late afternoon he moved to the smaller area of the lawn in the back of the cottage, the lawn that the deck, a floor above the ground, supervised grandly and greenly, and Eldritch moved there after lunch to breathe the new thick layers.

"Ah, brown mulch!" she seemed to murmur, her dark countenance expressing her profound content as the ripe smell rose around her, her spiky hair leaping from her brow. To her delight it rained that evening, slow and steady. When we slept that night the smell was no longer as powerful as it had been that afternoon. The brown mulch was seeping into the lawn, intimately and deeply.

For three days, off and on, it rained—sometimes a mist in the morning, through which the sun attempted to shine, and then once more a gentle, soaking rain. We did what one does on the Cape when it rains: we shopped, we went to the movies, we read and played Scrabble. Kirsten, my beautiful wife, trounced me regularly.

On the second day the man who was going to trim the trees called to say he could not make it until the fourth or fifth day; his work would be simply too backed up, even when the rain stopped. But at last the rain stopped.

I put on my old boots and stepped out on the mulch. It trembled. I know; you want to point out that when ground is so wet it always trembles. I agree. But this trembling had a quality about it such as a sentient creature might have when it trembles, shudders, and shivers. Think of a horse, still being trained, when you place your hand on its flank. Its skin shivers; it thinks you're a fly that it can brush away. Its tail goes swat, swat, but the horse still trembles. The lawn trembled for ten seconds, fast at first, then more slowly, and then it stopped. I stepped carefully back to the stone tiles and smelled the brown mulch, its smell for a short time redolent of fear. And I think that I smelled like fear also.

"There, there," I said.

As I thought of the horse, shuddering, shivering, trembling, no help for it but our presence, I looked more closely at the brown mulch and saw that like a horse it had a definite musculature, peculiar to the species. Not like the musculature of a horse, no, nor of any other creature that I knew, but there it was. The mulch, the magical brown mulch, had become, or so it seemed, some kind of dazzling new creature.

It was so new. Fear beset me on every side, and I fled into the cottage, locking the front door behind me. The creature squelched—that was the sound of it. Only later did I realize what that squelchy sound had been. The brown mulch, reaching deeply into whatever passed for a stomach in its life, had burped, a great, rich, long, burbling burp, with the promise of so much more behind it. That burp, perhaps more than anything else, convinced me that the lawn was alive.

As I realized all this, so piecemeal at first, the tree doctors arrived with their chainsaws, raucous and deadly. Eldritch, in a purple and gold kimono from which one breast peaked discreetly, stepped out on the deck to direct them. Monmouth followed her with a careful tray of his breakfast, a double espresso and a heavily buttered croissant. The gold pin on his black sweater glittered in the new sun. Much that was Confucian and pithy brewed in his forehead.

I was fearful, and more than that I was afraid, but since I had no idea truly what I should be afraid of my fear was obscure. It had no object I should recoil from. The lawn had begun to quake, no doubt from my short walk, and it surrounded us. It burped a few more times, but none of us, high on the deck as we were, were afraid of its burps. The tree men had looked down on the odd behavior of the lawn and laughed good, hearty laughs as they positioned their ladders and climbed into the limbs and branches that spread out that thick green foliage as their first goals.

Hanging on the central trunk, the first man ripped his saw alive and set it to the branch.

At first it was all as anyone would have expected. The man cut the branch clean and it fell in a rush to the earth, followed then by one after another, clattering and flapping. The men were doing their job, just as they expected.

Then one branch, just as it fell, preparing itself for its fall, flapped below, reaching a small branch around the neck of the man, just as he did not expect it, and ripped him off the trunk to fall with it. Having no idea that he would fall, he fell and in a most ugly, awkward fashion wrenched his neck. The brown mulch seemed to welcome him, gobbling and gobbling for his heavy body, which soon vanished into it. It had no mouth—I had no idea what "it" was—that I could see; perhaps it had thousands of mouths, and each had its toothy bite.

The two men on the top trunks of the pin oaks and maple were stunned. They had no idea what had happened. Their friend, they thought, must have had an accident, though he was not at all the sort of person who would misplace his hand or his foot. He had been doing the job for ten years; he was in fact their boss. So one man clambered down to look after their friend—he had not realized that the man had vanished—while the other brought his saw alive once more to bring down some more branches.

It was not a good idea. Eldritch and Kirsten clutched me as I clutched them, and as Monmouth set down his tray and said something like "No," or "That's not right." The tree had gripped the man's hand, the man who held the buzzsaw, holding it firmly, but the tree gripped the handle of the machine as though it knew perfectly well what to do with it, flourished it on high, and brought it across the man's neck. Kirsten clutched her eyes and rushed into the kitchen to call 911.

"911," she said, "911." But you can imagine the response she received from the operator. "Murderous trees?! Is it mushrooms or what or too much Tolkien? I don't understand what we can do for you."

My wife took a great breath. "Two men are dead here, and the other is in danger. The number here is 7 Pin Oaks Avenue, Crows Walk."

"We'll have someone there in five minutes."

And so they did, a police car with two officers, but there was no sign of the three men other than their truck, the blood on the trunk of the maple, the man who was spared, and the two chainsaws on the thick mulch. As they gathered up the saws and took our depositions we tried to say in as clear a language as we could what we had seen, and of course what we thought it was best to have not seen. The man on the ground said much more, because for him the danger had been so much the greater, but the police discounted all that. Then the man became frantic and tried to make Eldritch in some way responsible because of her loose kimono. The officers tipped their hats to her and winked at the man. An hour passed before they could persuade him to leave. Heaven knows what they wrote in their report! I think it was the officers who started the rumor that a small earthquake had visited the area.

The first person who spoke in the dust of their departure was Eldritch. "The trees are alive."

"You're right," Kirsten said, "the trees are alive." She so seldom asserted anything so forthrightly that we had to accept her statement. Besides, I had seen the muscles of the creature, and I had no doubt that what held with the lawn held with the trees also.

"How do you know?" asked Eldritch.

"In the late morning, after I heard Jacob's story about the musculature of the lawn, I went out to the trees and walked my hand up and down the bark. I walked my hands up and down, and then my fingers. The bark liked what I was doing—don't ask me how I know. I kissed the bark, and it kissed me. You don't mind, I hope?" she asked, looking at me, and I waved my hand in a vague permission. Love a tree if you like. Kirsten was very given to the salvation of the ecosystem.

"The police will not come tomorrow," said Eldritch, "so it does seem to be up to us."

"Have you cast a horoscope for tomorrow?" I asked.

"In the manner of Manilius," she said.

"Of course." During the reign of the rational Caesar Augustus, Manilius was an influential astrologer who wrote a didactic poem on the subject of horoscopes. Augustus did not approve, but he had an itch for it. I was not impressed by Eldritch's decision for the poet, but she did have flare.

"My husband and I have discussed this creature that lies under the lawn, that seems to have been excited by the amount of brown mulch we laid down over it—"

"Yes, we did seem to lay it on," I said.

"We did, and now I am utterly terrified of that creature."

"Why?" my wife asked gently.

"It has reached into the trees, so how much further might it have reached? To the foundations of the cottage, to the pond? If it has reached to the foundations of the cottage we are not safe here, not at all. If it has reached to the pond we may be even less safe."

"You don't know what you're talking about," I said.

"My wife," said Mr. Monmouth, "frequently knows what she is talking about. That is what banished her from Salem." She looked slightly embarrassed by this admission. "So what she is talking about is ineluctably true, more than true, and we would be well advised to listen to her."

"Please," I said, "if you must, do a bit more with Manilius." I laughed but she did not.

"I can do that," she said, and we sat down to a frugal lunch.

During the day we did our best to ignore the events of the morning. We each did our usual affairs. Monmouth did figures, Eldritch did intricate horoscopes that blossomed under her long fingers, horoscopes such as Manilius would have drawn, and Kirsten worked on her necklaces. I continued reading a recent history of the Civil War. It was no use, we thought, to make sense of the lawn and mulch and trees.

There was one difference, however, in our usual day. Every two or three hours Eldritch would suddenly break into tears, sobbing, wretched. Monmouth would rub her shoulders—but no, she would pull away and return to her horoscopes. She was inconsolable. She shivered and bit her hand. Three times we heard her say, "Those poor men," and we could not but agree with her.

Our conversation that night was much more strained than our talk with the officials, a conversation I began with a mammoth Manhattan. Eldritch and Monmouth were teetotalers, but they always allowed for my weakness, especially on this day. But now Monmouth and Kirsten had a stiff green tea. As for Eldritch, she told me to make her a double Manhattan, and she drained her first shaky, cheerless drink to the halfway point. I had looked at her long and steady, as though to ask her whether she really wanted that drink, but there was no doubt as she downed the rest of the glass and set it in front of me.

"Another, if you please." I looked at her husband and he nodded with more *te* than Confucius ever mustered. I placed the Manhattan before her, which she left untouched as she began to speak.

"The cautious people of Salem had reason to suggest that I should leave. I had learned enough there to satisfy even the Chaldean masters. What I learned led me on to the ancient horoscopes, of which Manilius knew only a small portion. If you pick him apart, however, you learn many things. And I learned the worst.

"In the first ice age, before the ponds of the Cape were formed, something flashed through the sky out of the Crab constellation as a thing of fire. It flared, but it was not extinguished, not in the power of its life. The autochthones of the time took note of it, after their fashion, and centuries later the Narragansetts passed the word along. The glaciers rolled boulders through the Cape, enormous weights that, when they came to rest, sank into the earth, leaving these inscrutable rocks upon which the later American tribes left the rubbing sign of their knives. And also, as the glaciers retreated they left enormous boulders of ice, some of them larger than three-story houses that sank into the sand and gave it these deep, round shapes, forming the ponds. We call them the kettle holes on the Cape. But one of the glaciers left this creature (I don't know if that can be the right word), a dampened crystal fire that cannot escape the bed of the pond unless we nudge the stars, just a tiny bit." Here Eldritch held up her long right thumb and long forefinger an eighth of an inch apart and then, as though embarrassed, took up the Manhattan and drank a good slug.

"Just a teensy bit," she whispered, setting down the glass, her dark eyes peering through her two fingers, "through a proper adjustment of their horoscopes, a global understanding of their meaning, for a horoscope you see is more than a simple record or foresight. Often a little nudge does more than help."

I was aghast. If I were to believe her, as I didn't want to do, she was playing with global madness like a happy child who has just learned arithmetic. My amazement grew as she sipped another quarter of her Manhattan and gestured as though in an appeal to Kirsten.

"Yes, we lied to you from the beginning. I had to work for you if I was to meet this monster, the one in the pond. And I persuaded Monmouth to follow my lead. In effect, we lied.

"There is more of course. This creature we have brought into being by laying down the law and the three layers of brown mulch." She giggled and drank the rest of her drink, sliding the glass over to me again. I filled it to the brim and then topped off my own glass. How much, I wondered, can this tall woman drink? "This creature in the lawn," she whispered, "is nothing to the creature in the pond. I brought the creature in the lawn to life"—she slapped her twin thin breasts and coughed—"because I knew that so and so much of this and that in the mulch would give more life, much more, than the desiccated landscape already possessed. Much more life. I was not thinking of the trees, and no, I never thought of the tree-men with their busy buzzsaws. The horror was that I thought the alien— this creature brought to life here—would be, I don't know, ethically neutral. But now I have two deaths on my hands. And who knows how the creature in the pond would behave!" She finished the glass in front of her and sneezed, looked at us with stunned eyes and sneezed again.

"But think," she said, "what the creature out there will be like, invigorated, vitalized, brought to life, as the various goodies, vitamins and herbs, seep down from your lawn to the pond. Think about it."

Her last words were blurred as she began to snore. Monmouth picked up her lank six feet, snoring and weeping, and carried her to bed. We three then ate a very quiet meal. At the dessert I pressed him about her last words, but he would say only that he never doubted her as an oracle.

"She is infallible," he said, "much more than the oracle of Rome." He laughed and stood up to his full height and stretched.

"Good night."

II

The next morning when we woke late Eldritch and I decided to venture out on the pond in the canoe. I'm not sure how it was decided that it was she and I who should take up the long paddles. Kirsten decided to stay in command of the cottage, as seemed at the time only right, and Monmouth decided—well, I don't quite know what Monmouth decided, but he was neither the deciding type nor the nautical type. He did help Eldritch and me as we hoisted the canoe onto the top of my car, strapped it down, with every bit of care that I could summon, and drove down to the boat launch. Eldritch, New Englander that she was, needed only to summon her dour familiarity with boats. At that moment it was better, we thought, to face the creature there, if it was as present in the pond as the other creature was in the lawn, than to cower in the cottage. Eldritch, after drinking a gallon of orange juice spiced with hot sauce, had cast the morning horoscopes according to the method of Manilius, so we felt reasonably safe. Ho-ho. Not that I believed in horoscopes, whether cast according to the method of Manilius or Master Hocus-pocus, but I felt that it was time to do something that the creature, if it was a creature, would not expect. So high-ho we said in our small craft, plunged our oars into the clear water, and moved out. I had taken the stern position, a bit to her chagrin but she silently agreed.

It was a lovely day, the sun clear in the sky and a light breeze blowing from the west, combing across the waters at ten o'clock. We were pulling one-two, one-two across the pond on our track, aiming our line-of-sight at a tall, scrawny pin oak that overtopped all the other trees around it. We meant to quarter the pond, watching for any sign of the creature that Eldritch believed dwelt in the pond and would soon come to life in it. As it was we were not the only people on the pond. Some were swimming on its beach on the east bank, fishing boats were put-put-putting along, various sailboats and speedboats were elegantly finding their way up and down the pond, and the jet skis were making a public nuisance of themselves, zipping to and fro erratically. Very popular in August, colder than most ponds, Ruggers Pond lay some four miles long and two miles wide, large for that part of the township; there was room for everyone, even a monster, I thought brightly. It was a brilliant, sunny day, not one on which I was about to pay serious attention to Eldritch's drunken words.

We came up under the scrawny pin oak, rested, and decided to cast a new track toward a high thin pine on the opposite shore, near the beach where the children were swimming. A few times as we paddled I looked into the clear water and saw, thirty feet below us, the bass and bluegills swimming along, unconcerned in their blind schools. Creature indeed! But even as I shrugged off the thoughts of something else in this pond, something unthinkable, I thought of the deaths of the two men the day before and confessed such thoughts as I just entertained were a sacrilege to them. Though the police could ignore our words, we could not ignore what we saw. Fortunately we looked up to the head of the pond in time to see the first indication that something was indeed badly wrong.

A jet skier had just made a sharp turn, followed by another sharp turn, forming a tight figure 8 and bracing himself to bounce across his wake, when the man flew to his right, twenty feet into the air, and his jet ski flew off to his left. It was as though he had hit a submerged rock, but there are no rocks in the pond. He hit the water hard, head first, and we learned later broke his neck, his descent was so ungainly. The jet ski came down near the beach, outside the safety rope, and almost hit a child.

The other jet skiers came roaring to the aid of their friend, floating dead in the water, and three of them were once more flung into the air. Two then, the only two left, came in more slowly. By this time the water was crimson—a soppy dead red. What struck us, however, was the appearance of a thing, driftwood intricately bound together as a raft, sun-bleached and white as a necklace of bones. Think of all the driftwood you have ever seen, bizarre artworks, polished and elegant, stabbing and cutting, saw-toothed. Think of logs piled chaotically one on top of another in a millrace, but white, bone-white, and the logs narrow like knives or spikes, sprouting out of the water in mad contortions—a snarl of white snakes.

"Eldritch!" I called, and pointed with my oar. She nodded and pulled with her paddle, not letting up to bring us to our line-of-sight, the thin pine tree that grew to the south of the beach. She had no intention of bringing us up to the gnarly collection of driftwood that had proved the death of the jet skiers. How could they not have seen it! The sun shone as brilliantly as before.

As we landed under the damp shade of the pine tree a speedboat came cutting into the waves where the bodies were floating, but wisely idled as it entered the crimson space. I was surprised to see the words Coast Guard painted on its bow. I had no idea the Coast Guard paid attention to the ponds, whether large or small, and it was a boat that I had never seen in operation on the pond. One of the men began pulling the bodies out of the water, attempted resuscitation on one of the men, and then gave CPR to him; the others were not to be saved, but neither was that man. The jumble of driftwood edged out of the scene, moving toward the northeast corner of the pond.

"There," Eldritch exclaimed, "that's the creature!"

"How do you know?"

"It can be nothing else. I don't know why it has wrapped itself in the driftwood, whether it thinks the wood is a camouflage or simply the newest style, monster chic, but that is the thing. Look at how purposively it moves—let's go!" She gestured that I should sit in the bow, and I did. Now it was her quest.

And the speed with which she whipped her paddle through the waves indicated how thoroughly the quest was hers. I had to pay close attention to my paddle so that we did not swerve. We had gone nearly halfway across the pond when she suddenly slowed the pace and asked, "What is in that corner of the pond?"

"Well, not far from it is the firehouse and the town hall."

"No, no, not on land. What is *in* the pond?"

"I don't have any idea."

"Huh!" She expelled air in disgust. "I have a good guess what's there, but we need to find out. Do you have a map of the pond?"

"Yes."

"We won't lose time, no precious time, if we consult it. We are turning back to the boat launch."

As we paddled back to the boat launch a mile away Eldritch did not say a word until she laughed and asked me, "If you were an animal, say a fox, with an enemy in pursuit of you, where would you go?"

"Back to my hole."

"Exactly, so tomorrow we will pursue this creature back to its hole—if we can say where its hole is."

Kirsten embraced me tightly when we returned, and Monmouth kissed Eldritch's hand. She did not, however, stand upon any formality but asked me immediately where my map of the pond was hidden; she was correct, you see, in thinking that I might not know where I kept the map. And I had no idea. Nevertheless, after two or three mistakes in opening this drawer and that I did find the map, a detailed and dusty topographic chart in which every height of the hill and depth of the pond was given with great precision.

"There," Eldritch said, placing her finger on the deepest spot, which lay in the center of the northwest corner, "there is the monster's den, and there we'll find it. I did see some snorkels and fins in the basement didn't I?"

"Yes," I assented. I was not sure that I wanted to follow her the next day into the pond. It was like sallying forth to confront the Loch Ness Monster, but now it was real. Good luck to them that they have still not found it! But I could hardly demur.

I was grateful for the Manhattan that evening. Eldritch tasted not a drop. I could not help asking her, however, whether Manilius had anything to say about monsters, or anything about the sudden presence of the monstrous upon our sweet earth.

I should not have bothered to ask, for she snapped back, "Astra novant formas caelumque interserit ora." I felt properly chastised but demanded a translation.

That was not a problem for her: "The stars create new forms, and Heaven seeds among us new faces. That is to say, she added, we cannot escape the monsters among us, at home in the most innocent places. And also, the verse seems to imply that Heaven is on the side of the monsters because they are so new—we will never see their like again. It is wonderful, it is horrifying, and we can't escape it."

"Well, good night then."

"Yes," she said, "good night, see you in the morning."

We kissed each other's hands.

I woke at 7:30 and peered out the window to see a broad, deep fog covering the pond, but I was not discouraged. So often the fog covered the pond at this hour. This was the season of mists and mellow fruitfulness. Down the road a man was selling local fruits, vegetables, and flowers, where I often bought tomatoes and melons, whatever my guests would choose. I did not mean to do so today. No doubt one or the other or the two of us would die in being guides for this new astral order. But I bet that Eldritch would come through whole, since it was her quest. That morning in the fog I admired her tremendously.

After we ate breakfast, eggs and sausage and toast, we drove the canoe down to the boat launch, where Kirsten and Monmouth helped us take it down and set it in the water. We were both, Eldritch and I, in swimsuits, ready to begin our search as soon as possible. Two snorkels lay in the floor of the boat. I was not surprised to see her take her position next to the stern as I sat at the bow. Who would argue that it was not her show? She pushed us out and hopped in; the voyage had begun. I had thought, as I said, that the fog would soon burn off, but I was wrong. It persisted, dripping off our hair and hands, chill and wet. It was the sort of fog in which you met an old man, all dressed in leather. Or you met a monster, driftwood like bones draped around its neck—if it had a neck—ready to suck whatever life you owned. We were paddling slowly, no need to meet the creature so fast. No need to be lost.

And it didn't matter at all because we had no idea where we were. Our only guide was the blur of the sun, smeared across the fog.

But that is not true in fact. I had my handy-dandy Boy Scout compass that I used to keep us in true, and so we were. In no long time we had paddled our way to the northwest corner of the pond and now found ourselves floating above the den of the monster. I nodded to Eldritch, who began to strap herself into her snorkel, mask, and fins. I did so also, but we had agreed the night before that I would wear them only to follow after her.

The sun came out in its full brilliance and we sank beneath the water. It was so easy. I floated above the bed of the pond, thirty feet beneath me in the dark green light, and saw Eldritch sinking down, an axe in her left hand. I had a spear in the canoe.

We had agreed on those two weapons the night before. We were too unsophisticated to have firearms available, and in any case we had no idea what sort of flesh gave life to this creature that we were dealing with. It came from elsewhere—that was all we knew. That may have been the reason that it had wrapped itself in driftwood, not simply in its countenance and head but, as we were to learn, upon every spot of its flesh—if flesh you could call it. The axe was for chopping through the driftwood we had observed the day before, and with it Eldritch could stab the creature through its armor. We hoped to be lucky.

Eldritch swam up, bringing with her a water that chilled me to the bone, clung to the canoe, and breathed deeply. She was experimenting with her ability to dive down so deep and stay at that depth. She shivered, gave me a thumbs-up, and once more ducked down. I also ducked down to watch her but once more remained on the surface.

Now I could see the spring toward which she was swimming with good, strong strokes. The map had told us true. It was difficult, however, to make it out from where I floated thirty feet above it;

and difficult because of the sun's dark green refractions shimmering across the bed. She found something, it seemed, and began once more to pull herself to the surface.

"Here," she gasped, passing to me a piece of white driftwood. "There's more of that down there, scattered around the spring. That is the monster's den, just as we suspected. And it's cold and deadly as a bath of dry ice."

"Do you have any idea how big the thing is?" I asked the question because I was becoming afraid. I had been afraid yesterday, but now the fear had grown in my tongue and lungs, almost shattering me.

She laughed and didn't answer. Size was not something that her horoscopes dealt in, only intensities. She breathed deeply several times again, put the snorkel in her mouth, and once again ducked down, pulling fiercely for the spring, the fins beating in time.

As I watched her long, lean body twisting down to the spring I rehearsed our conversation of last night.

"What did we do to make this thing come out? Did we wake it up with the drip, drip of the mulch?"

"It's very hard to say," Eldritch answered. "Did we wake it out of a deep slumber, or did we rouse it from a daydream? Or do these words have anything to do with the actual state of its alien mind and flesh? Or is it simply that the stars have moved into a new configuration, black holes and pulsars sending out gravitational waves to which it is sensitive? In any case, I am certain that what happened yesterday with the jet skiers will quite likely happen again, aggravated and bloody."

"Meanwhile, what are we to do about the lawn?"

Stirred out of his Confucian quietude Monmouth had a practical answer: "In a few months it will not be dangerous." A few months, the man says! "Seed it with grass that will soak the herbs and vitamins into itself, and meanwhile the concoction will also be soaking into the pond. The monster will grow more and more powerful, but that will not be your affair. The best thing would be to sell the cottage."

Eldritch edged into the opening of the hole. She could not have had much oxygen left. Suddenly she stabbed into the hole, turned in a flurry, and rushed to the impossibly distant surface. Behind her the creature, a great, disjointed pile of dead-white driftwood (human bones stuck in it too), stepped through the hole, like an elderly, disheveled gentleman stepping through his Palladian front door, his senility disturbed by a horrid salesman and ready to do battle. And such a senility, half hidden in a sick-green light, was more horrible than I could have imagined, having only seen a small part of the creature yesterday in the bright sun. We must, I thought and giggled, have aroused it.

You shouldn't giggle in a snorkel.

Eldritch erupted across the surface of the pond, ripping her snorkel off and gasping. She caught her breath to say, "Yes, it's there, and it's enormous." She might have said that. As she panted, still out of breath, I put my head beneath the water and saw it coming.

It was enormous, jagged, provisioned in jagged bright blades. Its shape made no sense to me, larger than a two decker bus, and trailing a pink tissue where Eldritch had stabbed it. And it was rising fast.

I tore the snorkel from my mouth, crying, "Eldritch!" but I was much too slow. Rising so fast, implacable, it caught us both, its wake flinging me aside but taking her, splayed in the midst of the sharp blades and spikes of the driftwood, and lifting her bloody body out of the water. She screamed once, two times, and three times, her great hands splayed against the sky, before it sank into the bloody water and dragged her down, sinking toward the spring. Perhaps she waved to me—I don't know—I doubt it. Seeing the six or seven spears of the burnished, sharp driftwood sticking through her dark body, I think she was dead before the waters had closed on her screaming mouth; and then I realized how bitterly, hopelessly I had come to love her.

Leaving the canoe behind, I swam slowly back to the shore and to the car. For half an hour I sat in the driver's seat shivering. Could it walk on land, I wondered—and I still have no idea. At last I returned to the cottage to tell Kirsten and Monmouth what had happened in as careful a language as I could. We took hours to think of it, of its horror. That evening we drank very little and ate very little, and that was the way we lived for the next few days. We saw no sense in reporting our loss to the police.

And we were careful not to walk outside.

I do not remember when in that rift in time Monmouth stood up and said, "I need to report Daisy's death to her employers."

"Daisy?"

"Eldritch was her professional name." He added in explanation, "She wrote the horoscopes for the day. For the newspapers. She was very successful."

For some time I considered buying a variety of explosive devices that would take fire underwater and destroy the creature, but gave up the idea. The Department of Homeland Security would have looked too closely into my innocent past and decided that my request simply made no sense. I was hopeless, and no one would have accepted my story. We did sell the cottage, with its wonderful green lawn and its partial view of the pond. We did well by it. Nevertheless, the cottage had a reputation on the street of being haunted. The police might consider the deaths of the two men an explicable, closed case, but the neighborhood knew better. As far as the neighborhood was concerned the case would never be closed because the guilty entity, being supernatural, could never be held in a police cell. And I was not one to argue with them; Kirsten and I were only too happy to have made the sale.

Three years later Kirsten read to me an account in the local newspaper of a certain James Monmouth who had died in an explosion in the Ruggers Pond. Yes, he died, and we attended his funeral. We doubt very much that the creature from the Crab had died. We keep a daily watch, and I draw the horoscopes of the day. I will know when the stars and planets are auspicious.

Soon it will be time for me to follow Monmouth.

CLICK

When he first saw her in the maze he heard a click, the kind of click you hear when the hammer of a pistol is cocked, ready to fire. He recognized, however, that this click meant no less than that this was she, that there was no other woman than she, click. He had felt the same for Jocelyn the first time he saw her. Well. He stumbled and almost fell. His hand caught a branch of yew at a turn in the maze and he walked on. The vertigo, he thought, was probably a residual effect of his jetlag.

He had entered the maze on a whim. Before that, like any tourist who has newly arrived in England and who has little idea what to see, he had investigated the castle of the nouveau riche Howards in which Anne Boleyn and her cousin Catherine Parr had lived as children. The second ill-fated bride of Henry the Eighth and the fifth ill-fated bride. They had seemed such beautiful, fascinating innocents, and one of them bore the signature of our curious pleasures in her extra finger. Two quirky, delicious ladies, almost mirror images the one of the other. Two heads for the king's block.

In the castle, armor that was meant for show lined the north wall of a long gallery, very interesting no doubt, but he began to suffer from vertigo, fourteen iron visors staring him down and twenty-eight iron gauntlets reaching for his throat; there is only so much armor to be endured in the halls of England. He was small, yes, no taller than little Johnny Keats had been. When at last he escaped the castle he found himself confronted by the maze, and on a whim he entered, slapping the post of the entrance with his right hand. Heigh-ho!

And became totally lost. The goal of the path and its several blinds was to discover the center of the world, but after five minutes he could find neither the center of the world nor the way out of the world. That was when he saw her, click.

She smiled at him through the stiff yew branches and walked on. On her left hand a friend was walking with her, perhaps a sister or a cousin; they seemed intimate. And three boys were walking with the two women, running ahead and running behind them; the boys were their own maze. He was dizzy watching the boys.

"Do you want to find the center?" one of the boys piped. They were so British, tallow-haired and rosy-cheeked; their knees in their gray flannel knee-high stockings, peeking out from their gray flannel shorts, were rosy-cheeked also, rosy-cheeked and shiny. Skin like butter. For the sake of the season and the holiday—he was rather fuzzy on the matter of English holidays—they wore white cotton short-sleeved shirts. Very spiffy.

Did he want to find the center? "Yes," he said, not so much because he did want to find the center but because he thought any conversation with the boy would have to lead to a conversation with the woman. She had smiled at him through the yew. Talk, child.

"Turn left twice, then turn right twice. That's the formula!" the boy said, nodded, and ran to catch up with the woman and her entourage.

He recited the formula three times and walked forward with a careful confidence that surprised him. He came to a turn and took it and the next turn left twice. He paused then, congratulating himself and breathing deeply, then walked into the next turn, careful, careful, and took the next turn right once and right again once. He paused, breathed very deeply ten times, and caught his breath. He had not exerted himself very greatly, but he needed to catch his breath, he needed to breathe deeply. She had smiled.

Leaning against the yew he tried to imagine her. Her body had nothing special about it. She had the well-fed body that she needed against the chill, wet weather of England. Her hair was very fine. It was spun quintessence, spun gossamer, yet there was nothing truly unusual about it. Her hair was a honey-white blond and hung rich and heavy except for every small breeze that found its way into the maze. She wore silver and pearl ear-rings that winked at him. And at the base of her hair, which was cut in a bob, a drop of sweat pearled upon the nape of her neck. A thin dark line crossed her neck where a heavy necklace had rubbed it almost raw.

Her face recalled Botticelli's Primavera, a soft and welcoming fox face, a smile that could never die because the edges of her mouth turned up. It was the smile of the Primavera that greeted him, the promise of spring. But since her flesh was well-fed, not narrow at the chin at all, it was not a fox face in fact; it would not stoop to the devouring spirit that lay within it. Her smile would not stoop. It was a devouring spirit, not a fox face, and that devouring spirit welcomed him, welcoming him so sweetly.

He stood up straight in the path and began to chant the formula that the boy had instructed him in. He did not feel so confident, however, in its charm, and after the next two turns that he took, left hand and left hand, he found himself on the outside wall of the maze. Aren't they the tricksy boys, and wasn't he the fool to trust them? Whatever gain he had laid up he had lost.

As he almost despaired, almost broke into tears, she and the boys and her close friend came past him on the inner wall and once more she smiled on him. No, she spoke.

"Hello. We're doing the best we can, aren't we?" She shrugged. "Here we are, lost going in and lost going out and the boys are simply no help at all. I love you." Click.

No, she didn't say she loved him. He knew he was making it up, it was a projection, but she was being helpful, more helpful than he deserved. No, it was he who loved her, but it was a despairing love, the same kind of love that Keats felt for the woman he saw in the Vauxhall, whom he knew in that instant he would never see again. Five years later he paid a tribute to her, never to be seen again, in a sonnet. In the delicious sensuality of one line, he was "snared by the ungloving of her hand."

He blinked. As she turned and walked away, her friend whispering in her ear, he saw that she wore gloves, very fine thin gloves. Where would they meet? At the way out, at the escape, or at the center? Oh, they must meet, they would have to meet, at the center. At the center of the world. That was his faith, and at the next turn he took the formula by faith again, twice on the left hand again. Then he stopped and began following any random path that pleased him.

In taking the random paths the images of his past, his recent past, began to arrest his attention, blotting out the maze. First, babbling as though he had a speech impediment, he had asked Jocelyn to marry him, and worse than her "No," for of course she said "No," was the look of surprise on her well-fed fox face and the sick prostration he had felt in his whole body upon realizing that she never imagined such a thing. He had known her for two years but she had never imagined he felt that way about her. It frightened her, and she said, "No."

He left her house awkwardly, as fast as he decently could, and walked the five miles home. In that walk he decided that it was time for him to take a long vacation, he would go to England. He was a teacher of English at a community college, but he had never been to England, so it was really time for him to go. More than time.

He turned onto another path in the maze, trying to remember how he had ever decided to come here. No, the moment of decision was lost to him.

Click. The woman and her entourage passed him on the path that once more lay on the other side of the yew. "Forget Jocelyn," she said. "Think about the world here, the world you chose to inhabit, and come to the center. I'll welcome you there and I love you." The boys jumped up and down, yelling, and her friend took her hand and led her back the way they had come. They seemed to grow smaller as they receded down the path, but the pearl and silver car-rings winked.

Well, what about the world here, the world of Anne Boleyn and Catharine Parr? Not very brilliant, they would say in the B&B where he was staying. The one had her head chopped off—and though her cousin had cared for the gouty old man who had done the chopping, her care had not saved her from the chopping either. It was not a happy family. Think of the resentment of the Howards. Think of that resentment contained in the castle that was now made happy for the tourists. Look at its dark windows that belied the sunshine and the sunshine that did not make its way into the maze.

Last night he had dreamed he was arguing with Jocelyn. He was in a rage. He did not know he was consumed with such a rage. When he woke he was certain it was a rage against her, but over his oatmeal he admitted it was a rage against himself. He should have known she could only say no to his proposal. He should have known. Click.

At this moment he perceived that music was in the air, no doubt coming from the castle. Wonderful the way the historians of times past get up these things, a simple melody from the time of Henry. They probably have dancers pacing off a gavotte to the recorders or a tempting and revealing pavan on the virginals. What did he know?

As he paused and listened to the music, so far away, the woman and her intimate appeared beyond the inner wall, one lane deeper toward the magical center, walking solemnly behind the three boys who now were acting the part of the horses pulling the carriage on which the ladies rode. As they passed him the woman brushed her honey-white hair from her brow and winked at him.

This was no projection. She truly winked.

The music ceased with no echo. Once more the entourage and the two ladies grew small in the distance, as though in time to the music with no echo, and vanished.

"Where am I going?" He stopped at another turning. No, the boys, the charming little painterly cherubim, must have given him the correct advice; and not aware whether he remembered the charm correctly or not, he began to follow it.

Oh, I am dead, I am "snared by the ungloving of thy hand."

Chanting the verse, "the ungloving of thy hand, the ungloving," he walked into a large space. Though the sun shone into it the yew still made it sickly-dark. He had come to the center of the world at last. A cast-iron love-seat, painted white, stood in the center; and upon the right-hand seat facing him lay an elegant pistol, chased in silver and pearl, and next to it a pair of fine, thin gloves. If he picked the pistol up it would fit his hand nicely. Yes, it did. The hammer was not cocked.

Click. Crack.

www.ingramcontent.com/pod-product-compliance
Lightning Source LLC
Chambersburg PA
CBHW051523050726
47503CB00014B/1013